≈ ASHES OUT OF HOPE

≈ASHES OUT OF HOPE

Fiction by Soviet-Yiddish Writers

Edited by IRVING HOWE
and ELIEZER GREENBERG

SCHOCKEN BOOKS · NEW YORK

First published by SCHOCKEN BOOKS 1977
First SCHOCKEN PAPERBACK EDITION 1978

English translation of "Joseph Schur" copyright © 1977 by Leonard Wolf.
English translation of "Civil War" copyright © 1977 by Seth L. Wolitz.
English translation of "Zelmenyaner" copyright © 1977 by Nathan Halper.
English translation of "Under A Fence: A Revue" copyright © 1977 by Seymour Levitan.
English translation of "The Hole Through Which Life Slips" by Reuben Bercovitch first appeared in *Art and Literature*.

Library of Congress Cataloging in Publication Data
Main entry under title:
Ashes out of hope.
   CONTENTS: Bergelson, D.   Joseph Schur.—Bergelson, D.
   The hole through which life slips.—Bergelson, D.   Civil
war.—Kulbak, M.   Zelmenyaner. [etc.]
1. Yiddish fiction—Translations into English.
2. English fiction—Translations from Yiddish.
3. Yiddish fiction—Russia.   I.   Howe, Irving.
   II.   Greenberg, Eliezer, 1896-
PZ1.A79974   [PJ5191.E8]   839′.09′3008   76-49731

NOTE: We wish to acknowledge our debt for factual material in the Introduction to Professor Khone Shmeruk of the Hebrew University, whose anthology of writings by the murdered Soviet Yiddish novelists and poets, *A shpigl oif a shtayn (A Mirror on a Stone)*, has become a classic text. His introduction to that volume, as well as his essay, "Yiddish Literature in the U.S.S.R.," in Lionel Kochan, *The Jews in Soviet Russia*, provides valuable material and analysis. Very helpful has been Dr. Elias Shulman's *Di sovetishe idishe literatur (Soviet Yiddish Literature)*, especially for the period of the early 1920's. We have also profited from the collection of essays by the leading Yiddish critic, S. Niger, entitled *Idishe shrayber in sovet rusland (Yiddish Writers in Soviet Russia)*.—Eds.

Manufactured in the United States of America

≈ Contents

≈ Introduction

BY IRVING HOWE
AND ELIEZER GREENBERG

On Russian fields, in the twilight of winter:
Where can one be lonelier, where can one be lonelier?
—DAVID HOFSTEIN

IN THE ENTIRE thwarted and scarred history of modern Yiddish literature there is no chapter more tragic than that of the Soviet Yiddish writers. Elsewhere in Europe scores of Yiddish writers were destroyed by avowed enemies; here, in the Soviet Union, a generation of gifted Yiddish novelists and poets came to its end in the prison cells or labor camps of the very state to which they had pledged themselves, sometimes with naive enthusiasm, sometimes with wry foreboding. Except to a handful of Yiddish readers scattered across the globe, the work of these writers is unknown and their fate hardly remembered. In this book we have briefly told the story of the Soviet Yiddish writers and then made available a representative—certainly not a comprehensive—selection of the short fiction that some of them composed. The bulk of their work remains untranslated in magazines and books increasingly hard to obtain, and our hope is that other editors, other translators will turn toward it.*

I

In 1912–13 there began to appear a new group of Yiddish writers in Kiev, an important city of the Ukraine and long a major center of east European Jewish culture. (Other literary groups arose in

* A modest sampling of Soviet Yiddish poetry can be found in our earlier anthology, *A Treasury of Yiddish Poetry,* and some prose fiction in still another of our anthologies, *A Treasury of Yiddish Stories.* In a collection edited by Ruth Wisse, *A Shtetl and Other Yiddish Novellas,* there is a short novel by David Bergelson, one of the major Soviet Yiddish writers.

Moscow, Kharkov and Minsk, but the one in Kiev seems the most important.) The "classical" fathers of Yiddish prose, Mendele Mocher Sforim and Sholom Aleichem, though sophisticated in their own ways, were still deeply tied to folk sources, myths, and styles. Rooted in common life, they served as spokesmen for an organic culture. By the early years of this century, however, Yiddish writers grouped around I. L. Peretz in Warsaw started turning to worldly themes, showing the influence of nineteenth century European writing, especially realism, and coming to think of themselves—this marks a major break in the Yiddish tradition—as literary figures somewhat estranged from their surrounding culture. And then, with the appearance of the Kiev group, led in prose by David Bergelson and Der Nister (The Hidden One, pen name of Pinhas Kahanovich) and in verse by Peretz Markish and David Hofstein, Yiddish literature in Russia took its first tentative steps toward modernism.

Tentative, because no Yiddish writer, as long as he remained Yiddish, could give himself entirely to modernism. Be drawn to it, profit from it—certainly! But always there remained the pull of his own pre-modernist culture, an unstable yet vivid mixture of religious tradition and secular rationalism. At no point was the development of Yiddish literature anything but cramped and compressed: literary movements, tendencies, impulses which would emerge among other peoples only after leisurely decades came to flower in the Yiddish milieu after only a few hectic years. Generations and groups crowded one another, amiably or roughly. Influences sped back and forth. For the stately fulfillment characterizing Western literature there was neither time enough nor space.

Still, the young poets and novelists who came together in Kiev had a perspective somewhat different from that of their predecessors. Most were well-grounded in Jewish learning. And some, like Bergelson and Hofstein, started their literary careers by writing in Hebrew—though at this point, writing in Hebrew could signify not merely an acceptance of tradition but a wish to reach an "elevated" Jewish-national consciousness rising above the provincialism of *shtetl* life.

As they turned toward Yiddish, the language in which they would do their major work, the Kiev writers created the beginnings of a literary intelligentsia, a group of writers choosing to separate itself from, even as it might maintain ties with, the larger Jewish community. Mendele and Sholom Aleichem, perhaps even Peretz, had not chosen to separate themselves; for Mendele and Sholom Aleichem it had hardly been a genuine option and for Peretz it was a possibility but forever a troubling one. The Kiev writers, however, had a "European" education or were struggling to acquire it—which means that they thought of themselves not so much as moral spokesmen for the Jewish community but as individual writers for whom Yiddish was a natural medium. They hoped to move beyond the folk character of earlier Yiddish writing, its preoccupation, fruitful but sometimes constricting, with folk motifs, references, and language. Gradually, as they settled into the life of the city, they fell under the influence of Russian and western European impressionists and symbolists. Though they had already published a good deal of work in earlier years, they came to fulfillment as a literary movement in a yearbook called *Eygns (Our Own)*, 1918–20. The very title is significant—*Our Own:* we are Jewish writers, but also, we write differently from our Yiddish predecessors. The historian of Soviet Yiddish literature, Khone Shmeruk, describes

> the poetry in *Eygns* . . . [as] noteworthy for its innovative metaphor, new rhythms, and an influx of prose elements—whether we are speaking of Asher Schwartzman or David Hofstein, Peretz Markish or Leib Kvitko. In all their work there is a striving to break with classic poetic forms and with the idyllic or melancholy lyricism which still reigned supreme in Yiddish poetry until World War I . . .
>
> [Extending into the early 1920's, the work of these writers] was seized with the afterpains of World War I, the Revolution, and the pogroms [especially severe in the Ukraine]. The unavoidable passing of the *shtetl* poured over into literal nostalgia; while, simultaneously, they were absorbed with urbanization as a personal experience and as an occasionally desired fate for Jews as a whole.

The break from both the Jewish past and the traditions of Yiddish writing could never be complete, since the Kiev writers continued to use Yiddish and, with whatever ambiguities or confusions, to regard themselves as Jewish. But if not complete, the break was still clearly visible. In Bergelson's early novel, *At the Depot* (1909), the decay of traditional east European Jewish life is depicted in a manner reminiscent of Chekhov, Hamsun, perhaps Andreyev. A new voice is heard, the voice of the post-1905 intelligentsia smarting from political defeat: dispirited, anxious, world-weary. In Der Nister's *Thoughts and Motifs* (1907), a visionary symbolism is linked with an immersion in the Kabbala, so that it becomes almost impossible to distinguish between the very new and the very old.

Over some fifteen or twenty years, these Yiddish writers carved out a path of their own. Some were sympathetic to the Bolshevik Revolution, though only a few of the younger ones, like Itzik Feffer and Izzi Charik, who had come to literary consciousness at the time of the Revolution, regarded themselves as doctrinal Communists. Those who had begun writing before World War I still had strong cultural and emotional ties with the older Jewish life of Russia, the life of *shtetl* and *shul*. Yet almost all were seeking fresh literary modes, strategies for yoking Yiddish past with European tomorrow.

By now we know the magnitude of disillusion and disaster that was to follow, but we should not let this knowledge keep us from recognizing that in the years of Revolution and Civil War many Yiddish writers saw reasons for hope. During the war the Tsarist regime had been especially severe in curtailing Jewish cultural life, but with the February 1917 Revolution, which for a few months brought democratic liberties to Russia, there began an upsurge of Yiddish cultural activity. In Kiev, the socialist Bund issued a daily in Yiddish, *Di folkstseitung;* another Jewish left-wing group put out a daily called *Di tseit.* About 850 Yiddish books were published in Russia during the years 1917–1921, a quantity quite remarkable when one remembers these were times of hunger and bitter fighting. In Petrograd, Minsk and Kharkov literary journals in Yiddish began to appear. Under the brilliant guidance of Shlomo Mikhoels, the Yiddish theatre would enter a period of first-rate work.

Together with veterans such as Bergelson and Hofstein, there emerged a remarkable number of Yiddish novelists and poets. Where, one wonders, did they all come from? It seemed as if in every Jewish town young men and women were rushing to take pen and paper: freed from the constraints of the past, buoyed by a vision of the future, enjoying the hope that national expressiveness could be linked with social transformation. Until about 1924, there was a flowering of Yiddish poetry and prose, as well as of critical and philological scholarship. Much of the writing in Yiddish had a strong political bent, and some of it, like a good deal of Russian writing at the time, was crude in its revolutionary gesturing; but as yet very little poetry and fiction was being manufactured according to party formula.

The atmosphere was still relatively free—partly because some Bolshevik leaders had enlightened attitudes toward culture, partly because the regime had more urgent matters to worry about than the political acceptability of Yiddish literature, and partly because the country as a whole was enjoying a lively moment of cultural experiment. A writer who attacked the Bolsheviks might get into trouble, but with a little ingenuity he could carve out some space for personal expression. If he refrained from praising the regime, this was not yet seen as proof of enmity. If he wrote about non-political matters, this was not yet taken as an act of hostility. And in any case, many of the younger Yiddish writers were genuinely swept away by enthusiasm for the Soviet cause. In the promise of socialism they saw not just an escape from Tsarist pogroms and *shtetl* disintegration but also a way of breaking past the dilemmas of the nearby Polish Jews who, despite strong political organization and cultural vivacity, were still trapped under repressive, sometimes anti-Semitic governments.

Writers in the Soviet Union could still employ "neutral" subjects. The problem of censorship was not yet unbearable. The distance the Yiddish-speaking community kept from Russian society made for some protection. But even as in the early post-Revolutionary years the Soviet authorities allowed some freedom to Yiddish, they began a harsh suppression of Hebraic religious education. If Yiddish literature was expected to fulfill "the tasks" which literatures in other languages were assigned in the Bolshevik outlook, these "tasks" were still relatively vague and undemanding. That Yiddish literature served, indeed, had no choice but to serve, as a voice of Jewish peoplehood or nationality, even though the Bolsheviks had steadily denied either status to the Jews—this would become a source of grief a few years later. But in the years immediately after the Revolution, a time of chaotic euphoria, there was still some breathing-space.

The growth of Yiddish culture was helped by the renaissance of Russian literature in the early 1920's, a modernist phase brimming with playfulness, impudence, and raw energy. The powerful chants of Mayakovsky, the dazzling stories of Babel, the brilliant work of Zamyatin, Olyesha, Pasternak and Pilnyak—these mark a period in Russian literature second only to that of the mid-nineteenth century. Some of the Yiddish writers were in direct relation with the new Russian poets and novelists; almost all found the Russian literary atmosphere stimulating, if also strange and unnerving.°

Inevitably, the Yiddish writers grew obsessed by the clash between Jewish tradition and revolutionary desire. Sometimes with a sneer, sometimes with benign crudity, younger Yiddish writers turned their backs upon the *shtetl* and the culture it had nourished. The Yiddish critic N. Oyslander asked: "Why continue to weave the threads of a universal Yiddish literature when the Revolution has shattered the whole traditional Jewish social structure?" Poets like Feffer and Charik launched sardonic attacks on clerical benighted-ness and *shtetl* idyllicism. With a kind of glee, Charik spoke about— and to—the remnants of the *shtetl:*

> Come, see with muted glance—
> The marketplace grows thick with rust.
> Each day a Bolshevik appears
> And each Bolshevik is our friend.
> As for us, rising out of need and woe,
> Emerging from the old and quiet streets,
> We will trample and forget you,
> Like rotted straw.° °

° Writers of Jewish origin who composed in Russian, like Ilya Ehrenburg and Isaac Babel, knew many of the Yiddish writers and exchanged ideas with them—though this area of Russian and Jewish literary history remains still to be studied. Ehrenburg has left a vivid portrait of the Yiddish poet Peretz Markish in these days:

"He was a handsome youth, with a great shock of hair that always stood on end and eyes that were both sarcastic and sad. Everyone called him a 'rebel' and said he was out to destroy the classics, to overthrow idols; but at our first meeting I was reminded above all of an itinerant Jewish fiddler who plays melancholy songs at other men's weddings."

° ° Except where otherwise indicated, the translations from Yiddish are by the editors. In the verse excerpts we have translated, no effort has been made to provide anything but literal renderings.

There were more complicated responses. One Yiddish poet, Leib Kvitko, tells the older Jews to be "on your way," get lost in the darkness of oblivion, but at the end pauses to murmur the wish that in their going they still "be well." Another Yiddish poet, Aaron Kushnirov, writes:

> In my soul there scratches a mouse
> With my father's or grandfather's tune,
> Though the door of my own Sabbath
> Has latched the week with a star.

II

In the first few years of the 1920's, Yiddish literature in the Soviet Union divides roughly into two main tendencies: the line of Kiev, supporting the Bolshevik Revolution while yet trying to maintain an autonomous Yiddish literature that will be varied in voice and technique; and the "proletarian" writers, some of them members of the Bolshevik Party, who seek to create a poster-like literature, militant in character, affirmative in tone, and accessible to simple readers. The major representatives of the former tendency are writers like Bergelson, Markish, Hofstein and Der Nister, as well as the critic Yehezkel Dobrushin; the major defenders of "proletarian" literature are, with occasional nuances and retreats, the poets Feffer and Charik, as well as the critics Yasha Bronstein and Moshe Litvakov, the last an editor of the Yiddish-language Communist paper *Emes* and soon to be one of the most irksome cultural commissars on "the Yiddish street." As early as 1919, sharp debates broke out over the differences between the two groups. Litvakov wrote an attack on the first volume of *Eygns,* charging it with a multitude of heresies, especially that its poetry and fiction appealed to cultivated readers rather than to ordinary people. Bergelson came back with a strong defense of literary autonomy. Other Yiddish writers oscillated between these two tendencies, sometimes out of uncertainty, sometimes opportunism. Perhaps the best that can be said for this moment is that the state did not force writers to choose.

Yet for the older Yiddish writers things seem to have become increasingly difficult in the years of "war Communism": material conditions hard, the trend toward party dictatorship severe. Bergelson, Kvitko, Markish, Der Nister left to become exiles in Germany; a bit later, Hofstein left too, living in Germany and for a time in Israel, where he wrote Hebrew verse. Among the remaining Yiddish poets and novelists in the Soviet Union, nevertheless, the authority of these men remained strong. In 1922, a group in Moscow—led by Aaron Kushnirov, Yehezkel Dobrushin, and David Hofstein—founded a literary journal *Shtrom (Stream)*. It lasted only two years but seems, in retrospect, especially important in the history of the Soviet Yiddish writers. For what *Shtrom* signified was that, if allowed a modest bit of freedom—not more, nothing so utopian as true freedom of expression—it might have been possible to create a vital Yiddish culture drawing upon the Jewish past while maintaining friendly relations with the new regime. That, in any case, was what the *Shtrom* writers wanted.

In its opening statement the magazine declared itself "a literary and art monthly . . . containing contributions from the best Yiddish writers, poets, and artists from Moscow, Kiev, Warsaw, Berlin, and New York. *Shtrom* aims to unite all responsible Jewish creative elements that are today forging the aesthetic values of our epoch." These seemingly innocent sentences contained the dark seeds of heresy. A Yiddish magazine openly declaring its solidarity with Yiddish writers in Warsaw (shades of Social Democracy) and New York (signs of petty bourgeois nationalism) and Berlin (home of the recent exiles)—this meant to recognize the reality of an *international* Yiddish literature with themes and norms not necessarily determined by either the Russian revolutionary experience or its "guiding" Party.

Shtrom was a serious magazine. The second issue contained a reflective statement by the editors concerning the relationships of literature to society, art to propaganda, and Yiddish culture to Soviet society. There were essays exploring the strain of plebeian rebellion in Yiddish folk materials. There were stories ranging in mode from traditionalist to experimental, drawing together old Russia and new. Marc Chagall contributed a pungent piece analyzing the distinctively Jewish sources of his art. Yehezkel Dobrushin wrote well on how Yiddish literature brought together yearnings of an oppressed nationality with sentiments of an exploited class. Peretz Markish contributed jagged and powerful expressionist poems. David Hofstein offered his lengthy "Song of My Indifference," subjecting Jewish sensibility to modernist devices. It contains a stanza he would live to regret:

> Listen!
> From the breast
> wrapped up in ancient fear,
> from shivering, chattering Jewish teeth,
> is torn a voice, a tempest—
> it speaks across the broad Russian land—
> Leib Bronstein! [Trotsky]
> *Translated by Allen Mandelbaum*

The contributions to *Shtrom* are often ripe with Yiddish sensibility and wit, Yiddish tonality and tradition. But everything is also responsive, eager toward the new Russia; nothing openly or tacitly hostile to the Bolshevik regime. Why then could not the authorities let it alone? As well ask why commissars are commissars, or totalitarians, totalitarians! True, nothing in *Shtrom* endorsed the arid formulas of "proletarian" writing; its contributors, who ranged in approach from realism to symbolism, went their own way as artists while constituting politically a stream of *nokhloifer* (fellow-travelers). But it was not to be. Litvakov wrote in *Emes* three attacks on the *Shtrom* writers, charging them with a failure to engage in explicitly political work and with "shutting themselves up in their own world and in their artistic problems." He ended with a veiled threat: "When *Emes* becomes established and has more time to remember 'old' accounts, it will do so with all the fiery spirit it can muster." Compared to the repressions of a decade later, this was mere child's play; but as a sign of things to come it was ominous. From petty bureaucrats, brutal commissars do grow. The *Shtrom* writers, not yet terrorized, answered with a statement insisting upon the distinction between literature and political journalism, which, they neatly jabbed, ought to be observed even in a paper like *Emes*.

Shtrom was doomed. By its final issues, a new group of editors had taken over and the "prolet" emphasis come to dominate. As

Elias Shulman remarks in a valuable study of the magazine, "*Shtrom* was the last independent Yiddish journal in the Soviet Union."

From the mid-1920's until after the Second World War, Yiddish literature was harassed with the same dull-witted fanaticism that the Stalinist state showed toward other literatures of minority peoples. If anything, the Party's hand fell more heavily on Yiddish. More insecure than their Russian superiors, the Yiddish sub-commissars sometimes forced themselves to act against their own inner convictions and therefore with a special venom. It is hard, from a distance, to estimate the extent to which the "campaigns of correction" suffered by Yiddish writers were a sort of charade to which critics drove themselves and the extent to which the critics genuinely believed their simplistic slogans. Probably both. When a "proletarian" critic like Burstein or even the more cultivated Litvakov went after one of the Yiddish writers, it was partly to save his own skin, partly to chastise his betters, and perhaps even to protect old friends from other, more brutal authorities.

"Petty bourgeois" and "nationalist" deviations were sought out; the Yiddish language was "cleansed" of its Hebraic component and religious references; and soon the literature fell prey to that dismal formula, "socialist in content, national in form."

Yet, precisely during these years, the Yiddish writers who had earlier chafed under less severe restrictions and gone into exile gradually came back to the Soviet Union. In retrospect this may seem perplexing; if we remember the tone of European life during the late Twenties and early Thirties, it is not. Everything in Western Europe had become gray, threatening, dangerous; men like Hofstein and Kvitko, Markish and Bergelson thought that the fate of the Jews in the Soviet Union might still be better than in Germany or Poland. Not necessarily their own fate. They knew they would have to bend to the lash of the party and its censors; but at least the fate of ordinary Jews. . . . Other gifted Yiddish writers, like the novelist and poet Moshe Kulbak and the critic Max Erik, immigrated to the Soviet Union and even became citizens. (A few weeks after arriving in the Soviet Union, Kulbak wrote an Aesopian postcard to a friend in Vilna: "I have come from the baths; one has to keep washing and purifying oneself here if one wants to avoid the extreme limits of life.")

And yet ... the human spirit turns and twists, struggling to survive, seeking avenues for honest testimony. Even during these wretched years there were significant achievements by Yiddish writers, theatrical companies, and scholars. The quantity of books published in Yiddish was impressive. The number of theatrical troupes grew, and some were very good. Yiddish scholarly institutions did first-rate work in linguistics and folklore. Writers like Der Nister and Bergelson turned to large-scale works of realistic fiction, hoping that, if they abandoned their earlier taste for experiment, they would avoid difficulties; their books of the 1930's, though streaked with obligatory Stalinist incantations, showed them to be novelists of the first rank. Even some of the "proletarian" writers, influenced despite themselves by the more sophisticated and alluring styles of the *Shtrom* group, produced lively work. If the role of a poet like Itzik Feffer within the Yiddish cultural community was unsavory, his work showed a genuine flair for satire—something of Mendele's acrid sharpness of voice remained with this hardbitten Communist who boasted, "It really breaks me up to remember/That I carry some famous rabbi's name."

Those who have experienced the torments of censorship describe it as consisting of several stages: first, the writer decides to withhold certain things he has written since he knows they might cause him trouble and cannot be published anyway; then he submits his work to the hard-breathing scrutiny of magazine and publishers' editors; and finally, if any political "deviation" or literary life has remained, the political censor lies in wait. With the passage of years these stages change in significance: more and more, perhaps to save his skin, perhaps out of mere weariness, the writer butchers his own work, making the task of the external censors almost, though never quite, superfluous. To have its people absorb its norms, as if by instinct, is an ultimate goal of the totalitarian state.

With the issuance of new Yiddish literary journals, *Nayerd (New Earth)* and *Oktober (October)* in 1925, the "proletarian" Yiddish writers and critics, backed by the authority of the Jewish Section of the Communist Party, clearly won out over the "autonomist" or Kiev group. Some of the latter even succumbed to the pressures of the time and began to write in favor of a propagandistic literature. In 1925 a Jewish section of the Association of Proletarian Writers was organized in Moscow, serving as a battering ram against those Yiddish writers who tried to keep an inch or two of autonomy. Two years later the Jewish Section of the Party intervened openly in the literary disputes and aligned itself with the "proletarian" group. By 1931, at a conference of Yiddish "proletarian" writers in Kharkov, the political assault against "rotting Yiddishism" had grown very fierce. Within a few years the issue was settled: all talk of Yiddish autonomy, or any other kind, ceased.

It is a lesson of twentieth century politics that the totalitarian dynamic must keep driving toward completion. A horde of cultural supervisors, some of them critics with a genuine Yiddish background, turned upon the writers, discovering endless heresies and deviations. It would be tiresome to chronicle this story in detail—a few instances will suffice.

In 1928, the critic A. Abtshuk offered a compilation of literary sins:

1) Cutting themselves off from real life and moving toward individualism and symbolism—Der Nister, L. Reznik.
2) Idealization of the gradually disappearing classes, with emotional participation in their fate—N. Lurye.
3) A passive attitude toward our reality—I. Kipnis.
4) Epicureanism, glorifying the passing moment—Z. Axelrod.
5) Lack of self-definition, neutralism, going along at a distance—a general evil.

When this catalogue was first made public, it must have provoked smiles among the Yiddish writers, especially for that delicious last phrase, "a general evil"; but within a very few years these writers would be fearfully scurrying about to prove their "innocence." And in a sense, as Shmeruk remarks, "A reading of the works of the writers under attack confirms the truth of all the accusations, if we take the 'proletarian' view. Indeed, from that viewpoint, almost all Yiddish literature from the second half of the 1920's lay outside the conformist trend in Soviet literature. . . ." And not because the Yiddish writers were especially bold or independent, but, as we now can see, because the very "Yiddishness" of Yiddish literature was incompatible with the reigning state ideology.

Attacks upon writers began to pile up—some absurd, some

sinister, many both. Peretz Markish, having published in 1929 two long poems about the October Revolution, was attacked by the critic Litvakov for making only Jews into revolutionary heroes and for letting his work be "restricted to a national point of view." Shmuel Halkin, a gifted poet, issued a volume in 1929 which met with a barrage of attacks because of its sorrowful, "negative" tone—and something of the later Stalinist savagery was foreshadowed when a group of Yiddish critics, the intransigents of Minsk, attacked Litvakov for "protecting" Halkin.

Still more serious was "the Kvitko affair." In 1929, the poet Leib Kvitko published a few poems satirizing cultural bureaucrats, one of them entitled *Der shtinkfoygel moyli (The Stinkbird Moy[she] Li[tvakov])*. This time the campaign against the poet took an organized form, as if it were a political faction fight. Meetings of writers were held to denounce Kvitko's "counterrevolutionary act"; a resolution of the Yiddish section of the Ukrainian writers organization attacked Hofstein for defending Kvitko, deploring the former's refusal to "liquidate his petty-bourgeois inclinations."

Writers of prose had it no easier. When Moshe Kulbak published his novel *Zelmenyaner* in 1931, he was attacked for applying the same tone (an affectionate irony) toward his youthful Jewish Communists as toward their traditionalist parents, clearly an instance of impermissible evenhandedness. When Der Nister published *Unter a ployt (Under a Fence)*, a symbolist story that is included in this volume, he brought down upon himself a shower of abuse for daring to write in so "non-proletarian" a mode.

For a little while, the Yiddish writers tried to resist. Markish pointed out at a public discussion that he was under no obligation to portray non-Jewish revolutionaries: "A Russian novel in which only Russian revolutionaries are described is not subject to such demands." During "the Kvitko affair," David Hofstein courageously sent out a letter entitled "Against Degradation." A few years earlier the poet Axelrod, a man of independent spirit, had declared at a meeting of Yiddish writers in Moscow that "all literary methods are acceptable as long as they are used with integrity."

But it was all really hopeless: the Yiddish writers, like their Russian and Ukrainian colleagues, had to bend if they were to continue to work, indeed, to live. When Markish republished his poems, he provided the necessary "corrections." Halkin radically changed his tone, from down to upbeat. Kvitko, dismissed from his editorship of a Yiddish journal, abandoned not only satire but writing for adults; he became a popular writer of children's poems in both Yiddish and Russian translation. Kulbak, in a second volume about his Zelmenyaner, added the prescribed "positive" elements. Der Nister turned to reportage, writing privately to his brother in Paris: ". . . what I have written until now aroused strong opposition. . . . Symbolism has no place in Soviet Russia, and as you know, I am and always have been a symbolist. . . . Here one has to turn one's soul upside down."

Translation of classics served as both escape and means of livelihood. Shakespeare, Goethe, Pushkin, Lermontov, Judah Halevi—putting them into Yiddish gave writers relief, pleasure and bread. But as the ghastly Thirties came to an end, there could be no escape. In 1937, the poet Charik was accused of the deadliest of sins: Trotskyism. Nor did it help that a bit earlier he had written "My dog, if I called him Trotsky or Zinoviev, would not cease howling with shame." Even Feffer came under attack for "Trotskyist-nationalist deviations" and for having published a poem in 1925 which praised Trotsky. In the late Thirties, Kulbak and Charik disappeared into prisons or camps from which they never would be freed; Axelrod died in prison; the critics Erik, Litvakov, Abtshuk, Bronstein (the last two only yesterday among the fiercest exponents of orthodoxy) were put to death. This was the first major stroke of physical terror against the Yiddish writers; it was not the last.

III

It may be worth pausing for a moment to ask ourselves: did the Yiddish writers suffer greater burdens than writers in other languages who also lived through the Stalin years? If so, why, and in what ways?

The mere fact of being Jewish made a good many of the writers feel uneasy. They might compose agit-prop verse or stuff their novels with uplifting Bolshevik sentiments, but memories of what Jews had suffered in old Russia and fears of what they might yet suffer in the new Russia could never be shaken off. The mere fact, too, of writing in Yiddish, a language notoriously entangled with national and religious traditions, was cause for nervousness. During the 1930's and 1940's, Yiddish literature, as Elias Shulman has noted, "became the only means of expression open to Jews" in the Soviet Union, at least insofar as they continued to think of themselves as Jews. Into their poems, novels, stories and plays, the Yiddish writers packed, or hid, all the intellectual pressures, moral quandaries, nerve-shattering anxieties and inescapable betrayals of the time. No literature could easily bear this, and an unfree literature least of all. Yiddish writers had to keep looking over their shoulders not only with the fear every other writer in the Soviet Union sooner or later felt; they also found themselves responding to the cultural authorities with the deep-rooted habits of an oppressed people. Yiddish critics had to be sure that not only did they hew to the party line but that as Jews they showed a little extra zeal, proof of caring more about "socialist realism" than about the writers who had been their friends for decades. It was an atmosphere that made for distrust, paranoia, and, sometimes, betrayal.

Special demands were made upon the Yiddish writers. In reality, they were being asked to yield their souls, abandon their being. Older writers like Halkin, Der Nister, and Hofstein felt emotional ties with the *shtetl* milieu, still more so with that complexity and pluralism of outlook which had flourished in Yiddish culture during the pre-Stalinist years. Even if they now turned their backs on traditional Jewish life, even if they kept hammering away at its social injustices,° their work was still imbued with its imagery, styles, feelings. Halkin wrote a clever poem, "The New Born," which spoke about the burgeoning Soviet Yiddish culture in a way that probably reflected the feelings of a whole generation:

> Let our newborn child be blessed.
> May it take in with mother's milk
> A thirst for bringing light to all mankind,
> Light that will also shine for us.
> But when it will discover a new star in the world,
> At least let not things grow darker for its own people.

° But what was new about that? Yiddish literature, starting with Mendele, is filled with harsh criticism of the social injustices Jews had to suffer in *shtetl* and city.

Some younger Yiddish writers saw themselves as far more militant; saw themselves as Soviet poets who "happened" to write in Yiddish because that was the language they "happened" to know, rather than as Yiddish writers emerging from the depths of Jewish life who had made a pledge to Soviet society. With the mounting terror of the Stalin years, only the strictest "proletarian" writers—and soon enough, not even they—escaped the blows of the Yiddish commissars who in every sentence found evidence of a tainted nostalgia for the old world, ties of emotion with the Jewish past, a failure to apply the "methodology of class struggle" to the life of the *shtetl*. Yet the truth is that this life had been so intertwined with Yiddish, it was almost impossible to write anything in that language without sooner or later employing Hasidic sayings, folk proverbs, and the imagery of religious belief.

Yiddish was suspect, inherently suspect. It contains, of course, a large component of Hebrew words, and to the commissars, not all of them Russian, this raised the spectre of heresy. But while the campaign against the Hebrew component was presented as a cleaning-out of clerical remains, in actuality it formed a kind of death warrant for the Yiddish language—not just a cutting off from vital sources, but a destruction of the very culture in which it had arisen. For, among the Eastern European Jews, religion had not been something that could be neatly separated from the rest of their lives; it had been entirely interwoven with daily speech and manners, with the ways people thought, felt, spoke. The secularist Yiddish writers knew, of course, that their language overflowed with references and metaphors of the faith they had abandoned. Where Yiddish literature flourished in freedom, or relative freedom, this fact was simply accepted as a "given"—you could not undo history. But in the Soviet Union, the campaign against Hebraisms led to a crippling of both language and literature.

Finally, there was another, perhaps more urgent reason for the suspicion that Yiddish aroused among the Stalinist authorities. Yiddish is an international language, part of an international culture. To write in that language is necessarily to be in touch with writers throughout the world. Despite the isolation to which they were subjected during the 1930's and 1940's, the Yiddish writers in the Soviet Union could not help being aware of developments among other Yiddish writers in Warsaw, Paris, Buenos Aires, and New York. They could not help knowing something about the energy and experimentation of Yiddish writing abroad. Almost unknowingly, the Yiddish writers in the Soviet Union were influenced by the work of, say, Leivick and I. J. Singer, even if they chose consciously to deny those influences.

During the 1920's, the Yiddish writers who had gone into exile had met or entered relations with colleagues from the West; Hofstein had come to know modern Hebrew writers in Palestine. Even now, despite the obligatory polemics against "bourgeois Yiddishists," they must have felt some kinship. Did not the mere fact that Bergelson and Der Nister shared a language—but more, a culture—with Mani Leib and Leivick create the grounds for heresy?

So, in a sense, the Communist *apparachniks* were right. Feffer might write

> When I mention Stalin—I mean beauty,
> I mean eternal happiness,
> I mean nevermore to know,
> Nevermore to know of pain.

Litvakov might try desperately to follow each twist and turn of the party's cultural edicts. But the very fact of being a Yiddish writer signified heresy and evoked suspicion. Not that the Yiddish writers were especially rebellious; far from it. It was simply that a literature extending backward to religious particularism and forward to cultural universalism was hardly the best stuff from which to forge a totalitarian mentality.

IV

A reprieve of sorts came to Yiddish literature with the Second World War. In response to the horrors of Nazism, and because the Soviet regime now allowed, indeed, encouraged the release of national sentiments in order to rally support for the war, the Yiddish writers felt freer to express again their Jewishness. Markish wrote long poems full of patriotic fervor; Der Nister, stories about victims of the Holocaust in Poland (it was easier to show traditional Jewish feelings if they were located beyond Soviet borders); Halkin, a play about the Warsaw Ghetto Uprising in which something like the full range of Jewish sentiment could be portrayed. Even Feffer produced a highpitched poem called "Shadows of the Warsaw Ghetto," and still more remarkable, a poem printed in the journal, *Eynigkeyt*, in December, 1942, and entitled "I Am a Jew." This was an astonishing outcry, as if a longtime convert to the gentiles had suddenly discovered an essential Jewishness within himself. Feffer spoke of "my people," identified with a range of traditional Jewish figures such as Bar Kokhba, recalled fondly "Heine's crooked smile," and ended each stanza thumpingly: "I am a Jew." (The poem was enormously popular among Soviet Yiddish readers, but while included in collections of Feffer's work abroad, it never appeared in his later volumes printed in the Soviet Union—by then the political climate had again changed.) Yiddish writers were active as war time journalists. One of them, Aaron Kushnirov, though over fifty, went to fight on the front; he survived the war, his son was killed. A Jewish Anti-Fascist Committee was organized, with the actor Mikhoels as chairman; this group reestablished ties with Jewish communities abroad, Feffer and Mikhoels touring the United States for support in the war against Hitler.

It is not easy to form a summary judgment of the work done by the Yiddish writers during the war years. At the very least, it seems utterly sincere in its hatred of Hitlerism and identification with the victims of the Nazis. Long-suppressed Jewish sentiments could now be brought into the open, especially if linked with praise for the Soviet regime. But this did not necessarily make for distinguished work. The earlier individuality of these writers, even their eccentricities, had been crushed; they had fallen behind the Yiddish writers of the West in technical and thematic sophistication; their work during these years, if not quite cut to measure, still must often seem crude, stilted, simplistic. The creative impulse is not a spigot that can be turned on and off by decree of the state.

During the war years and those immediately afterward, the situation of the Yiddish writers was often painful, always troubling. The more successful among them lived on the lower levels of the materially privileged Soviet elite—privileged at least by comparison with most Soviet citizens. Spiritually, however, the Yiddish writers felt increasingly isolated. They were isolated not only from Western culture and the Yiddish writers living in the West, but also from the Russian literary world. In the 1920s, some of the free-spirited and experimental Russian writers had befriended their Yiddish colleagues, but now the dominant Russian literary figures, usually conformist hacks, cultivated a provincial outlook. So the Yiddish writers lived in a kind of limbo, inwardly always ill at ease even if sometimes materially comfortable.

Their isolation led them to see Western society not as it had developed over the decades for both better and worse, but as it had congealed in Bolshevik dogma. It was not so much that the Yiddish writers believed the Soviet propaganda; it was that, in order to maintain a bit of dignity and hope, they *had* to believe that if things were bad at home, they were still worse abroad. Worse spiritually and culturally, if not materially.

Did they still believe in Communism, those, at least, who had ever believed? There is no easy way to know. There is no easy way to probe inner thoughts, or words kept only for the dark of night, or words never spoken at all. Transport the Yiddish writers to the West and they would probably sigh with relief; but since they were clearly going to spend the rest of their lives in the Soviet Union, they sought rationales for saying what they had to say.

Yiddish writers from other European countries, arriving in Russia as wartime refugees, would meet and become friendly with Bergelson and Markish, Hofstein and Halkin. To these "petty-bourgeois" colleagues the Soviet Yiddish writers were often very generous: the bonds of language and all that language embodied were still strong. In talking to the refugees, the Soviet Yiddish writers would repeat the official party line, more, perhaps, to convince themselves than anyone else. In rare nighttime conversations, some would let out a groan of Jewish yearning. But they were trapped and they knew it. Not even the solace of evasion, or the balm of silence, was within their reach. To survive they had to keep speaking and writing as they were bidden, and hope that within these limits some fragment of their talent might yet show itself.

The end is terrible. In January, 1948, the actor Mikhoels is murdered by the secret police. A campaign begun by the Soviet regime, under the cultural dictation of Zhdanov, turns once more against "manifestations of nationalism" in literature and, with still

more sinister overtones, against "cosmopolitanism." The writer
Kipnis is forced publicly to confess his errors: he had written about
his pleasure in hearing Yiddish spoken in Europe. Hofstein writes a
poem that includes a traditional Hebrew phrase, "For learning issues
from Zion," and for this he is mercilessly attacked. At a public
gathering called to denounce the heresies of Yiddish writers,
Kushnirov is called upon to speak, but upon reaching the platform is
struck dumb: his lips move, no words come.

   In the late 1940's, all Yiddish publications are closed down. The
Jewish Anti-Fascist Committee is dissolved. Scores of Yiddish
writers—the historian Elias Shulman estimates some 500—are sent to
concentration camps, where many of them, no longer young, meet
death. Der Nister dies in prison. And on August 12, 1952, the secret
police execute a number of Yiddish writers—including Bergelson,
Markish, Hofstein, Kvitko, Feffer, and Shmuel Persov.

   Why? What could have driven the regime, even during the days
of Stalin's worst paranoia, to such terrible acts against men who
represented no danger, some of whom had long been broken in
spirit? We turn again to the historian of Soviet Yiddish literature,
Khone Shmeruk:

> One wishes to find some crumb of logic even among these fantastic
> and heavy-handed crimes. There is no doubt that an important role
> was played by the deep-rooted anti-Semitism which revived during
> and after the war, and the warm feelings that Soviet Jews expressed
> toward the state of Israel at its very founding. The fatal mistake of
> Soviet Yiddish writers apparently consisted in forgetting the lessons of
> the Thirties, and assuming that the temporary liberalization of the
> war years was an enduring condition that allowed them to express
> their Jewish national feelings somewhat more freely.... As bearers
> and representatives of a "dangerous regression," they had to be
> silenced in the most effective manner....

   About the writers themselves in the last years we know a little.°
Some behaved with courage, one or two with deceit. In 1951, the
Yiddish literary critic S. Niger published an article in which he

---

° A memoir literature is accumulating in Yiddish, scattered in various journals
published in the United States, Israel, and the Soviet Union. The reader confined to
English will find a vivid and stirring portrait of the murdered writers in Chaim
Grade's "Elegy for the Soviet Yiddish Writers," translated by Cynthia Ozick, in our
anthology, A Treasury of Yiddish Poetry. Grade, a Yiddish writer raised in Vilna, lived

compared the Yiddish writers of the Soviet Union with the Marranos, those forced converts to Christianity during the time of the Spanish Inquisition who tried to remain secret Jews. Niger repeated a story told by a Yiddish writer who met Aaron Kushnirov in Vilna in 1944. Seeing a pile of Yiddish books that had been rescued by Jewish partisans, Kushnirov surprisingly asked for a Bible, but one with a Yiddish translation, so that he could follow it. He said that he was working "for himself alone" or as we would say "for the drawer," on a poem about the Sabbatai Sevi period: he was drawn back, this Red Army captain, to old Jewish themes. There were also rumors, more difficult to believe, that Bergelson had turned to religious interests—this lifelong skeptic in whom no faith, apparently, could remain unqualified. And hardest to believe—but what in our century cannot be believed?—is the recollection of a Soviet Yiddish writer, Abraham Kahn, that during the war years Feffer had taken to studying Hebrew in order to find his way through the Bible and the learned commentaries.

Toward the late 1950's, a few Yiddish books were again being published in the Soviet Union. A literary journal, *Sovetish heymland (Soviet Homeland)*, began to appear, printing some of the literary remains of the destroyed writers (a few were "rehabilitated") and the generally ashen work of the few dozen Yiddish writers who survived. No doubt, writings in Yiddish remain buried somewhere, in forgotten caches or the files of the secret police; others are lost forever. But it is all too late. An odor of death lingers over Yiddish in the Soviet Union. What Hitler had left undone, Stalin completed.

V

We have provided here some material about the historical circumstances of Yiddish literature during the Soviet era, but while these circumstances crucially affected the literature, they did not

---

in the Soviet Union during the Second World War and befriended the writers there. His poem starts with the memorable lines: "I weep for you with all the letters of the alphabet/ that made your hopeful songs."

In a novel by the Russian writer Lydia Chukovskaya, *Going Under*, there is a touching portrait of a Yiddish writer, perhaps based on Leib Kvitko, who knows that his days are numbered.

fully determine its nature. Even in the worst moments, strands of individual sensibility and personal talent could be detected. Even under the most brutal repressions, lines of continuity with traditional Yiddish writing and of connection with modern Yiddish poetry and prose were flickeringly visible. To attempt a comprehensive critical description of Yiddish literature in the Soviet Union these past fifty or sixty years would be beyond both our powers and the scope of this essay. But it may be of some use to say a few words about the fictions translated in this book, as well as their authors. Apart from helping readers make their way into works likely to contain some points of unfamiliarity, this may also cast a ray or two of light on the literature as a whole.

David Bergelson (1884–1952) is one of the three or four most important figures in Soviet Yiddish writing: prolific, gifted, an intelligent and self-conscious artist. In all his novels and stories, but especially the earlier ones composed in conditions of relative freedom, he brings to bear a sensibility threaded with both modernist skepticism and a sardonic Yiddish irony that recalls Mendele Mocher Sforim.

Bergelson is a superb stylist. His Yiddish has been freed of the fatty bombast and tinkling folksiness which afflict a good many writers in that language. His style is refined and nuanced, even when dealing with coarse figures or situations—even, say, when writing about the stagnation of *shtetl* life, the vulgarity of arriviste merchants, the decay of religious feeling. Rich in impressionistic pictorial effects, subtle in cadence, and severe in structure, Bergelson's prose helped to make Yiddish into a fluent literary medium.

In his early work—novels like *Arum vokzal (At the Depot)*, 1909, and *Noch alemen (When All Is Said and Done)*, 1913—he evokes moods of tedium, aimlessness, drifting: what might be called the passions of weariness that overcame the Yiddish-speaking intelligentsia, or at least the politically oriented portions of it, during the years after the failed 1905 Revolution. Bergelson is a master at depicting the break-up of the old Jewish ways, the greenness and confusions of the emerging secular intelligentsia. Comparisons with Chekhov and Turgenev are inevitable and, at least if we confine ourselves to the relation between a provincial culture and its aspiring writers, there is even a limited comparison to be made with

Faulkner. In short novels like *Joseph Schur* (1913) and *In a Backwoods Town* (1914)—the former appears on p. 29 of this book, the latter in *A Treasury of Yiddish Stories*—there hangs over action and characters a languid, somnolent atmosphere, the atmosphere of moral twilight. Some of the leading characters have been touched by urban manners yet cannot enter the urban world; they slide back, in their sloth or avarice, to the crumbling *shtetl*, there to rot and talk and dream away their lives. A few do break away: they go, so to say, to Moscow. Bergelson's major figures are marked by what his colleague Jacob Sternberg calls "a Jewish Hamletism, feeling themselves superfluous both in their own world and in the surrounding world. . . ." In many of these novels and stories, like a leitmotif in a minor key, there keeps recurring a phrase or sentence spoken by the central character: "the world is so much muck," in *In a Backwoods Town;* "the hole through which life slips," in the story of the same name (see p. 74).

Joseph Schur is a finely wrought fiction dealing with pre-revolutionary life among the Russian Jews. Mild yet taut, repelled both by the disintegrating Jewish past and the grubby Russian present, the voice that narrates the story is clearly that of a sophisticated mind. There is a good deal of stylized repetition, a refusal of mere noisy bustle, and a strong reliance on rhythmic effects to communicate the story's vision. The central figure, a distracted son of wealthy merchants, does not even appear until the fourth section of the story. Before that we see the old Jewish milieu, its figures going through their traditional motions but without the traditional self-assurance. When Schur takes over the narrative, the *shtetl* characters drop away, and through his eyes we encounter "new" Jews: a harassed, wealthy merchant, young artists and writers, independent young women. Schur is drawn to them, he hardly knows why; but they ignore or rebuff him and then, his matrimonial hopes disappointed, he returns to his small-town sloth.

Both in *Joseph Schur* and *Civil War* (see p. 84), Bergelson has worked out a narrative technique of considerable originality, what might be called the "relay method" of narration. The central or inner action of the story is a movement of history as it looms behind and weaves through the lives of the characters. Individual figures count mainly as they are swept along for a moment by an historical current, or are stranded in historical eddies. A figure will carry the narrative a part of the way, seeming to be emblematic of a phase of Jewish experience, and then drop out, his future undisclosed, while he hands on the action to another character. "Loose ends" are often left as they are.

Joseph Schur himself is present through most of the story but, unable to act, is acted upon. He serves mainly as a somewhat torpid but by no means foolish observer, watching the "relay" of Jewish figures move past his life, from old-fashioned matchmakers writing florid Hebrew to modern artists chattering in a parlor. He is there, but as an enfeebled contrast to the movement of historical progress or historical retrogression. (Bergelson is hardly certain which it is: perhaps both.) In this mode of narrative, the characters are secondary to, temporary enablers of, the twisting course of action. On some level, all of this may follow from a Marxist perception of the relation between individual and society, but it surely has its roots deeper in Bergelson's own experience, in his sense that he is a latecomer in relation to the traditional Jewish past while too much of an outsider in relation to the revolutionary future.

The tone of futility, doubt, and weariness comes through again in the story, "The Hole Through Which Life Slips," where the balance between activity and withdrawal, energy and retreat is so fine that one cannot be certain, as perhaps Bergelson himself was not certain, where his sympathies lie. As for *Civil War,* a powerful and enigmatic novella published in 1927, Bergelson is clearly trying to whip up a certain enthusiasm for the revolutionary idea, perhaps trying to whip up an enthusiasm that he partly feels; yet what finally strikes the reader a half century later is the depth of his skepticism, distancing, and questioning. There are patches of verbal impasto in *Civil War,* flares of rhetoric, which may be a sign of Bergelson's straining to transform himself into a writer of positive belief; but these can also be seen as tokens of the chaos which is the single strongest impression left by the novella. (Some of its specific circumstances are elucidated in a note on p. 84.)

After his return to Russia in 1933, Bergelson tried to produce the kind of uplifting portraits of Jewish life that were required by the Soviet regime. Many of these are characterized by the technical finish intrinsic to his work: a first-rate writer can do well what he knows in his heart he should not do at all. Yet these works do not exude inner conviction, certainly not with the strength that his earlier fiction does. Two volumes of an unfinished trilogy, *Baym Dniepr*, deal with the pre-revolutionary period, juxtaposing the required ideology in which Bergelson partly acquiesces and his own brooding sense of human loneliness and division.

Examples of Bergelson's, or anyone else's, enforced "agit-prop" writing do not appear in this book. It has seemed pointless to waste space by printing what Yiddish writers had to compose during the worst years of the Stalinist period—these should be familiar enough to anyone who has read equivalents in other languages. And there are some things it is better to leave in the past.

The highly gifted poet and novelist Moshe Kulbak (1896–1940) was born near Vilna, the son of a lumber dealer; some of his most vivid poems evoke the rough life of Jewish woodcutters and farmers. Kulbak studied at various yeshivas; he went in 1920 to Berlin, living in severe poverty but absorbing the excitement of postwar German life; three years later he returned to Vilna, becoming a teacher of Yiddish; and then, in 1926, apparently out of genuine idealism, he moved to the Soviet Union, declaring himself a Soviet Yiddish writer. Until about 1936 Kulbak published widely, both in prose and verse, but always with a personal tone bound to irritate the authorities. His poetry carries a heavy sense of the Jewish past, as in his long poem *Vilna,*

> You are a dark amulet set in Lithuania.
> Old gray writing—mossy, peeling.
> Each stone a book; parchment every wall.
> Pages turn, secretly open in the night,
> As, on the old synagogue, a frozen water carrier,
> Small beard tilted, stands counting the stars.
>
> *Translated by Nathan Halper*

But there is also a sharply satirical feeling for modern chaos, as in his sequences about postwar Berlin, *Childe Harold.* None of this endeared him to the cultural oxen ruling the Soviet scene.

When Kulbak's novel *Zelmenyaner* appeared in 1931, S. Niger, writing in New York, praised the book highly while noticing again that it was not a work likely to be accepted "with open arms" in the Soviet Union. "It is hard [for the party-liners] to rely on him. He is too intelligent. . . . He tries with all his creative powers 'to serve the revolution . . .' but the so-called proletarian critics are correct in not rushing to accept him. . . . Kulbak strives honestly to 'orient himself' toward Minsk [then the center of the 'proletarian' Yiddish critics] . . . yet there remains about him an aroma of Vilna [then the center of traditional Jewish learning and Yiddish culture]. It is not his fault."

Isaac Babel, the great Russian writer who was "liquidated" at about the same time as Kulbak, once spoke at a meeting of Soviet writers in behalf of "the right to write badly." What he did not say must surely have been clear to all his fellow writers: without the right to write badly it is impossible to write well. Kulbak, in his *Zelmenyaner*, seems tacitly to be pleading for, or perhaps celebrating, something equally precious: the right to live oddly. Oddly means here living in accord with ingrained ways, justifiable by nothing but the heart's desire, and thereby without any need for social rationale.

All those delicious, eccentric uncles in *Zelmenyaner* are rooted in a tradition—a decidedly "backward" one—which in Kulbak's view reveals its full strength only at the point of its going. And the sons of these uncles, good solid Bolsheviks, are eccentrics too, for like it or not the Zelmenyaner heritage has burned itself into their souls. They are full of the family's stubbornness and passion, akin to their fathers in character if painfully different in custom. As for opinion, there Kulbak fudges a trifle, or has to fudge. He tries to show the older generation slowly edging into "the new world," something that is no doubt possible but not, even within the limits of what he has portrayed, very persuasive. Yet one can readily imagine the pressures that led Kulbak to do this. And he is artist enough to show that even those of the older generation who group themselves hesitantly under the red flag still wonder why the Bolsheviks fail to appreciate, or at least respect, their religion.

Still, at close to the surface of their consciousness, they realize they are doomed, though they don't quite know why. After all, they are not rich or religious Jews; they are workers for whom Jewishness has gone deeper than mere belief, indeed, formed the very substance of their lives. And they try to think, to keep their minds open, at least as much as they can bear to. In a quizzical, uneasy sort of way they are even somewhat proud of their Bolshevik children, in whom they see oddly shaped versions of themselves. These younger Zelmenyaner, having something of the family toughness in them, will not easily bend to the forthcoming Bolshevik orthodoxies.

What is so lovely about Kulbak's treatment is the delicate balance, the mixture of humor and good feeling. He laughs at all of them but loves them too; they are his friends. History may be on the side of the young ones, the modernized sons and daughters bristling with slogans and electrification, but the heart finds virtues of character in the older ones. If, as Scott Fitzgerald once said, the mark of a first-rate intelligence is its ability to hold two ideas in the mind at once, surely that is one reason for the pleasure Kulbak's fiction yields. In its playfulness, its kindliness, its delight in the absurdities of what we are, *Zelmenyaner* was not the sort of fiction that could readily thrive in the Russia of the party-state dictatorship.

With Der Nister (1884–1950) we come to a Yiddish writer of rare distinctiveness, perhaps uniqueness. Profoundly drawn to the roots of Jewish pietism, both Hasidic and Kabbalistic, he produced symbolic fictions quite justifying his pen name, the Hidden One: fictions secretive, subterranean, symbolic. Behind his work there hover stories and parables, commentaries and maxims from the Jewish past, all devoted to elucidating the unknown, illuminating the invisible. Together with this strand of the darkly esoteric there is a lively feeling for the folk experience of the Eastern European Jews and a certain kinship with the methods of modernist symbolism, apparently the result of an absorption with recent Russian literature. Past and future come together in Der Nister, bridging or eradicating the nineteenth century realism which forms a major component of Yiddish literature. Reading some of Der Nister's symbolic stories, one might be tempted to compare him with Kafka—perhaps more because of a glimpsed community of sources and traditions than a similarity of method.° In any case, though hardly a writer for the populace, Der Nister is an original figure, serious and pure-spirited.

The kind of response he evoked in the Russia of the 1920's and

---

° Anyone comparing Der Nister's "Under a Fence" with Kafka's "A Hunger Artist" will be struck by similarities in outlook, tone, and even references (the circus, etc.) We do not know whether Der Nister was familiar with Kafka's work; it is possible that during his stay in Germany he learned about Kafka from writers he encountered there.

1930's can easily be imagined. By the late Twenties he had ceased publishing symbolist fiction entirely; in the early Thirties, to feed his family, he turned to reportage; in the late Thirties he made an astonishing turn by issuing the first volume of a large realistic novel, *The Family Mashber;* and during the war years he wrote some effective stories about Jewish martyrdom.

It seems clear, however, that Der Nister's most original and deeply felt work was that of his earlier years, and we have included in this volume a story called "Under a Fence," first published in 1929, which is notable in its own right as a symbolist fiction, and also as an oblique but dramatic comment on the situation of Yiddish writers under the Communist dictatorship. A note preceding the story offers a few remarks about its possible implications.

In this volume, we have barely touched the resources and range of Yiddish writing in the Soviet Union over the past half century, and it bears repeating that we make no claim to providing a comprehensive selection. That would require a much larger book. By now it would be foolhardy, and mere rhetoric, to speak of justice being done to the Soviet Yiddish writers—there are situations beyond reclamation or even retribution. At the least, we may try to preserve their work and remember their fate.

≈ *Joseph Schur*

BY DAVID BERGELSON

I

AT THE BEGINNING of spring, the Talmud teacher Jacob Nathan Viderpoller of Great Setternitz wrote a letter in Hebrew to Mokher-Tov of Brashek "inquiring whether my kind friend will be good enough to write to me in such detail as he can whatever he knows about Joshua Heschel's son-in-law, Moishele Levine who died a year ago—the same Moishele Levine who, together with Joshua Heschel's rich son, inherited the immense sugar factory in Brashek. I know, of course, that my honored friend Mokher-Tov was an intimate of Moishele Levine's household, and yet I believe, dear sir, that I can count on you not to mislead me but to tell me frankly and sincerely all that you know."

Some two weeks later, there came a letter in reply, also in Hebrew, and written in a tiny script. The whole first part of this letter was devoted to the salutation and much of the rest of it was composed in the pompous style of Rab-Shakeh,° the Assyrian prince, haranguing the Jews from the walls of Jerusalem a couple of thousand years ago.

"Why should I not," asked Mokher-Tov, "tell you sincerely and frankly all that I know? Is it possible that I could conceal anything from my worthy friend? And what is there that one would wish to hide about a dearly beloved man who walked in the ways of truth and righteousness?"

The second part of the letter was proof that Mokher-Tov could employ all the skills of secular learning while writing in the holy tongue. One caught glimpses in it not only of Moishe Levine's life, but of Moishe Levine's face itself—its fair features; of his blond beard

° 2 Kings 18:28

which grew, not from his cheeks downward, but in a narrow band between his neck and chin. The letter also described what Moishele Levine had looked like years ago when he was imported from abroad to be a son-in-law. In those days he had been considered an ornament to Talmudic learning and quite worthy of being a rabbi. But he only smiled at such notions, because his belief in Providence was curiously secular; and he had committed a number of the German poets to memory.

The letter went on to say that "he very quickly squandered his fortune, after which his wife began to lead him a quarrelsome life. They quarreled because of the money and not, God forbid (as was rumored) because she was still grieving for her girlhood lover in Riga. At that time, Joshua Heschel of Brisk was still living—a vigorous, generous father who loved to do things spontaneously and on a grand scale. He gave his son-in-law, Moishele Levine, a second dowry and built him a luxurious house near the sugar factory in Brashek where he settled him, making only one condition, that the dowry must be invested in the business, while any sums Levine would need for expenses would come from the sugar factory's daily flow of cash."

Mokher-Tov's letter reached Jacob Nathan around Passover, when Jacob Nathan had a good deal of free time. He wrote a second, longer letter to Mokher-Tov in which he expressed himself, at length, as being amazed. "My friend Mokher-Tov," he wrote, "perplexes me. He is regarded by all the world as a greatly learned man. Surely he knows that our sages have written, 'A word to the wise is sufficient.' Then how does it happen that Mokher-Tov, missing the whole intent of my letter, fails to write so much as a word about Moishele Levine's only daughter about whom I have certain serious concerns?"

This letter received no reply. Clearly, the learned Mokher-Tov was nobody's fool. It was one thing to honor Jacob Nathan, on whom all the gentry of Great Setternitz fawned, with an ornate letter written in the holy tongue, but it was quite another to take Jacob Nathan's "serious concerns" seriously. Nor, evidently, did he feel obliged to gossip over the affairs of a family with which he had been on intimate terms for many years. Rebuffed, Jacob Nathan held his peace.

During the middle days of Passover, when the weather was warm and dry, Jacob Nathan obeyed a sudden impulse to pay a visit to the Hasidic Rabbi of Skvir with whom, he said, he had various matters to discuss. Before leaving, he argued the absurdity of making the trip to Skvir by train. "Anyone who does not travel from Great Setternitz to Skvir by horse and wagon is simply out of his head, because the train makes endless detours all over the landscape."

The road to Skvir, winding south from the hilly, prosperous town of Great Setternitz, turns quickly ill-kept and overgrown. Dreary, dilapidated, it crosses the railroad tracks, then winds for a while among the three cobbled streets that carry the cheerful bustle of the town away in all directions; after which it descends, like an impoverished man, into the valley past the ruins of a brick factory huddled amid heaps of bones of such dogs as have been shot there or that simply came to die. Later, the road is joined on both sides by the endless sameness of the fields—the broad, gray-green, dry fields of the steppe expanding outward, perpetually ready to swear that if perfect silence was to be found in the world it would be near *that* solitary tree bending over a well at the horizon's edge.

A wagon driver from Great Setternitz took Jacob Nathan the first thirty versts along this road until they came to Kozlov, that dismal, God-forsaken town that stood with its back forever turned to the mined clay pits on the mountain behind it; forever waiting for the Sabbath, or a Monday fair, or the coming of the Messiah.

From Kozlov, he rode on to the larger, more prosperous town of Brashek that boasted, among other things, a sugar factory, a water mill, and a Polish church. Since it was nearly noon when he arrived in Brashek, and since there was no wagon driver from Skvir to be found, and because Mokher-Tov had been called away from home that morning, Jacob Nathan made his way to the only decent inn in the town which, as it was owned by Mokher-Tov, was known in the neighborhood as "Mokher-Tov's Inn."

He ordered a substantial lunch and treated himself, when it came, to a generous Passover measure of wine. His meal done, he prepared himself expansively for an afternoon nap, as if he were paying for everything with the proceeds of years of coupon-clipping rather than with the charitable twenty-five ruble notes he had "touched" various of his wealthy patrons for in Great Setternitz before leaving that town.

As he was saying his after-meal prayers there developed a silent interplay between the middle-aged, broad-shouldered Jacob Nathan and Mokher-Tov's niece, who was clearing the dishes from the table. Each time she felt his dark, burning eyes on her, she experienced a strange chill at her heart. Surely, there was something wrong with him, this Jew with the carefully combed black beard and the fine Hasidic garb. And yet, she found herself coming frequently into the room—again and again until she assured herself she had been mistaken, that her dark suspicions were unfounded.

Later, before his nap, Jacob Nathan lay on the couch, a strong-smelling cigarette in his mouth and thought how fine the day was— warm and bright. Almost a summer's day. And thought too how both Brashek and Kozlov had declined in recent years. There was not left a single disciple of the Rabbi of Skvir whose home one could visit. As an instance, he recalled how some years ago Hayyimel Weintraub had left Kozlov for Palestine. His fine whitewashed house had been bought by some sort of wealthy grocer; and Weintraub's blond, moody son, the one who once ran away from home, was now, it was said, a famous painter in Paris or in Berlin. And here in Brashek, Joshua Heschel's children had rebuilt the inherited sugar factory and packed it with secular Jews—bookkeepers and engineers.

Reminiscing, he smoked his cigarette down to its stub, then rolled over on his side. The glass of strong wine together with his previous night's restlessness demanded the sleep to which he now yielded himself.

Sound asleep though he was, he could not shake the feeling that somewhere outside the thin-walled, curtained room, important events were taking place. One would have sworn that all of Brashek was celebrating a wedding—a strangely elaborate and wealthy wedding; but a couple of hours later, when he started from his nap, Brashek was as quiet as always. Nothing had happened in the interval except that Mokher-Tov, driving his son's horse and wagon, had returned from visiting a land owner for whose timber he had found a buyer. It was the wagon wheels clattering over the old boards of the entryway that had disturbed Jacob Nathan's sleep; and it was the sound of Mokher-Tov knocking at his door which, later, Jacob Nathan heard in his sleep as the beating of a drum.

When Mokher-Tov returned home and learned from his wife who it was that was staying in room number three, he blew the dust off his peaked cap and stroked his dark gray beard which grew so thickly at the neck that he wore it tucked under his collar to make it seem shorter. "So ... so ... Jacob Nathan Viderpoller," he said cheerfully, then toyed with his coat buttons and smiled to himself. Mokher-Tov was inclined to be friendly. Once, when a young couple in Brashek who had fallen in love came to him for help, he went to their parents and lectured them at length on the number of holy precedents there were for falling in love, citing romantic tales from the Bible—"And Jacob loved Rachel"—as well as quotations from Ibn Ezra. He had known Jacob Nathan in Great Setternitz where he, Mokher-Tov, had owned a hardware store and thereby had become acquainted with the prosperous Jews of that town. There it was well known that Jacob Nathan, perhaps some eight years before coming to Great Setternitz, had deserted a wife in a village somewhere to whom he never sent so much as a penny for support. Yet he was treated with respect in Great Setternitz and was a familiar figure who went from one wealthy Jewish home to another giving lessons in Talmud. Those rich Jews showered Jacob Nathan with gifts: sometimes twenty-five ruble notes, sometimes a handsome traveling bag from abroad, sometimes a fine silver cigarette case. Their justification for these presents was always that Jacob Nathan was a learned man, and as proof they cited the story of the great Talmudic scholar who, when translating the Talmud into Russian, could not make a move without consulting Jacob Nathan about the difficult passages.

Mokher-Tov smiled at his wife's innocence regarding Jacob Nathan. She seemed not to know that Jacob Nathan had remained a disciple of the Rabbi of Skvir simply to spite the world's opinion; and she actually believed that Jacob Nathan was on a journey to visit the Rabbi. Mokher-Tov flattered himself that he knew the true purpose of Jacob Nathan's travels as well as his reason for stopping at their inn. Nevertheless, Mokher-Tov, as he toyed with his coat buttons, resolved to be as gracious to his visitor as he usually was to his more important guests.

Jacob Nathan, his face freshly washed, was pouring himself tea from the boiling samovar on the table when he answered Mokher-Tov's knock at his door. "Ah ... Mokher-Tov," he said, as if surprised to see a visitor in his room. "My learned friend, Mokher-Tov."

Mokher-Tov bowed politely, then bowed again as he extended his hand and said, "And how are you?"

"Fair ... fair...." One would have thought from his genteel bearing and from the way he stood slightly bent and attentive, that it was Jacob Nathan who had for years been the host in this place and that Mokher-Tov was no more than a casual visitor. And indeed, Mokher-Tov was momentarily so disconcerted by Jacob Nathan, this Jew on whom the wealthy Great Setternitz families fawned, that he failed to understand Jacob Nathan's first sentences—though he grasped that they all began with the stressed word *I* and that they were spoken by a man not easily interrupted.

"*I* recognized your Brashek at once. *I* said to myself, 'Brashek, with its new tiled roofs, always has the look of a town after a successful market day in which everyone has made money and all are happy.' "

Mokher-Tov heard a creaking sound coming from the cloth-covered table that held the samovar and winced at the misbehavior of the warped boards he had noticed yesterday. Then, something Jacob Nathan was saying reached him and he shook his head in gentle denial as he remembered certain charitable (and secret) projects of his own undertaken to help an unfortunate shoemaker and another indigent Jew in the town. As if he were apologizing for Brashek, he said, "Just the same, we do have ... poor folk in Brashek."

"Poor ... ha, ha ..." Jacob Nathan offered it as his opinion, of which he was not ashamed, that "poor" was a despicable word. Did not Mokher-Tov agree that it was formed of the ugliest letters in the alphabet? He, Jacob Nathan, preferred to talk of wealth. "Who are the wealthy folk in Brashek?" He leaned his head against the upholstered back of his chair and inhaled the strong-smelling smoke of a freshly lighted cigarette, demonstrating thereby first his contempt for the notion that rich folk were rare in Brashek, and second that he knew how to sit in an upholstered chair. When he gestured with the hand holding the cigarette, one could see how hairy it was inside its cuffless sleeve—like the hand of a *shochet* ° or a *dayyan* °° accepting a tendered question. As for rich folk, they hardly concerned him, though he was willing to say that in general only among the Jews were the wealthy so eager to become somebodies; "and that, among no other people did they so stubbornly remain nobodies as among us Jews. Ha . . . ha . . . ha . . ."

Mokher-Tov, embarrassed, lowered his eyes and shrugged his shoulders ambiguously. "As to that . . . that's as may be. I only meant to say . . . there are wealthy Jews . . . have always been Jews noted for their charity. The family Schur, in Great Setternitz, for example."

"Charitable people! No!" On this matter, Jacob Nathan was at swords drawn against the rest of the world. In his excitement, he seemed ready to leap from his chair and would not let Mokher-Tov speak. "*I* know about Jewish wealth. *I* was well acquainted with the grandfather of the Schurs of Great Setternitz." The grandfather, according to Jacob Nathan, was nothing more than a haughty old man, a fool, and illiterate to boot. He spent all his life imitating Joshua Heschel Rappaport of Brisk—the one who built the great sugar factories here in the neighborhood—imitating Rappaport even to the point of importing sons-in-law from abroad, and German governesses for his grandchildren. He imitated Rappaport's charities, too. And what of Joshua Heschel Rappaport—who was *he?* He would tell him. It would profit Mokher-Tov to know.

Mokher-Tov shook his head to indicate how much he disagreed and would have gone on to say something, but Jacob Nathan, out of all patience, would not let him begin.

Jacob Nathan took a long time venting his spleen against the rich families in the region who had any reputation at all. In his excitement, he managed finally to confuse the Rappaports with the Schurs. "They're all alike," he cried. "All."

° *shochet*—a ritual butcher.
°° *dayyan*—a rabbi charged with deciding questions of ritual cleanliness.

Mokher-Tov smiled and looked away. Clearly, there was a method to Jacob Nathan's diatribe; and he thought he could guess what purpose it was meant to serve. It seemed wiser, then, not to quarrel with him or to rub him the wrong way.

Later, as Mokher-Tov took polite leave of his guest, he found himself being detained by Jacob Nathan, who wished to confess that he did indeed have an ulterior motive for coming to Brashek. He begged leave to remind Mokher-Tov of a letter that he, Jacob Nathan, had written some time ago. "The long and the short of it is— what can you tell me about Moishele Levine's daughter?"

Jacob Nathan was puzzled by Mokher-tov's equanimity. He had expected a surprised response from that naive Jew. Instead, Mokher-tov replied in the even tone of a man answering a long expected question: "The daughter . . . of course . . . the daughter." He drew abstracted lines with his finger on the tablecloth. It would seem that images of the young woman and her family were passing before his lowered eyes; that Mokher-Tov was struggling to decide whether to speak of her or not. The uncertainty lasted a considerable while, then he said, "She is hardly twenty years old . . . and already there are romantic tales . . ." Then he added, with a smile, that he used the word "romantic" not in its usual simple sense; that he had read in a Hebrew book not long ago that the word "romance" did not need to mean only a work in which a man and a woman fell in love.

As he spoke, Mokher-Tov's voice drifted toward tenderness as if he were telling a tale of pious Jews of long ago and far away: "As all the world knows, the young woman's mother, Joshua Heschel's daughter, was married this *Lag b'Omer*° to that fellow from Riga, and lives with him there. The marriage distressed all of the Rappaports because the mother had not bothered to wait the usual year after her husband's death in order to remarry. So once again there was a love story to gossip about."

"Now, while there is some reason to raise the question of propriety, the matter itself, in my opinion, is quite simple: That fellow from Riga was rumored to be worth more than three million rubles—and was a bachelor into the bargain; while she who was equally rich was herself not quite thirty-nine years old. As for her

---

° *Lag b'Omer*—A holiday in the period between Passover and the festival of Shavuoth.

daughter . . . the whole thing affected her strangely. Very strangely."
Mokher-Tov stood thoughtfully for a while, then said, "To be
precise—the daughter had to leave the country."

Mokher-Tov went on to speak of the Rappaport family and of
how fond they all were of the young woman; he mentioned as well
her uncle Abraham, Joshua Heschel's older son, who lived in Kiev
and was also said to be very rich. He said, too, that the young woman
had come back from abroad just before Passover and that she was
staying—not in Brashek—but with her uncle Abraham's family in
Kiev.

Then Mokher-Tov was gone and Jacob Nathan was left alone in a
dark room heavy with the smell of many smoked cigarettes and
oppressed by the swirling presence of living and dead shadows.

Later, the door opened abruptly to reveal Mokher-Tov standing
in the deep gloom like one of the shadows. He begged Jacob
Nathan's pardon, but there was one thing more that needed to be
said. Again, he excused himself at great length, then came finally to
the point: "Not so long ago, there was a marriage broker here. Not
really a marriage broker—actually, he was a primary school teacher.
He came to propose Joseph Schur as a match for Moishele Levine's
daughter. That Joseph Schur who was the only son of Isaac Maier of
Great Setternitz. The Joseph Schur who, it was said, was descended
from the not quite respectable side of the Schur line and who, not
long ago, had inherited from his father a vast property that included
the sacking factory of Great Setternitz as well as its surrounding
houses.

"Now . . . God forbid that I should ever meddle in other people's
business. Still, I am an old friend of Moishele Levine's family. At the
same time, I happen to know that young Joseph Schur is a former
student of yours. And so, I want to say that if you, Jacob Nathan, are
toying with the same notion as that other matchmaker, then it is
wrong of you. Very wrong."

For one instant, Jacob Nathan found himself perplexed, even as it
struck him that this Jew, this Mokher-Tov, knew more about the
young woman than he would ever tell. Perhaps he knew whom she
went to see on her frequent visits abroad; but his perplexity gave
way at once to a rush of Viderpoller pride and he sneered at the
effort of that amateur matchmaker, the witless Brashek schoolmas-

ter, who had no notion how to go about his business. *"I,"* said Jacob Nathan, *"I* am on my way to Kiev. *I* will propose the match. *I,* Jacob Nathan Viderpoller."

II

Some time later, on one of the middle days of the Passover holiday, Jacob Nathan paced the platform of the small wooden railway station eight versts distance from Brashek as he waited for the train to Kiev. He was desperately bored. There had been nothing worth looking at inside the station; out on the bare, clean platform, there was a solitary passenger, a priest, pacing, like himself. Jacob Nathan yawned and looked the priest over indifferently as he passed by: a corpulent, dark fellow, wearing a double cassock. He had the clean look of a man who spends a great deal of every day washing and combing his hair. "And this they call a holy man, fit to be compared with a rabbi!" Jacob Nathan shrugged and felt pity for the non-Jewish world.

When the train came at last, Jacob Nathan found a place in a spacious, whitewashed car filled with secular, clean-shaven Jews of various ages—the sort one sees traveling from one large town to another. Jacob Nathan felt himself a stranger among them. For the most part, they sat in separate, shirt-sleeved groups, their teapots and their food spread out around them, and in cheerful conversation with a number of females who gave every indication that they were camp followers travelling constantly from market fair to market fair. The more he studied these Jews the more Jacob Nathan wondered at them. In this crowd of secular Jews eating forbidden breadstuffs in mid-Passover he, Jacob Nathan, was the only one dressed in pious black and wearing a silk hat. The only learned man among them. Jacob Nathan, though he exchanged small talk with them, could not help looking upon them as anomalies. It was as if one were to say of them, "Look. They have mouths. They speak Yiddish like everyone else."

Later, it developed that some of them came from Kiev and were familiar with the man on whose account Jacob Nathan had undertaken his mid-Passover journey. Abraham Rappaport, they said, was a Zionist who had large land holdings in Palestine; he owned sugar mills worth millions; and his only daughter, a hunchback, was a sculptress who studied in the Petersburg Academy.

"A hunchback? So." Jacob Nathan was sad to hear it.

He scratched an ear and considered all that he had been told: that Abraham Rappaport was a wealthy Zionist; that his daughter was a sculptress. Bad omens for his venture, since rich, freethinking Jews always made him uncomfortable. More uncomfortable even than true gentiles, born and bred.

The matter was indeed so worrisome that he wandered about Kiev for several days driven nearly out of his mind. He was staying at the home of a prosperous Hasid from Skvir to whom he confided that he "had a terrible burden to bear. To have conceived such an important notion; then to come all this distance on its account only to find that it was all likely to be for nothing. A terrible burden."

But three days later as he was standing among the East Wall ° benches of the local synagogue where he had gone to say his holiday prayers, he noticed a nickel plaque inscribed with the name "Abraham, son of Joshua Heschel Rappaport." He studied the plaque for a while, reading it over and over again. Then he inquired of an idler standing nearby whether the Abraham Rappaport of the plaque was the famous Rappaport of Kiev, and was pleased to learn that he was the very man. That, in fact, he occasionally came to this synagogue's services and that, no doubt, Abraham Rappaport's prayer shawl was in the keeping of the sexton there—the old Jew saying his prayers near the holy ark. Jacob Nathan further learned that Abraham Rappaport kept a kosher kitchen; that his father, Joshua Heschel, had, on his death bed, made his son swear that he would continue to maintain the family charities; and that he would wear a prayer shawl and phylacteries during his morning prayers. Altogether, it would appear that Abraham Rappaport had not turned entirely secular. For all anyone knew, he was still quite capable of delivering a handsome piece of Talmud commentary.

Later in the morning, Jacob Nathan joined a circle of Jews presided over by a wealthy congregant which was arguing the merits

° East Wall benches are usually held by the congregation's prosperous members.

of a Mishnaic commentary. Jacob Nathan very quickly showed them that their discussion was without merit since it was based on a corruption in the text which none of them had sufficient Hebrew to recognize. He was immediately treated with the greatest respect.

When, later, a toast was proposed to the health of the Rabbi of Great Setternitz, who was said to be gravely ill, Jacob Nathan had already become the dominant member of the group. He held the wineglass in his hand and, staring down a Jew who had interrupted him, he praised the Rabbi in the voice of a man speaking to the greatest potentates of the world: "*I*, he said, "*I* am the living witness that the Rabbi of Great Setternitz is a pious, learned, God-fearing man."

In the course of that same day, Jacob Nathan paid a visit to the Rappaport home where he learned that Abraham Rappaport, though he had returned to Russia from abroad, was delayed somewhere between Rovneh and Brisk visiting one of his sugar factories, but that he was expected home that night. Jacob Nathan breathed more easily, and began to believe that his project might yet prosper.

Leaving the Rappaport house, Jacob Nathan paused to appreciate the silent wealth of the street into which chauffeur-driven automobiles occasionally turned. Near Rappaport's gate, there stood a tall, uncouth looking Jew, a man with the forehead of an ape, a flattened nose and sparse, patchy, red hair on his face. "You're a Zionist preacher, too?" the man asked bleakly, speaking with a broad Lithuanian accent. It developed that he too had business with Rappaport, whose house he visited frequently without success. Jacob Nathan caught a whiff of the man's bad breath as he answered Jacob Nathan's questions in unwilling monosyllables. He stood buttoning and unbuttoning the short, worn topcoat that covered his still shabbier jacket; then, his eyes avoiding Jacob Nathan's, he grubbed about in his cigar case for a cigar, muttering that Abraham Rappaport was "Yes. A hard man to find. Yes."

On the last evening of the holiday, in Jacob Nathan's lodgings in the home of a prosperous Skvir Hasid, one of the Hasid's relatives, a clever, freethinking young man who worked in a local bank, came to visit. He was a bachelor who, finding himself suddenly with a free evening had, in desperation, chosen to squander his witticisms in his pious uncle's house. He took note of Jacob Nathan's interest in the

Rappaport family and of his desire to meet Abraham Rappaport. Abraham Rappaport, he said, would be attending a director's meeting at the bank the next day at twelve. "You'll recognize him at once. A man of medium build, slightly stooped, wearing a closely trimmed black beard."

Jacob Nathan turned his quick, dark eyes on the smiling young man. "A closely trimmed black beard?"

"Yes. And he has a receding hairline."

Later, when the young man's uncle left the room, the bank clerk entertained the other guests with a performance in which he mimicked the way Abraham Rappaport walked through the bank, moving slowly, hunched over as with fatigue, stealing away like one who is afraid of being recognized. While the other guests laughed, Jacob Nathan looked on with distaste.

Just the same, before he went to bed that night, he arranged with his host to be wakened at dawn the next morning.

III

On that same morning Abraham Rappaport woke earlier than usual. Slowly, his eyes took in the heavy furniture of his shaded, pleasant room. A gleam of light glancing from a mirrored door startled him, as did the sight of his wife sleeping in the bed next to him. Everything around him looked strange, as if the house had turned sullen and would not recognize its master who had been absent for two months.

Still tired and stiff from his late night arrival, Abraham Rappaport dressed slowly and went into his study where he raised the blinds. It was a damp, cool morning, so overcast that it promised to be a thoroughly dismal day. Nevertheless, Abraham Rappaport had important business to conclude. As was his habit lately, he delayed putting on his prayer shawl and phylacteries and skipped altogether the shorter form of recitation of his morning prayers. Instead, he paced the floor of his study and worried about the stock he had lately bought and forgotten about, which now pressed fearfully on his mind.

A servant girl came into the study and said something to him which, because he was so preoccupied, he failed to understand. "What . . . what?"

Later, in the electrically lighted bathroom to which the girl had summoned him, he found his barber waiting. There, sitting under the barber's hands, he felt that he was immersed in a curious glow of good feeling produced, perhaps, by the silence of the still sleeping household. Whatever the reason, the music of the scissors seemed to bring a genteel, pious message from the barber welcoming him home, acknowledging Rappaport's importance to the entire town and to the many people who were dependent on him.

Rappaport sat hunched over, dozing a little. Then he recalled that he had to be at the bank for a meeting with the director; and remembered at the same time the foreign professor with the long beard who sat listening to Abraham Rappaport read his speech at the conference of Zionists, nodding his head from time to time as if to say, "Right. Right. Precisely to the point."

Now that professor's face appeared with a strange clarity in his mind, even as, half dozing, he thought of the sugar factory in Brashek whose affairs could never be quite straightened out, complicated as they were by the problems of the inheritance; and he thought about the factory in Great Setternitz which he would have preferred to own outright rather than be involved with partners. Then he thought of his wife with whom he had lived happily for so long. He remembered how, when she hugged him yesterday at the train station, he had felt that she loved him more than ever; then he recalled her fragrance which, he concluded, must have come from the powder which she had brought back from her journey abroad last summer.

He closed his eyes against the sharp smell of the eau de cologne with which the barber was rubbing his face, making his cheeks glow. When Rappaport left the bathroom, he felt that the barber, trimming his left sideburn, had snipped off also a bit of his beard; and, as he considered the matter, he recalled the two money gifts he had made just before he left Palestine and wondered if perhaps he had not been too generous, and made a mental note to look over his books to see if he had kept a record of the gifts.

In the dining room, his wife was already at table. She was a plump, blonde woman whose oval face Abraham Rappaport studied intently. It had once been beautiful, but now she had to use powder to hide the red blotches on her skin. In honor of her husband's homecoming, she had risen fully an hour earlier than usual. She sat now, still sleepy, her entire body swathed in a great shawl. "Abraham," she inquired, "is it you?" Then, as if wide-eyed with wonder, she said, "How good that you're home." She drew the warm shawl more closely around her, leaned her head on her elbows and smiled up at him. Her eyes glowed with love, making her look almost young. She was just at the age when women begin to lose their attractiveness to other men and seek to bind themselves more closely to their husbands. Now, she told him that the house without him had felt empty; that Sarahle Levine, his niece, had been living in the house since before Passover; that their daughter, Nessie, had written from Petersburg to say that she was very busy and would not be home until next week; and that if Abraham planned to go abroad again soon, she, his wife, insisted on going with him.

As she spoke, she poured tea for them both, letting her bare arm escape from under her shawl. It was a bold maneuver, since her arms were still fresh and young. Rappaport loyally stood near her, his hands deep in the pockets of his jacket, trying to remember what it was that he ought to be writing down in his study. Each time she moved a bare arm, he remembered how he had loved her once; and when he looked at her face he was aware that now he respected her. He ought to be going to his study, but respect dictated that he stand quietly and listen while she talked.

He had good reason to respect her because, though she was descended from a notable family of which she might well boast, she had always gone to great pains to make clear to the world that her husband too was well-descended. Now she sat before him pouring tea and talking trivia, but in her youth, when she was an heiress and an orphan, any number of important Russian and foreign marriages had been proposed to her. And she loved importance. To this day, she delighted in tracing the intricate ties binding Europe's great Jewish families to each other and finally to the Frankfurt Rothschilds and the two Jewish barons. And yet, how pleased she was that he had come home, and how proud that she had married *him*.

In the dining room, the first sounds of the business day could be heard from below. A telephone rang. The gate at the entryway.

squeaked on its hinges. In the counting room, voices were raised inquiring whether the boss was likely to be down soon.

A while later, the chief bookkeeper, notepad in hand, appeared in the dining room. A young Zionist bachelor, he was so eager to put his questions to Rappaport in Hebrew that he had memorized them.

Rappaport listened inattentively and paced back and forth, his head down, his shoulders rounded, trying to give the impression that he was thinking of the matter at hand; but when he stopped his pacing it was not near the bookkeeper but beside his wife—where a sudden thought struck him. He grimaced, and ordered the horses hitched to the phaeton. He had remembered his meeting with the director of the bank, as well as the imprudently purchased stocks which might yet endanger the sugar factory in Brashek.

His wife, because she wanted him to appear youthful, had urged him to wear a dinner jacket, but when he put his top-coat on, he could not remember if he was wearing it; nor could he remember anything else that she had said.

Slowly, heavily, he descended the stairs which led through a long corridor to the second of the street doors. He paused on a step, remembering that in the bathroom some idea had occurred to him that required action, but what it was escaped him. Just the same, he retraced his steps, but more slowly than he had descended them, meeting, on his way, the bookkeeper at whom he glanced without a word.

Back in his study, he remembered—not what it was that had made him return—but something else. Taking a notebook from his desk, he went with it to the telephone and called his chief clerk. "Ah? That you? Good." He opened the notebook, leafed through it myopically, then dictated the details of the various business ventures he had undertaken while en route. When he hung up, he stood, suddenly dazed and could not recall a single thing about the busy day yet to come. It was a curiously gratifying disorientation because, despite his freethinking ways, he had retained a superstitious streak in his nature and this made him regard his present confusion as a sign that his success as a businessman had so overwhelmed him with work he could hardly think straight. It was the same streak of superstition that made him renew the annual thousand ruble stipend his father Joshua Heschel of Brisk used to send the Rabbi of Great Setternitz.

Still bemused, he made his way back toward the street door, passing, on his way, several people who waited for him in the corridor. One of them, who caught his eye, was the gentile tenant who lived in one of the wings of the building. The tenant rose to make his petition: He wanted one of his cellar walls rebuilt—but Rappaport continued on his way without reply. The tenants' affairs were his wife's concern. As for the Jews waiting there, their business could as easily be handled by his bookkeeper.

Outside, the Lithuanian Zionist preacher stood near the street door rolling a cigar. Had he gone up promptly to Rappaport, he might have been able to detain him, but he was so awed at the sight of the stylish team of horses waiting there that he forgot to raise his hand. Rappaport had taken his seat in the phaeton and been driven off by the uniformed driver before the preacher could recollect himself. The patient black horses were already trotting toward the other handsome carriages and automobiles moving about at the far corner of the street.

As Abraham Rappaport got down from the phaeton near his bank, he recognized the aged Madame Bernstein's automobile parked nearby. He recalled how, some five years ago, she had helped him with a hundred thousand rubles at a time when he had not been quite so rich as he now was. She had let him have the money for more than a year, and in secret. To this day she still regarded him as her protégé. These days, she was closely involved in the affairs of the local Jewish hospital to which she contributed a great deal of money each year. She believed that the personnel of the hospital hated her, and it was certain that Rappaport, once inside the bank, would be made to listen to new stories of all her feuds.

And indeed, she was in the bank—an aging woman who wore an old-fashioned hat over her dark gray upswept hair. She stood beside a table studying, through her lorgnette, the face of the portly man who spoke respectfully to her. At her side, there stood her usual companion, a plain young woman with the features of a seamstress.

Rappaport sidled by, hoping not to be noticed. It was still a few minutes before noon when he was stopped by an acquaintance who insisted on talking to him. No sooner had he shaken him off than he was stopped a second time, right beside the bank director's door, by a Jew in Hasidic garb who introduced himself as Jacob Nathan Viderpoller. He was struck by the man's penetrating, impudent dark eyes. He would have turned away but found himself instead trying to sort out what the man was saying about Sarahle Levine, his sister's only child, who was presently staying in his, Rappaport's home. He tried to concentrate on the match the fellow was evidently proposing for his niece, but he found himself thinking how strange Jacob Nathan looked with his hat off, and of the contrast between his close-cropped hair and his thick side curls. The man's haircut looked very fresh.

Jacob Nathan talked on, but Rappaport no longer understood what was being said. Rather, he was thinking that he, Rappaport, was his father, Joshua Heschel's older son, the one who maintained his father's traditions; and he remembered that it was his father's custom to take all matchmaking offers very seriously. Then, he remembered something else: five years ago or thereabouts, before he had attained his present prosperity, a money broker had arranged a loan for him from Joseph Schur's father.

The consequence was that Rappaport handed Jacob Nathan his visiting card, saying, "I make no promises. But . . . who knows. Let the young man come. Let him come . . . on Saturday night."

It was midnight, and Rappaport's house was dark, except for his bedroom where the lights were still on. Ethel Rappaport lay in her bed while her husband, sitting at the edge of his bed, took off his shoes. He set them carefully down, then said diffidently, but with a smile, "Sarahle has been offered a match."

"Sarahle?" His wife sat up at once. When she heard who it was that had been proposed for Sarahle, her eyes narrowed and she wrinkled her brow. "Who?" she said. "You don't mean it. That's dreadful." But her husband, buried in his comforter, was already asleep, and she was left lying there restless and terribly awake to consider just *who* were these Great Setternitz Schurs. Nobodies. Parvenus. Little people who lived mean, stingy, narrow lives; who came from a dismal place somewhere. The Rappaports had always been amused at the ways in which the richest of the Schurs were always imitating the Rappaport's, down to their charities and imported sons-in-law. And now, a Schur was being proposed for Sarahle! God pity the girl.

Ethel Rappaport's left eyelid throbbed and she could not get to sleep. She had a clear vision of her sister-in-law living this moment with her second husband in Riga. Oh, that woman had managed things just fine. Not a year gone by from the time of her first husband's death and she married the rich bachelor whom she had loved as a girl. The whole world had buzzed with that romance, and now see what sort of match was being proposed for her daughter, Sarahle. God pity the child.

When Rappaport woke the next morning at eight, as usual, she turned to him saying, "Abraham. How could you bring yourself to sleep? I haven't so much as closed an eye all night.

"And that filthy matchmaker. Did you send him packing? Oh no. No. You gave him your visiting card; and now Schur will come here; to this house. How scandalous!"

IV

Meanwhile, Joseph Schur had received Jacob Nathan's first letter from Great Setternitz urging him to be ready and promising that "with God's help the match with Moishele Levine's daughter will be made."

In fact, the match was already the talk of the town. On the last day of the Passover holiday, the men at the East Wall benches of the synagogue watched Joseph Schur attentively as he sat in the place his father had occupied before him. They noted how well his new overcoat fitted his somewhat portly form; they commented on the way his trimmed beard framed his dark, youthful features; and they talked of his swift rise in the world as they considered what might yet become of him if the match should come to pass. It was exactly the sort of alliance toward which the Schurs had been reaching for years.

Joseph Schur, meanwhile, sat in his departed father's seat in the synagogue, his thin lips forming dutiful prayers. Occasionally a thought would strike him, and his dark eyes acquired a new, very

tender look—the look of a young man, too long a bachelor,
contemplating the unexpected good fortune that was about to bring
an overwhelming change in his life. Then suddenly the real world
surrounding him seemed a strange jumbled place.

But there's another tale that needs brief telling here: At about
this time, an intelligent, wealthy young woman named Mina
Moreiness came home to Great Setternitz after a long sojourn abroad
where she had turned the heads of various rich or famous men. On
the day after her return, she passed Joseph Schur in the street and
had been so moved by the look in his dark eyes that she had set
about immediately to learn what she could about him.

The rest of the story could be heard among the synagogue's East
Wall benches as it was told by the genial local matchmaker whom
old Moreiness had invited to the wine-blessing on the first day of
Passover. "Mina Moreiness," so went the tale, "sat in the dining
room, her hair as disheveled as a gypsy's, wearing house slippers on
her bare feet. Who knows whether it was laziness or indifference? Or
whether it was because of the free life she had lived for so long
abroad, where none of the famous or rich young men whose heads
she turned had pleased her." In any event, at some point in the
conversation, she turned to the matchmaker and, drawing her shawl
more closely about her, said, her voice raised as if she were speaking
to the deaf, "Make me a match—with Joseph Schur."

Looking back on the matter, the idea of a match between
Moishele Levine's daughter and Joseph Schur seems entirely natural.
He was easily the most capable of the well-to-do local young
bachelors. The sacking factory he had inherited was in full
production beside the deep narrow river half a verst away from the
town, where it was a landmark to passing boats with its smokestacks
impudently pouring black smoke into the clear blue sky and its
electric illuminating system adding an exuberant, if totally unneces-
sary, holiday brightness to the broad light of day.

Not to speak of the factory, there were also his two very aged
and wealthy aunts living in the hills of Great Setternitz where they
resolutely refused to have anything to do with the other prosperous
Jewish families of the town. They had married off their own
daughters to various foreign sons-in-law, and now they lived far from

the town's teeming center in two vast homes which chilled the rare passer-by with their air of melancholy old wealth.

They were the elite of the town—these two aunts, Esther and Hodel, who would not countenance marriages into any rank inferior to their own. It needs to be said here that Joseph Schur did not vaunt himself as descending from the loftier side of the Schur clan. His father, Itzik Maier Schur, had been a fanatical and stingy Hasid, famous for his rages; a man on whom his employees fawned in his presence and whom they mimicked the instant he was gone. While still young, he quarrelled with his two sisters, Esther and Hodel, over an inheritance and ever after had asserted loudly that they—his sisters, their husbands and their children—were his enemies to the death. He was harsh to his first wife, the barren one. After her death, though he was already an old man, he had, to spite his own family, married a young divorcee who wanted no more from the marriage than to "improve herself" and to dress well. Joseph Schur was born of this spite-marriage—the well-mannered, cultivated Joseph Schur into whose twenty-four years had been packed a world of Jewish as well as secular training. He was, then, the son of a haughty, intransigent father; a father who, for more than thirty years, would not let his own sisters into his house; who, a few hours before his death, turned suddenly tender-hearted and wept because he had lived an ugly life. And Joseph's mother, as we have seen, was a divorcee who wished only to "improve herself" and to dress well.

The reserved, silent young Joseph Schur had such considerations as these well in his mind, no doubt; but there was the further fact that he had once encountered Moishele Levine's daughter and that the meeting had roused in him, for the first time in his life, a yearning for marriage. And yet it had been a strangely inadvertent coming together, with none of the trappings of respectability that should be present at such an important event.

It happened a couple of weeks before Passover, as Schur was returning from a visit to his younger aunt Reisel in Warsaw—the same Reisel who, as a girl, had been unable to put up with her brother, Joseph Schur's fanatically Hasidic father, and who therefore had run away from him to Paris.

No one ever quite believed that Joseph Schur's aunt Reisel had all the troubles she complained about because the two favorite themes of her life were her sorrows and the huge acquaintance she had among the famous people of the world. As a young woman, she had had many romantic encounters, though in the end she married a rich husband with the conventional help of a matchmaker. Her husband turned out to be an even greater windbag than she—a man whom the world could never surprise. He claimed to know everything and everyone and was, by his own account, a man of nearly godlike achievement. Schur's aunt Reisel held her peace as her husband poured into her nephew's ears endless tales about himself.

In truth, his aunt Reisel was not very happy, as Joseph Schur could easily confirm after the few days he spent in her home. On their way to the train station to which she insisted on accompanying him, he felt himself moved by her situation. Had he not been raised in his father's rigidly reticent home, he might have taken her hand in his and said: "Suffer in silence, so that no one will know. Silence gives dignity." His aunt Reisel sensed his unspoken sympathy and was touched by it. When she kissed his eyelids, as she used to do when he was a child, the tears rose in her throat at the recognition that he had become her friend. "A friend is all I ever wanted," she said. But when the train pulled into the station something she glimpsed in one of the cars made her assume the wanton, gossipy look of a female matchmaker. "How lucky you are," she whispered. "You'll be travelling with a rich and beautiful woman. With Moishele Levine's daughter."

At that point Joseph Schur was not yet clear what that might mean, though he had heard in Great Setternitz that she was involved with someone abroad, or why would she leave the country so frequently?

The thought was immediately painful to him, and he found himself studying with glistening eyes the blonde young woman in the seat opposite him. Moishele Levine's daughter! She, for her part, sat throughout the course of the evening with her head back against the seat pillow, her eyes closed and her hands folded over her breast. Joseph Schur watched her intently, reminding himself from time to time that she was said to be in love with someone who lived abroad. He fancied that she kept her eyes closed and her hands folded the better to accommodate herself to a dream in which her lover leaned his head against her shoulder. A yearning dream.

There was one instant when she opened her sleepy blue eyes and rested them on his face, as if she were trying to recall something; then, evidently disappointed, she let them lapse again into indifference. He noted the change and was assailed by a spasm of heartache that quickly subsided as it was overwhelmed by the tide of a suitor's passion: "She is beautiful."

Taking out a Hebrew book, he turned its pages as if he were reading by the yellow light that escaped from under the yellow silk shade of the standing lamp; but eventually, he gave that up and went out into the corridor, hating himself for having gone through the pretense of reading. He despised pretense. It was pretense that had made his visit to his aunt Reisel difficult for him because, as he saw it, she was constantly pretending things. He resisted pretense with all the force of the Schur pride that seethed in his veins; and decided, therefore, that he would not look at Moishele Levine's daughter. On the other hand, he could hardly stand in the corridor forever.

Back in the compartment, he was surprised to find that the electric lamp was burning too brightly. Walking on tiptoe, he turned it off, afraid that its glare would disturb the young woman's sleep. But no sooner did the lamp go out than a bare blue bulb high in a corner of the compartment went on. It was the signal for the train to assume its nighttime character. The wheels of the train kept up a continuous suppressed muttering. In the carriage, everyone slept.

Joseph Schur, deeply withdrawn into a corner seat of his compartment, rocked with the motion of the train and presided over the young woman's sleep. She reclined as before, but her wavy blonde head leaned now against her hands. Her long dress reached to her feet, covering all but the toes of her child-sized lacquered slippers. Her black striped shawl enveloped her from her innocent young shoulders to her waist. Schur watched her: "Moishele Levine's daughter."

After this encounter Joseph Schur returned home transformed. He slept for days in a row, like a musician after a wedding. A sweet and easy sleep in which he expected at any moment to see the pampered young woman at his door come to say, "It's not true. I do not have a lover abroad."

These events took place while it was still spring. The ice in the river flowing by Great Setternitz melted early and the thaw was followed by days of light frost. It was a time of deep attentiveness: as if nature was trying to discover what further changes might yet come over the stunned region.

In Great Setternitz, it was a time of flickering small fires, extinguished early. Wearied by the pre-Passover scurrying and matzo baking, the confused streets and alleys of Great Setternitz dozed off early; and the enthralled dusk, like a long held breath, vibrated silently to the rhythm of the express train crossing the iron bridge. The train, as if appalled by the abyss over which it was crossing, scattered the silence and rushed on, returning to the place to which, only a few days ago, it had carried Moishele Levine's blonde young daughter.

In the course of those spring days, Joseph Schur felt that the very air was fragrant with betrothal, with the scent of young women, with his own fragrance; and with whole passages from the Song of Songs. It was a mood that stayed with him as he went daily to his work in the factory he had inherited, and which, even before his father's death, had employed dozens of workmen. On his way home, he frequently cut through the great square just outside the town. There, he often noticed a couple of young women taking their afternoon stroll who playfully tested the thickness of the snow with their galoshes, and cast friendly glances at him as he went by, as if they were old acquaintances of his. One of the two was Mina Moreiness, old Moreiness's attractive daughter. Each time that Joseph Schur appeared, Mina Moreiness whispered something into her friend's ear. Every day, it seemed, she had a different secret to confide, but the real secret was to be found in the warm look in her dark eyes as they followed the handsome twenty-four year old Schur. He, for his part, also guarded a secret. As he passed the two young women and studied their faces, he could not, for the life of him, tell which of the two reminded him more of Moishele Levine's daughter.

Schur was not a man with intimate friends in whom he could confide. He had been born and raised in a prideful, reclusive family that was not particularly well regarded either by its neighbors or by the townspeople at large, and the family pride and reserve were deeply ingrained in him. Here, in the town, he rarely paid visits; not even to his aunts who were revered for their wealth and who loved him dearly for making no claims on them for money, and because he was better bred than his father.

One evening, as he was making his way down the noisy street, he had the impression that Moishele Levine's daughter was walking before him. He was on one side of the street while she, moving away from him, was on the other. She went as if she were leading him on—stopping to wait, then hurrying off the moment he drew near, until, at a dark intersection, she made a sudden turn and disappeared. Joseph Schur came to a stop and looked around him at the faces passing in a dusk so intense one might have thought the sun had been eclipsed. He stood and heard a strange sound—like the rushing of waters through the sluice gates of a vast dam.

What could it all mean? He went home slowly and spent the entire evening telling himself that Moishele Levine's daughter must have arrived long since at the home to which she had been returning from abroad. That perhaps, wherever she was, having made up her mind not to go out for the evening, she was, at that very moment, quietly pressing a white dress to wear for the Passover holiday.

The next day he could not resist the temptation to tell what was happening to him to Itzikel, his only friend in the town. Itzikel, the son of the Rabbi of Great Setternitz, had been Joseph's childhood friend in the years when they had both been pupils of Jacob Nathan studying Talmud together in the Rabbi's court.

V

The court of the Rabbi of Great Setternitz had been in decline for some time now. Every room in the spacious house had its painful secrets and could tell of hidden spites and quarrels. Renowned for his scholarship, the Rabbi had grown more and more orthodox with the advancing years. He had no inkling, moreover, that he was fatally ill and persisted, behind locked doors, in his customary fasts of expiation. It was some years since he had given up the practice of accepting petitions from his constituents and of presiding over their festive evenings. He ignored entirely the consequent loss to his income and went on believing that his family actually lived on the three thousand rubles he earned as the Rabbi of Great Setternitz. He did not lack enemies who argued that the Rabbi was not quite the holy innocent he pretended to be, and that the real reason he no longer accepted petitions was that there was no longer any profit in them. Meanwhile, the Rabbi's wife, endeavoring to uphold the honor of his court, borrowed large sums of money from those Hasidim who had once studied with him—whether they were still believers or not.

Joseph Schur moved through the silent, half-empty rooms of the Rabbi's house, fearful that he would be noticed by the Rabbi's wife who, mistaking him for a former disciple, would insist on confiding the family's troubles to him.

In the ascetic room in which, long ago, Joseph Schur and Itzikel had studied together and in which Itzikel had once compelled him to listen to a romantic tale involving a winter's evening in the Rabbi's court, a marriage canopy and a young woman's perfumed hand creeping shyly into his own in the dark . . . in that room, Joseph Schur now sat, reserved and dignified, and listened as Itzikel constrained him once again to be attentive to the latest tale he had to tell.

Itzikel still retained the pale, saintly complexion that seems to yearn all week long for the silken garments of the Sabbath day. His eyes still kept their light-struck look from the years in which he secretly read Heine and Ahad Ha'am. Though he had recently returned with his father from abroad where the doctors had pronounced the Rabbi's doom, he had something else he wished to tell. He held Joseph firmly by the arms and described something he had seen from the train window on their way home. The train was hurrying through the flat Russian landscape, spreading a gloomy smoke across the evening sky. He, Itzikel, was standing alone at a window, looking out at the passing Jewish villages. They seemed so isolated, so empty—as if it were the Sabbath and all the inhabitants were inside having their afternoon naps. He caught the gleam of a mud puddle before a house that faced the railroad tracks. Geese were probing the mud of a discolored courtyard when a young woman, a young woman in white, came running and stopped short on the porch. A young woman in white.

And now, Itzikel confided, he was in love with that young woman. The glimpse of her had disordered his life. He was, according to himself, a lost soul. He had dark circles under his eyes and claimed he could only keep himself calm with the frequent use of cigarettes. And he could not bring himself to pay attention to the affairs of the rabbinate of Great Setternitz which, after his father's death, would come to him.

Joseph Schur, who had come to confide in Itzikel, felt how little he could help his friend. He was preoccupied with his own new experience and could offer no advice.

Back in his home, there was nothing to do but wait.

One afternoon, Jacob Nathan Viderpoller, Schur's former Talmud teacher, paid him a visit. On the face of it, he just dropped in to inquire how things were, yet Viderpoller, decked out in his Hasidic finery, sat at Schur's table and led the conversation—sometimes impertinently—into matters involving Joseph Schur's inheritance. At one moment, he came abruptly to the point: he wanted to propose a match to him. "A match with Moishele Levine's daughter."

"With Moishele Levine's daughter?" The coincidence filled Schur with wonder. How had it come about? Was it a notion that had occurred to Jacob Nathan all by itself, or was it the consequence of a letter from Joseph Schur's gossipy aunt Reisel?

As for Jacob Nathan, Schur had little confidence in him. It was widely known that this pious fellow in the fine Hasidic garb had, some years ago, abandoned a wife for whose support he never sent so much as a penny. Schur, in his reserved and formal way, sat and watched Jacob Nathan toying with the hundred ruble note in his fingers, as if it were an ordinary piece of paper. The hundred rubles were toward expenses in this marriage project, and, as he turned the bill over he said, for the second time, "There is, of course, the matter of her trips abroad." Then he added, "It may be necessary to inquire about those frequent journeys . . . yes."

Long after Jacob Nathan was gone, Joseph Schur turned over in his mind the question of those trips abroad. To learn what they might mean, he would have to visit Itzikel once more, because Itzikel's mother, the Rabbi's wife, was related to one side of the Rappaport clan. She might know.

Schur never made that visit. What happened instead was that Jacob Nathan, during the middle days of Passover, made a journey to Brashek from which he sent Joseph Schur a letter advising him to hold himself in readiness because, with God's help, "the match between you and Moishele Levine's daughter will be . . . a match." He added that it appeared "there is nothing to those frequent trips abroad."

The news stirred Schur to fantasize: he would rebuild his father's house in Great Setternitz, he would evict the tenant who occupied the two stores in the lower left corner of the building. The entire entryway stank of the shoemaker's trade. There was another reason for remodelling the building—too much of it reminded him of his stingy old father.

Jacob Nathan's second letter came from Kiev where Moishele Levine's daughter was staying with her uncle, Abraham Rappaport. Schur was advised to hold himself in readiness for a telegram summoning him to Kiev. He was given to understand that the marriage had been broached in Rappaport's house. Schur concluded that the young woman must have been a party to those conversations and that she had agreed to let them proceed. Perhaps she remembered him from the time they shared a compartment together on the train.

The receipt of the second letter prompted Schur to order several new suits at his tailor's; at the same time, he stopped going out in the evenings.

While he waited for the promised telegram, he led a hermit's existence. To make the time pass more quickly, he immersed himself in his books, feeling, as he turned the pages, that Moishele Levine's daughter was standing at his shoulder; that, as his eyes came to the bottom of a page, she said "Turn the page, dàrling." He remembered the melancholy, yielding look in her blue eyes as if he were still sitting in the train, watching her as she raised her head from the pillow to look for an instant into his delighted eyes—trying to remember something.

He continued to turn the pages of his book, but his mind dwelt continually on her. Then he thought how wrong it was of him to have been pleased because she would bring wealth to their marriage. Very wrong, because he, Joseph Schur, was rich enough without her wealth.

One evening he prepared an elaborate bath for himself, and sat for hours in the tub, as if, by washing frequently, he were sanctifying himself. Later, that same night, he was wakened by a servant who handed him Jacob Nathan's telegram: "All progressing well. Will meet evening train, Kiev, day after tomorrow. Jacob Nathan."

He stood, endeavoring to be calm, beside the lamp as he held Jacob Nathan's telegram, but his nostrils paled and he breathed hard: "The day after tomorrow is Tuesday. A lucky day."

VI

The morning of Schur's departure smelled of the fine silvery rain that was still coming down after a torrential night. A smell of good fortune; a betrothal smell. Schur sat behind a taciturn, respectful driver who whipped his team up dextrously so that they passed a whole line of phaetons carrying people in a holiday mood hurrying, like himself, to the station to be in time for the nine o'clock train. Schur, as he was driven by, thought he caught a glimpse of faces he knew from somewhere; and hatboxes perched precariously on drivers' seats; and a woman looking out at him from under her veil, her eyes studying his newly trimmed hair and beard. Whose eyes might they be? Schur, still exhilarated by last night's news, and the sense of his imminent good fortune, did not dwell long on the question. Later, however, it turned out that old Moreiness of Great Setternitz was also travelling to Kiev with Mina, the daugher of his old age. They occupied the second compartment in the carriage, where the old man sat performing tricks and treating his daughter with the air of a cavalier.

No one, seeing this sophisticated Moreiness who had a whole chain of rich dead grandfathers in his ancestry, would have guessed that the broad-shouldered old man's smelting mill had for the past three years sustained very heavy losses; that, indeed, the mill was now shut down and birds were nesting in its tall chimneys. Old Moreiness and his daughter travelled in great style, with imported suitcases and a huge box of chocolates from which to nibble; even a specially designed cigarette case to hold the interminable cigarettes the old man smoked. The gray hair where his moustache met his broad beard was tinged with yellow, like the attractive amber cigarette holder between his lips.

He joined Joseph Schur in the corridor, and immediately lighted one more cigarette, as if obeying a doctor's prescription. "Tuesday," he said, "is always a lucky day." Like any well-bred man, he pretended not to know why Joseph Schur was travelling to Kiev. Schur, who had been idly watching the train stations pass by, moved aside to give old Moreiness space at the window.

It was not long before their talk turned comfortably to Great Setternitz themes. Old Moreiness remembered both of Joseph Schur's grandfathers. He could recall when Great Setternitz was still a small town. "Not even paved."

"That must have been a long time ago," observed Schur.

"So long ago that 'four kings were fighting against five and one of them was called Chedorlaomer. . .' " °

They both laughed and Schur felt a thrill of pride because his grandfathers were well known. Suddenly, the old man's daughter, Mina, stood before them, and their laughter stopped. She swayed in the open doorway of the compartment, holding on to both handrails, looking like a slight, frail creature that was poised to leap away, yet studying the two men as if she were imagining them together as father- and son-in-law. Then, lowering her eyes, she came toward them with slow, submissive steps and whispered to Joseph Schur, "Mina Moreiness," as she put out her hand. There was something strange about her; though it was said that abroad she had turned the heads of the greatest and wealthiest young men, that several of them had followed her to Russia from Switzerland and Germany.

Old Moreiness brushed aside his daughter's interruption. Looking fondly at her, he told her that they were speaking of Joseph Schur's grandfather on his mother's side, Samuel Reb-rabin, who came from central Poland long ago, who bought himself a prominent home, and built important limekilns in the region. That grandfather, Reb-rabin, Moreiness wanted his daughter to know, had been a uniquely intelligent man. A friendly fellow, with a blond beard and a clever Polish head on his shoulders.

He never let his business weigh him down. During the course of

° Genesis 14:8–9.

the long summer days, he could be seen wandering about his house, dressed in a long linen caftan trimmed with embroidered velvet, smoking a longstemmed Polish pipe while he read *The Duties of the Heart* with a look of such pleasure in his eyes that one could suppose he was reading a novel and not a work of piety.

"A novel!" The idea enchanted both Mina and Joseph. They laughed together and old Moreiness joined them, laughing so hard that the cigarette he was puffing on enthusiastically brought on a coughing fit. Even that pleased him—he had made his "children" laugh. Then he grew serious once more. "In Great Setternitz," he continued, "Reb-rabin had been tremendously admired. He was a learned man who never put on a display of learning."

His family, too, was interesting. Samuel Reb-rabin had come here from central Poland—a man without a wife, bringing with him his widowed daughter who, not much later, married Joseph Schur's father; Reb-rabin also had with him his nine or ten year old son, a somewhat unsettled boy, but with a good head on him—perhaps even cleverer than his father.

It was this nine year old pipsqueak that old Moreiness remembered clearly to this day. He, old Moreiness, had been reckoned one of the best chess players in Great Setternitz, yet the boy, Jonah, used to come frequently to Moreiness's house and beat him, game after game. "Jonah left Setternitz when he was very young. He must be . . ." Here Moreiness performed some swift calculation; then, "He must be thirty-two years old now, give or take a year. Right?" he asked Joseph.

Mina Moreiness too had something to say on the subject. While she was living in Berne, she had been part of a small colony of Jews there—Jews with political convictions of some sort. One day a young man visited the group. A man with boyish features and gray hair whose name was Jonah. She remembered that there had been a party at which some gentile woman had taken such a liking to Jonah that she had turned her own lodgings over to him.

As Mina talked, she smiled at Joseph in the friendly way of a woman hoping to please a suitor. She was not sure, in fact, whether the Berne Jonah was the same one of whom they were speaking, but she was happy to have added something to a conversation regarding Schur's uncle.

Then, the Moreinesses grew abruptly aware that Schur had a withdrawn look on his face. Regretfully, they allowed the conversation to die. He evidently had his share of the Schur reserve and family pride and was not pleased to be talking about an uncle who, from childhood upward, had withdrawn himself from the family and who, as an adult, had cut his ties with it altogether.

It was evening when they arrived in Kiev. From the window of their car, they looked out on a freshly swept chilly-looking station and, on the platform, an equally cold-looking crowd of strangers. Inside, the Moreinesses and Joseph Schur parted from each other in a mood of estrangement.

On the platform, standing beside his porter, Joseph Schur felt again his morning's sense of excited anticipation as he waited for Jacob Nathan, but when Jacob Nathan failed to appear, a depression settled over him. He felt the glances from the Moreinesses and the other travellers from Great Setternitz as they went by, taking him in: Joseph Schur, dressed in his brand new clothes, like a bridegroom. Waiting.

Eventually, he took a droshky and drove off to a hotel. It was clear that Jacob Nathan's matchmaking scheme was not proceeding smoothly.

Jacob Nathan showed up the next morning in Schur's hotel room where he sat like a gloomy in-law and reported that, for the moment, he had no news. Not a word.

He sat there, smoking one cigarette after another. Then an idea occurred to him and he asked Joseph Schur to give him one of his visiting cards. "I'll tell you what I mean to do. *I'll* take the card to Rappaport's house. Right now. *I'll* do what's needed."

Schur looked at him mistrustfully. He paced the room, beating his fist into his palm as he debated what to do. Finally, he gave Jacob Nathan the card and it was left that Jacob Nathan would contrive an invitation for Schur to visit the Rappaport home. The invitation should reach him no later than the following morning; but more than forty-eight hours were to pass while Schur, furious and humiliated, waited alone in his expensive room, interrupted only by bleak visits from Jacob Nathan who slipped in to inquire, "Well? Anything yet?" as if the invitation which Jacob Nathan was supposed to have arranged would somehow appear of itself in the hotel room.

At long last, a sweating, haggard Jacob Nathan showed up carrying one of Rappaport's engraved visiting cards—an expensive, embossed affair, with gilt Russian script which, when it was set on the table, seemed to breathe an air of coldly distant wealth; as if it were letting one know that it had not been given freely.

Joseph Schur prowled the room, unwilling to approach it, but at last he forced himself to reply, "All right then. I'll be there— Saturday night," after which he refused to hear another word concerning the Rappaports. Instead, he withdrew deeply into himself. Himself, Joseph Schur: the proud, reserved, stubborn Schur waiting until Saturday night in the calm, glazed mood of a man who intractably and passionately refuses to think about a thing. "It's all the same to me."

When he finally roused himself from his torpid state, it was Saturday evening. A gloomy, portentous, strangely sluggish time when the sun went down at the edge of town in a chill, red haze; after which there came the sound of the wind blowing through the pale dark, slapping at the town's high roofs as if at something foul.

A week was over. Where had it gone?

Below, in the streets, the city's life flowed as usual making its haunted, yearning sounds. It was just before the Christians' great holy day and gentiles were returning home from their churches with lighted candles in their hands and the streets resounded with the music of the bells.

VII

Schur made his way along the noisy street, not at all sure that he was going in the right direction to find the Rappaport house; nor, in his stupor, was he willing to think about it. He moved slowly, almost aimlessly, until, turning a corner, he came upon a dimly lighted theater entrance before which stood two signboards describing, in Russian, a lecture on a Jewish theme. The place had an aura of shy intimacy about it; it was a sort of Jewish hiding place amidst the tumult and probing of Christian bells and candles.

The entryway was empty and Joseph Schur, after hesitating for a moment, went in. It may be he went in out of indifference; or else it was an act of stubbornness, to prove he was in control of his life; or that he was in no hurry to go anywhere. Standing in the half-dark, he found himself looking down over rows of backs turned to him and sensed the presence of young women in knitted jackets. Someone—a woman with a flushed face and feverish eyes—stared at him. On the brightly lighted, bare stage, a redheaded young man of medium height who looked older than his years stood beside a podium, wearily wiping his face with a white handkerchief. He was wearing a student's uniform with brand new buttons and seemed to be working very hard as he spoke to his audience about the problems Jews had in Russia and in other countries. All that the student said was true, but Schur felt himself a stranger to that audience and aloof from their concerns. He stood for a while longer, then left the hall.

At the corner of the fashionable street where Abraham Rappaport lived, Schur felt once more a twinge of his family's stubborn pride and hesitated to go on. He stood watching a nearby street lamp giving off its cold light. The lamp appeared to be steady, but when he looked closely at it, he could see that it was trembling in the breeze, even as it shed a frosty calm over the rare passers-by. As it happened, there was someone there at the moment—a man much taller than Joseph Schur. He had an actor's shaven face and swollen, sleepy looking bags under his eyes. The man appeared so suddenly that it was as if the night had given him birth—a creature fully clothed, with hands deep in the pockets of his short jacket, his shoulders hunched and a general demeanor of haughty isolation. Like Schur, he was approaching Abraham Rappaport's street door.

"Pardon." The two men arrived together at the frosted glass door which opened into the corridor that led to the second floor. Each man raised a hand to press the doorbell: Joseph Schur who, though he had rested all that Sabbath day, could not remember at what time in the evening he was expected to pay his visit; and the other man, a not-quite-young poet who wrote in Hebrew and who, two years ago, had entirely given up writing and, as if to spite himself, had accepted a job in a partly social, partly Zionist organization almost entirely underwritten by Abraham Rappaport.

It was the poet who was startled by Joseph Schur's "Pardon."

As he entered the handsomely lighted dining room, Joseph Schur, apparently calm, gathered that the topic of conversation was a pogrom which, rumor had it, was being readied to take place in the town just before the holy day.

"It's a fact."

A flushed and weary Madame Rappaport made a grimace. As she leaned forward toward the person speaking, she caught a glimpse through her dining room window of a gentile in the street hurrying homeward, protecting a lighted candle from the wind. In the exhausted voice of a newly delivered mother, she complained, "Didn't I ask to have the shades drawn?"

Joseph Schur, now seated not far from Madame Rappaport, looked about him reflectively. There were not many people sitting around the table—perhaps half a dozen chiming their teaspoons, crumbling cake as the tea darkened in their glasses. There was a burst of laughter nearby which infected everyone at the table. Except himself, Joseph Schur. Already, he was beginning to regret that he had come. Then there came the slow surge of another mood: a bridegroom's sense of exhilaration, happiness flooding his heart as his brain seized on the idea—*"She* is in the house . . . Moishe Levine's daughter. She may show up at any moment. Perhaps, on my account, she is even now dressing herself in her room."

Joseph Schur was received as warmly into Rappaport's house as the other guests. He was constantly introduced. Each time someone new came in from the cool outdoors, Schur was required to bow politely; to press someone's hand; to murmur, "Joseph Schur." But Moishele Levine's daughter did not leave her room quite so readily.

The poet who wrote in Hebrew, a clean-shaven man with heavy circles under his eyes, sat facing Joseph Schur, but Schur could find nothing to say to him. The daze in which Schur had wandered earlier in the evening was entirely dissipated, and he sat now entirely aware of the motive that had brought him here and alert to every detail of his surroundings. He was conscious of the arrival of each new guest who came in bringing with him a whiff of the cold outdoors. The newcomers, however, were all intimates of the household and, whether intentionally or not, seemed hardly to notice him; and if, finally, they did manage to shake his hand, it was done as if in passing, and they promptly forgot about him. Schur observed the warmth with which they clustered around Abraham Rappaport's only daughter, Nessie, the sculptress who had come from Petersburg to spend Friday and Saturday at home.

Nessie was a slender young woman, almost as diminutive as a

child. She had been born a hunchback and, as a consequence, had very soon lost her youthful looks. Because of her deformity, everyone forgave her her studies abroad. And everyone loved her, as was clear from the way the guests crowded around her, caressing her tiny hands as if they were petting a child.

And yet, there was a maturity in her. More maturity, indeed, than in those who surrounded her. She peered up at them with eyes that seemed at once friendly and compassionate—the eyes of a woman who long ago had come to terms with herself and who forgave life the worst that it could offer. She kept herself aloof from her parents, though Schur observed the way in which, without looking at her directly, they had her very much on their minds and were distressed by the not quite respectable life she had chosen to live. As an instance they offered, without quite complaining about it, the way in which she had come abruptly home without a word of warning. Not a word, not a telegram.

A guest who sat near Nessie took almost too great a pleasure in telling the story of Nessie's late night arrival in Kiev. The guest had come upon Nessie as she was being driven home from the train station by an irritable cab driver. The night was cold, the road uphill; and all of Nessie's pity was for the horse whose lean haunches writhed in the traces. "No," she pleaded with the old driver, "No, don't drive so fiercely."

Nessie ignored the story. Schur noted how Nessie stood beside the seated Madame Koireh and stroked the woman's hair with her tiny hands, putting questions to her all the while about Madame Koireh's husband who was away on a journey.

"She's not a bad sort, that Nessie," thought Schur. And yet, how did she concern him, Joseph Schur? He sat in his chair, a well-fleshed young man tightly buttoned into his new suit and emanated polite patience. The whole intention of his manner was to keep those present from having the remotest suspicion that he, Joseph Schur, saw anything in the room as remarkable. He too came from a wealthy background. Most decidedly, he had not come here to learn anything. Looking at him, so clean, so fresh, so new, one would have thought that the very soul inside him was as thoroughly soaped and barbered as his body. Just the same, despite the reserve of his manner, he would have been glad to join in a conversation that would turn on him, and on his motive for being here. He looked about the room, hoping for a sight of his host, but he was not there; as for Madame Rappaport, she deliberately avoided his eyes and called, "Madame Koireh." She wanted the young Madame Koireh to move her chair closer.

Again, she called, "Madame Koireh," and was vexed because she could not be heard above the sociable chatter around her. Finally, Madame Koireh noticed that she was being called. Her thin nostrils flared; a flush spread over her translucent features and she smiled as she edged her seat closer to her hostess. Madame Koireh was the daughter of an aging poet who wrote in Hebrew. Lately, she had received considerable sympathy because her father, who had been financially independent as a young man, was now quite sick. He lived in Switzerland where, rumor had it, Abraham Rappaport supported him directly or through one of Rappaport's many charities.

Abraham Rappaport now emerged from his study in the company of a bespectacled old man wearing a shabby jacket. He had the stoop-shouldered look of a big-city rabbi. He had been speaking Hebrew but, as he ended what had evidently been a long speech, he changed to Yiddish: "And that's my advice; without it, the journal cannot survive." Clearly, he had sweated a considerable while in Rappaport's study; he sat wearily at the table, drank his tea and rested. Then, noticing Madame Koireh, he peered at her over his glasses in his schoolmasterish way and asked her if it was true, as he had recently read in a Hebrew-language journal, that her father was feeling better and was thinking of returning to Russia.

Rappaport, meanwhile, stood alone, not far from the table, engrossed in thought, as if he were a neglected guest. It would have been impossible to surmise what he was thinking: perhaps he was considering whatever it was the old man had been droning on about for so long; or he might have been thinking of the glass of tea on which his eyes were strangely fixed; or his thoughts might have been of himself and the complex business affairs in which he was involved. When someone spoke to him, he turned with a start and listened with a sour expression on his face as he was told of the pogrom which, rumor had it, was being talked of in the town; then he moved off like an ill-humored in-law shuffling away from people who wished to entertain him. Then, recalling something, he turned again to face the table and said, feeling guilty, "Wait a minute. Aren't you . . . he . . . the young man from Great Setternitz who has come to . . . to look over . . . to see Sarahle?"

When Rappaport told Sarahle that Schur was coming to the house on her account, she had only smiled. Then she had gone off to spend the evening with a friend who brought her greetings from abroad. Gone off, in fact, with that blond young fellow who thought so highly of himself because various newspapers and journals had recently given the world to know that he existed: Joel Weintraub.

Abraham Rappaport blinked his eyes and seated himself on the empty chair beside Joseph Schur, then, leaning his head on the palm of his hand, he studied Schur's freshly-barbered face as if he were asking himself, "What sort of features does a rich young bachelor have to have these days that would make a marriageable woman unwilling even to be seen by him?" Out of deep fellow-feeling, he leaned forward, grasped the arm of Schur's chair and engaged him in conversation: "So? Is it true that you don't manage your factory by yourself? Is it still leased to those tenants?"

Joseph Schur, feeling that his time had at last come, answered his host's question in a voice that was fully an octave higher than normal. He said that he had no intention of directing the mill on his own just yet, but that, soon after Shavuoth, when his renters' lease ran out, he would make some changes. "Remodeling."

"Extensive remodeling?"

Schur shifted in his chair. He felt awkward and believed himself to be speaking nonsense. Wanting desperately to amend what he had said, he would have added that he meant, among his other plans for remodeling, to replace the metal smokestack with one made of masonry, but Rappaport was called away and Schur left to his own devices.

Just then, the other guests turned to greet a newcomer. Schur looked toward him and recognized him at once. It was the red-haired student with the prematurely aged face, the fellow with the brand new buttons on his jacket who had given the lecture. The Rappaports' guests expressed considerable interest in the meeting at which the student had spoken, but the student answered their questions meagerly—as if unwilling to talk about it. Then, something

Schur saw out of the corner of an eye drove everything else from his mind—the red-haired student, the lecture, Schur's awkwardness in the conversation with Rappaport.

What happened was that Madame Rappaport and Madame Koireh, finding themselves alone at the table had pushed their chairs together as if at a signal. Madame Rappaport whispered something into Madame Koireh's ear; the younger woman listened intently, smiling all the while as she turned her slightly reddened eyes in Schur's direction. It was all too obvious: they were whispering about him. Schur felt himself grow rigid with offended pride; every ounce of the Schur blood that flowed in his veins rushed to his face just as, behind him, someone spoke the name of Moishele Levine's daughter.

It was the red-haired student. He had been standing not far from Schur—to whom, so far he had paid not the slightest attention—turning a teaspoon between his fingers, evidently still engrossed in memories of his lecture, when he looked up and asked vaguely, "Well? And where is Sarahle?"

Just then, Abraham Rappaport rejoined Schur and they resumed their conversation. Schur was pale and breathing hard, but he managed to maintain his reserve and his formal manner as Rappaport led him into an adjoining large white room. Once again, Schur felt a rush of anticipation. Surely Rappaport was leading him off this way for some weighty purpose; surely he meant to say something confidential to him.

VIII

But as it turned out, they were not to be by themselves in the white room where the shades had been lowered and the chandeliers dimmed. Shadows moved mutely, dreamily, over the surfaces of darkened mirrors; and chairs in their white slipcovers huddled piously against the walls. The room was nearly dark, except for the light that came from a rose-shaded lamp in a far corner where half a dozen people sat so deeply ensconced in their overstuffed chairs as to seem enervated with fatigue. They were listening to Nessie telling them that she would absolutely refuse to hear a word said against the painter, Weintraub. Nessie spoke softly, very softly, smiling all the while a friendly, patient smile as if she were tolerating her friends' foolishness. Lowering her long eyelashes, she said, "No, darlings. You don't understand."

Nessie had an embroidered yellow silk reticule in her lap from which, with her dry, child's fingers, she took out reproductions of paintings her artist friend had made and passed them around to be looked at. One of the reproductions showed four blind horses, but it was not the horses that moved Nessie as much as the thoughts about the artist's life that rose in her mind as she studied the picture: a boyhood in a Godforsaken village where the soul-destroying summer days dragged on their endless way; a village in which even cockcrow sounded the world's grief.

He was the son of a hard-bitten querulous father, a man with a whiplash for a tongue who was quick to scold the boy: "Good-for-nothing, ne'er-do-well, scamp. Off with you now. To school, boy. To school. Whatever's to become of you?"

To school which, for the boy, had long ago become a place of torment where the rabbi made the boys repeat endlessly the weekly Torah portion.

"Good-for-nothing. Ne'er-do-well. Scamp." The boy leaned against the fence surrounding his father's house and heard the words, while above his head the thick branches of an acacia creaked. Sometimes he wandered into the back yard where the flies buzzed over their chosen filthy places; sometimes he went off to the village and poked about in its back alleys; sometimes he visited the mill and watched the grinding of the grain and the four blind horses dragging the vast grinding wheel as if a circle were their road to heaven. They strained their necks; they flared their nostrils; their blind eyes glistened but their route was a circle still, and they remained where they had always been.

And this is what that boy—now grown—had drawn. These blind horses. With a couple of hundred of his father's rubles, the boy had somehow made his escape. He had run away from home; gone abroad; and now he had come back. Now he was the subject of newspaper articles. A painter, recognized. Famous. Great.

"Great," Nessie agreed, and added, "There are some lucky people in the world."

One of the company pointed a connoisseur's finger at the

swaybacked black horse and calling attention to the way in which the forelock fell over its eyes, he sniffed, "Jewish horses."

Schur took a second look at the picture. He was evidently expected to say something about it. Looking about him, he observed unhappily that Abraham Rappaport was no longer in the room. Left to his own devices he said, "I'm sorry but I know nothing about paintings."

The things people talked about in Rappaport's house were never mentioned in the Schur home, nor in the homes of his two rich aunts. Schur, trying to understand the conversation, sat and listened attentively. As it happened, nothing very profound was being said. The red-haired student with the strangely matured features and the brand new jacket buttons did most of the talking. Earlier, he had been asked about various of his published essays which dealt with Zionist themes but now, on the subject of Weintraub the painter, he had grown lugubriously earnest. Sunk deeply into his chair, the student absolutely denied Nessie's contention that Weintraub deserved to be called great. "No," he said. "Nessie will have to forgive me. To be great, an artist must have . . . substance."

"Substance?" It was the poet who wrote in Hebrew, the reticent fellow with the pouches under his eyes who, looking dumbstruck, had turned to question the student.

"And one thing more," the student said, ignoring the interruption, "There is such a thing as an overblown reputation." The student, it developed, had had a personal experience with Weintraub. It had happened just before Passover, when the student, having finished his exams in Petersburg, was traveling home, and sharing a train compartment with one of his friends, an interesting young woman. As it happened, Weintraub, too, was there. Throughout the entire journey, Weintraub displayed all the tricks of a village wit—a peasant grossness, so to say.

Schur watched the student's display of ill-temper and was perplexed. The student went on to berate the Petersburg intellectuals who kept singing Weintraub's praises, and heaped scorn on the women students who pursued the painter on every occasion. Evidently the student took Nessie's and the newspaper's praise of Weintraub as a personal insult to himself. Schur thought the whole thing very strange.

Someone interrupted the student's diatribe and in the discussion that followed several things became suddenly clear: the young painter, Weintraub, was presently in Kiev; he was on very good terms with Nessie and came to the house often to visit her. And one thing more was now terribly clear to Schur: Moishele Levine's daughter had gone off to spend the entire evening with this Weintraub.

Schur's heart sank—or, to put it better, it actually died for an instant. Then there was a numb feeling, after which his reason asserted itself, though he felt a lingering dissatisfaction for allowing himself to be upset by the whole thing. After all, Schur was visiting Rappaport's house for the first time. How did Moishele Levine's daughter concern him?

Then, to avoid thinking of her, Schur made a devoted effort to pay attention to the conversation. Again, the redheaded student was doing the talking. He was describing the trip home from Petersburg and how Weintraub, throughout the journey, had freely helped himself to the young woman's chocolates and oranges, while keeping up a constant monologue about himself, Weintraub.

It would appear that the young woman and the student were by no means coincidentally in the same compartment. Indeed, the student had had to wait a day or two for her in Petersburg before they could travel together, and he had looked forward to their train trip, hoping to answer various questions that she had about some of the articles on Zionism he had lately published. But Weintraub, the blond, longhaired painter, sat facing them, constantly interrupting their conversation with flip remarks as he swayed back and forth to the motions of the train. His tongue was in constant motion as he looked into the young woman's eyes and talked on and on—about himself.

Telling them that he, Joel Weintraub was returning home after an absence of many years. He was going back to Kosloveh, the little village near Great Setternitz where he had spent his boyhood. There, in Kosloveh, he was called Yoelik, simply Yoelik. His father had been both a Skvir Hasid and a Zionist who had finally left for Palestine after selling his property in Kosloveh to a wealthy shopkeeper. The well-built, whitewashed house had octagonal yellow window frames, and there were old acacia trees in the front yard. Not only acacia trees; there were also three huge craggy stones. Joel Weintraub said he was haunted by the stones. Often, he started up from his sleep at night and felt compelled to draw those stones whose every crack and contour he could still remember. When, having drawn the stones, he tried going back to sleep he was unable to do so but lay, wherever he was, with his eyes closed, seeing himself again in Kosloveh, sitting on the porch of his father's house behind whose closed shutters there now slept the strange shopkeeper and his family. Sometimes he imagined that he sat on the porch steps late at night and listened to the hushed murmur of the acacias as he had heard them once, long ago in the course of a summer. He could still hear his father shouting, "Good-for-nothing. Ne'er-do-well. Scamp." And now Weintraub was going back to Kosloveh. He had sent the shopkeeper a telegram offering to buy back his father's house.

The red-haired student was taking far too long to tell how Weintraub had bored them in the train compartment. "I never in my life," he said, "heard anyone go on at such a rate, or be so boorishly in love with himself, with the sound of his own words." But the student had lost his audience. No one was listening. One by one, the company had scattered.

Schur was touched by how frail and forlorn the waiflike Nessie looked sitting in the weak glow of the lamp. He remembered how, when she was being driven home yesterday, she had pleaded with her driver, "No, dear, no. Not so fast." And now she sat looking unhappy in her father's house. It was hard to know what she was thinking . . . perhaps of Weintraub of whom she had spoken so much in the course of the evening. Or perhaps she was imagining a tale about herself—a sad tale of a hunchbacked sculptress. A tale that began, "Once upon a time a weak child was born to a respected and wealthy father . . ." Wanting to make Nessie feel the warmth of his sympathy, Schur bowed and engaged her in conversation. "Can you tell me, perhaps," he said, "how old the painter is . . . Weintraub?"

"How old he is?" Nessie mused. As she looked up at Schur, her long eyelashes quivered. Her slightly crossed eyes had resumed their usual gentle good humor. "How old is Weintraub? I really don't know, dear," she said. "Young. He's still quite young." As Nessie turned her mind to other thoughts, Joseph Schur found himself grateful for the word "dear."

"But you," he persisted, "you too are an artist. A sculptress. Why don't you talk about your own work?"

"Me," she said. "Ah, me. No, dear. I'm no more than a simple craftsman, and not a very skillful one at that." She was not offended, but spoke gently to him, as to an equal and thereby earned his gratitude. He would have liked to forget all that had happened that evening; he would have liked to go on sitting with her; to ask her why she spoke so negatively of herself; but all about them, the company had scattered. The hour was late and the last guests were saying goodbye.

Outside, at the street door, the redheaded student and the poet who wrote in Hebrew stood talking to each other with considerably more intimacy and candor than they had inside. They were making plans to go somewhere and though Joseph Schur was standing nearby, they paid him no more attention than if he were a stray cat passing by. Schur wondered what they would have thought had they known what had happened to him that evening in Abraham Rappaport's house. Then it came to him that the whole point was that no one there had thought about him at all. He felt the insult of it as a sharp, convulsive pain. Then he moved on.

At the corner of the quiet, expensive street, not far from the street light he came face to face with Moishele Levine's daughter and the young painter, Weintraub, who was seeing her home. There was a moment during which she looked closely at Schur as if she were trying to remember where she might have seen him before; or as if she were puzzling out how it happened that he stood there before her now, at this late hour. In that instant, Schur gazed once again into her intelligent blue eyes and noted the firm line of her mouth that reminded him strangely of something remembered, something deeply intimate.

Joseph Schur had no memory of his mother who had died when he was a child of four. And yet, his mother might have had just such a mouth. Schur felt his heart contract. Though just then he could not be certain whether Moishele Levine's daughter had recognized him or not, he felt himself drawn by that mouth until a surge of family pride overwhelmed him and he became once more Itzik Maier's only son who had been raised in an aloof household in Great Setternitz. There, in Great Setternitz, at any rate, he had never been made to feel as utterly worthless and dejected as he now felt. There, in Great Setternitz, he was still the owner of two important houses . . . and the mill. His . . .

Schur heard the painter Weintraub somewhere behind him laughing at something he had just told the beautiful young woman he was seeing home, but the laughter made no further difference to Joseph Schur who walked with firm, quick steps, thinking of his houses and his great mill.

"Ah, yes. The mill. My mill. That's something."

Translated by Leonard Wolf

≈ The Hole Through Which Life Slips

BY DAVID BERGELSON

HIDDEN IN MIST, unseen cankers feast on autumn dampness.

The city is Kiev.

Broad, sprawling.

Along the brows of her hills churches spread. Above, the overcast drips bombs.

Furtively, Yana Grigorievich stands near the window of his upper story apartment. Yana lives alone in the dusty, cobwebbed four rooms. He is tall and broad; a hulk. His hair as well is overgrown; head, mustache, beard. The unrelenting frost in the empty apartment has numbed and reddened his hands and face, swelling them beyond their normal ampleness. Peering out over Kiev, Yana suffers the ache of a prisoner. His memory plucks at another morning; young, sunny.

She'd been bustling since sun up in the bedroom. On the soft rug in the book-lined study, he submitted to the languid roll of the rocking chair. Once, when she passed through the library, he smelled fresh talc.

He would swear it happened this way:

She was humming. To him—tufting at his neatly shorn brown beard—the moment seemed important, requiring solemnity. Rocking soundlessly, he wished to probe the following thought, "Odd . . . when I married her elder sister twelve years ago, I knew, even then. . . . I was attracted to her, the slip of the family. I've loved her since."

Although he knew she was past first flowering, her fresh, young fragrance teased his nostrils.

Between them—husband and wife—the following conversation took place:

"You're leaving me, Eva?"

"I'm leaving you, Yana."

"For good, Eva?"

"For good, Yana. Be well."

"Stay well, Eva."

This was the morning his memory plucked.

But the truth is, she had not said, "Be well," and he had not answered, "Stay well."

The truth is this:

Less than a year ago—after the Bolsheviks had seized power in Petersburg—two misfortunes befell Yana Grigorievich, graduate engineer and practicing publicist (his caustic lampoons had marked him, in the eyes of the Czarist regime, a radical Marxist):

In the midst of a spiralling demand from the Left press for his services—each newspaper outbidding the other to hire him—he was struck with an odd languor. As if the will to write had been drained from him forever, he set his pen aside.

Shortly thereafter, his wife Eva cast him off without a "be well" to join her family—brothers and brothers-in-law—who were deeply involved in the Petersburg uprising.

She deserted him because Kiev was tasting only the backwash of the exciting events in Petersburg and Moscow. Restlessly, Eva rattled like a machine gun:

"In Petersburg, they did . . . what must be done."

"Things are just beginning to get lively."

"In Kiev's nationalist swamp, you need hip boots."

She left him also because he was twelve years older (he, forty-three; she, thirty-one); and she, childless. What else, other than children and love, could hold a marriage against the tremors of a shaking world?

That was that. Yana did not seek solace even in the thought that her leaving was no less banal than her rat-a-tat. Moreover, his first misfortune was more serious than her departure.

Introspective, quiet—admiring, as he did, organization—Yana disdained to upset his way of life over Eva's desertion. Both

externally, in his four room apartment (laid out neatly and func-
tionally to serve a writer) and internally, where he'd learned to
control thought and emotion, Yana desired to maintain his accustomed stability. Here he drew on his childhood training, instilled
abroad. His mother, a widowed emigrant, had given Yana a German
education in order to teach him discipline.

It would be accurate to say that Yana sat through the whole
morning Eva left him, rocking in his chair on the deep-piled rug,
unperturbed. His eyebrows, arching over the dark horn-rims of his
glasses, and his lips pressed tight to distention, conveyed, clearer
than words:

"Well yes . . . what other way . . . you can't cross swords with
nature. . . ."

In short:

His balm that day—his accommodation with fate—was the
repetition of his own philosophical formulation:

"Misfortune will have its way."

Therefore protest was frivolous and resistance farcical. He was
content, with these convictions, to rock the days away in this chair
on the carpet of his book-lined study. Languor was less farcical than
sword-crossing.

Paradox is, after all, an exercise in defining conflicting congruities
through logic. Life, however, scorns logic and pulverizes congruity.
Thus paradox is both life and truth, and he, Yana, as validly definable
as a paradox as an individual.

In totidem verbis:

Since all individuals, including Yana Grigorievich, are paradoxes,
if you lose a three-ruble note, the urgency is not to find the bill, but
the hole through which it slipped.

In those days, Yana went about, seeking the hole. . . .

Yana remained with the maid. She carried on in the spirit of the
old days, puttering in the apartment, as if Eva was still overseeing.
Each morning, as usual, she shopped, waiting patiently in the queues
for bread and other foods.

The city in those days:

Ukrainians in yellow and black headbands cruise the streets,
piled on requisitioned automobiles.

The boulevards swarm.

The faces are dour. Occasionally, one or another of the crowd will stop, as if just roused from a nightmare:

"Look at them."

"Fiends!"

"So that's our sovereignty! . . ."

The Kievers jeer the queues, the bad bread, the wagons trundling off the corpses of the executed along the streets at dawn.

An airplane churns the bilge overhead. A mother in a breadline, stretching her neck as if to the slaughter knife, says, "Come. Kiev's a cow. Whoever grabs an udder, draws milk."

That autumn was its own burden. Sog hung, unable to drop rain or snow; heavy, pasting to the eyelids like spit.

In short:

The weather suited Yana Grigorievich. Rocking in his chair, he probed. . . . Where is the hole, through which life slipped?

"Why have I stopped writing? Ideas flowed. Now, I've dried up. Why?"

A few weeks later, Yana's maid abandoned him. Suddenly, without a word. Crudely, as maids can. She left the week the regiments of the new regime arrived and fanned out behind Kiev. Overhead, airplanes appeared and spilled bombs, and the queues broke and scattered. Yana, whose apathy kept him from a newspaper or the street—to discuss the identity of the new sovereignty (although he assumed it to be the Bolsheviks)—was too numb to think through a conclusion on why the maid had left him:

"Was she uneasy living in the apartment with him, unchaperoned? Were all women contemptuous of a deserted husband? Or was she as fearful of the airplanes overhead as the crowd in the queue, and as hopeful that the regiments fanning out would bring peace?"

Several days had gone by before Yana noticed the maid's departure, so absorbed was he by his determination to avoid any move that might appear absurd.

He felt:

The sympathy of the populace for the new regime, his wife's desertion, and his inability to write, had all been woven into one woof, and he could heard the weaver whispering in his ear:

"A snare, Yana Grigorievich . . . a tangled skein."

He answered slowly; too slowly and overcomposed.

Outside, cankers hidden in mist continued to feast on autumn dampness, and bombers to fly overhead. His hands stiffened and reddened in the unrelieved frost filling the dusty, empty rooms; swelled. Yana put on weight, puffed out, grew ruddy. He drew specious pleasure from his isolation, and the opportunity it gave him—without a maid intruding—to observe the snarl in the city below. He prowled the rooms for tinder. In the kitchen, fetid with mice droppings and unremoved garbage, he found several boxes. With slow, swollen fingers Yana splintered the wood and fed kindling to the fire in his room. When ashes only remained, he continued to sit opposite the fireplace, gross and overgrown, snug beneath his layers of fat. He lifted his horn rims to his forehead and pursed his lips, as if to whistle. Yana was on the verge of finding the hole through which life had slipped. . . .

With the last bomb, sun broke through the overcast like shrapnel.

A new regime took over the city.

Yana Grigorievich's face, a question:

"Bolsheviks?"

Strangely radiant, the maid returned with a girl friend on the third or fourth day for her forgotten possessions. They chattered, loudly, as if Yana were not at home. Their babble grated him out of a deep afternoon nap. He thought, "The maid is marrying today. Her girl friend also. Each will stand as the other's bridesmaid."

To no purpose, the day was clear, sun frosted. The newly hung-out red flags snapped jauntily. Festivity throbbed in the city.

The squares filled with rallies.

Stillness hovered only over the dead. Quiet tears. Church bells mute.

That afternoon Yana observed:

"Setting aside reason, I feel fit physically. Festive, stimulated, as if all sorts of delights are returning with the Bolsheviks. My wife, Eva Abramovna, for instance. Any moment, she might call on the phone or step through the door."

But reason is clever and the body an oaf.

To prove to his flesh that its anticipations lacked logic, Yana dressed in a short fur jacket and a pair of boots, holdovers from the beginning of the War when he'd worked in a factory as an engineer. To quell the eruption in him, Yana forced himself into the street, strolling without zest, as if he were pushing a perambulator.

In the city, skeins of light link the holiday to the populace. Individually, each face in the multitude is nothing, an idle poppy-seed cruncher. Yet the mass is solemn and imminent. Hard with determination. Eyes ominous.

The crowds in the squares grow raucous. At midday, when the hoarseness can be weighed, Yana shuffles still, as if behind his perambulator, from one rally to another. It seems this is possible: in a leather jacket, cheeks flaming, he will find his Eva Abramovna haranguing a crowd.

"And why not? She's a clever woman. A politcom!"

Yana knew, this was hope appeasing restlessness and reason. He started to limp under the exertion of shuffling from square to square, rally to rally, trudging in grief and anticipation, but without rancor. At every square, he called his body's attention, as if it were a child:

"See? No Eva."

"Convinced?"

"You're tired."

"Come home."

His weary body surrendered. Yana turned back to his apartment to take up his task of finding the hole through which life had slipped.

Events intervened.

Yana had wandered to the bank of the Dnieper and there as well a rally clustered. The throng: in short jackets and frayed boots, unstable, resembling the eddying waters nearby. The river: unfrozen but colder than ice; alternating confluences of still and scudding tides; heavy and angry, its black pitch too dismal to shelter either shadow or reflection.

From both rally and river a cold wind bit into Yana.

At the edge of the crowd, a knurl of rivermen, youngsters and idle poppy-seed crunchers watched the speaker, a spitting frump dressed like a parson's spinster daughter: shabby, with a dusty ostrich feather waving over her broad-brimmed hat. From the knurl someone shouted:

"What's she talking about?"

"The Czarina. Heard her mention the Czarina."

"A pity? Did she say, 'a pity'?"

The poppy-seed crunchers cackled. One shouted, "Crown her!" A calloused hand reached out from the crowd and plucked the ostrich feather. The hat spun in a circle and then wafted off to the nearby Dnieper. Whooping and laughing, the crowd forsook the speaker and scuttled to the bank after the hat.

The wind ruffled the short gray hair of the abandoned frump. She wept. Sobbing not only accentuated her meagerness—drawing her cheeks in—but emphasized her one fullness as well. Her thick lips bulged, whimpering independently of her eyes and watery nose. One young man approached the frump hesitantly, shuffling to her side without a greeting. He spoke, apparently in consolation, placed his palm on her elbow and led her down a side street as if she were the widow at a wake.

To Yana, the profile and carriage of the young man suggested Eva's family. Having no wish to meet her relatives, Yana turned away. He felt lonely as an orphan. If he nursed any desire, it was to drag his body to the apartment, certainly not to face acquaintances. While engaged with this thought, Yana became aware that a new speaker had attracted a new crowd. He plodded to its edge and his face strained toward the harangue, as if asking:

"What's he want? What's the point?"

Some moments later, Yana turned, and saw the young man at his elbow. The youth's gaze was uncertain. Stubble spattered his face like ashes. His fur coat, its worn skins no longer identifiable, flapped unbuttoned, although the whipping wind hunched the young man's shoulders. Between his parted thin blue lips, attractive even teeth showed. His smile would be as engaging as Eva's. Owing either to insufficient sleep or the pressure of conflicting thoughts, around his gray eyeballs the whites were mottled pink. He gaped in artless astonishment at the speaker, glancing sideways into the crowd to seize each random comment and examine with wonder the by-stander who had made it.

The orator, thickset and square, with a cloak falling from his shoulders, thrummed powerfully to his peak. His pumping arms hovered over his coat buttons, primed, if necessary, to rip the cloak off to emphasize a point.

The young man strained forward, cupping his ears to snare every word. Distractedly, he blurted to Yana standing nearby:

"Did you hear *that?*"

"He's raining hail."

"Each word. . . . You're right. He flings more granite than the River Sambatyon."

The youth turned, and slowly distraction gave way to attentiveness, and a fresh expression seeped into his eyes.

"Ach! Yana? Yana Grigorievich! Didn't recognize you, I swear. Let's look at you. I've been asking, hoping someone'd seen you. For spite, no one's crossed your path. Come, let's stand here. No, we'll walk. I was certain you'd left too. These last weeks, the whole city's scattered. . . ."

This is just a thread of the sleave of talk with which the young man entangled Yana Grigorievich.

"Today the basic question is, who's alive? Pardon? . . . Yes, out of work. That is . . . look at them."

The youth stopped and waved his hand at the crowd on the river's bank.

"See them? When we're both dust they'll still be fodder for historians. . . . Eva is in Petersburg I know. A Bolshevik. Well yes, *my* family, but no surprise. I remember Eva . . . a firebrand even as a child. Dragged her young brother Volodye into her cell. And then at eighteen–nineteen, when you met her, she turned shy. That happens often you know. Responsibility confronts immaturity. Marriage and motherhood. Some face up. Others turn back. . . ."

As the young man paused for breath, Yana lifted his gaze toward the sky, peering through his horn rims in search of light. Pressing his lips together, he prepared to say, "Of course we can't change nature." Instead he mumbled, "Well, yes, . . . Eva . . . lately she'd been restless, tense. . . ."

The youth ignored him and resumed his chatter:

"Just last week a woman, a Communist, said to me, 'These times are more interesting to live with than any man.' I told her, 'Firstly, if you weren't pretty I'd accuse you of frustration. Secondly, an attractive woman doesn't live with interesting times. She whores with it.' My word, I said it. Today I learned Eva's younger brother, Volodye, is a key Bolshevik, a policy maker. A head he always had on his shoulders. A temper . . . live embers. Fire! Inherited. A family of daring merchants. Remember this rule: a bold merchant makes a bold revolutionist. Don't laugh. They're comparable. Just this morning I ran into . . . guess who? Zolotonash. Moscow ordered him to Kiev. A risky delegation of power. . . ."

The young man glanced sideways at Yana. Here Yana is, he thought, idle. A pity. During the war he showed promise. Wrote with bite and to the point. Wait a minute, wait. . . . I wonder. . . . "You know what I think?"

In his distraction, the youth stopped suddenly, and Yana was forced to retrace several steps. The young man lay one finger across his nose, deliberating whether to confide in Yana.

"You know what I'll tell you? It just occurred to me, why you stopped writing. Listen now. Simple. What pinched you all these years? Society. Capitalism pushed you to invective. 'The devil take you!' Since you're a man of delicacy and vulgarity's foreign to you, your feelings channelled themselves into a stream of perceptive articles. Now that the Bolsheviks are here, it's clear: perceptiveness is irrelevant. Did you hear that speaker? Short and vile and up his mother's. . . . Why do you look at me like that? . . . Is it my loss of weight you notice? . . . Yes, I am drawn. . . . Three months I spent in bed, half dead . . . my old ailment, leukemia. . . ."

He'd entered a sanitarium, he told Yana, when the German retreat began, and left when the Bolsheviks came.

"Pardon? . . . Yes, pure delight. I missed a regime or two. . . . True, the sanitarium serves as a refuge. On the other hand, it becomes the haven of neither the sick nor the healthy. Rather a madhouse. The sights! Generally, the atmosphere. . . . Listen, Yana, give me a hand. Please. . . . Here's a coach. . . . I beg you. Help me up and take me home. . . . For some reason, my head's spinning. . . . Maybe I left the bed too soon. But I'm restless. . . . Here, here. . . ."

Eyes shut, the young man sat in the coach all the way to the

sanitarium. Although his color turned the dead gray of ashes, his lips
continued to twitch, and dribbled weak, feverish phrases:

"If it hails granite.... Sambatyon!... The sights!... In the
sanitarium, you're driven by the emotions of others, not your own
... or you clutch at the past.... You saw the frump lose her hat?...
A pauper.... Ugly.... Not her emotion. I mean, pity for the
Czarina. Someone else's sorrow, not hers. Out of the past.... Not for
me. Live with your own emotion.... Your own.... Are we near ...
eh?... Are we near the sanitarium?...

At dusk, Yana Grigorievich came back to his apartment.

Of all the young man's chatter—he turned out to be a first cousin
of Eva's, named Muni—Yana could remember only his words as he'd
stopped suddenly, forcing Yana to retrace several steps.

"What pinched you?... Pushed you to invective. 'The devil take
you!' You channelled your feelings into a stream of perceptive
articles. In vain. A waste. Did you hear how they say it now, short
and vile and up their mothers'?..."

Working his eyebrows, his lips pressed tight, Yana plodded about
his apartment deep into the night. He seemed on the verge of saying,
"Of course ... well, we can't change nature."

He could not convince himself. "Did Muni speak the truth? Is
that the hole, through which my life has slipped?... Can it be ...
that simple?...

Translated by Reuben Bercovitch

≈ Civil War

BY DAVID BERGELSON

Introductory Note

When David Bergelson published the novella *Civil War* in his collection *Storm Days* in 1928, the artistic recreation of the Russian Revolution and its aftermath dominated Soviet literature. In 1926 there had been several notable events. Eisenstein had presented *Potemkin* on the movie screen; Bulgakov had offered his play, *The Last Days of the Turbins*, on the Moscow stage and won critical acclaim; Babel's *Red Cavalry* had been hailed as a masterpiece of the new literature.

Civil War was one of Bergelson's first efforts to show the Revolution through the lens of his impressionistic prose. The story relates the experiences of two gentile workers, Botchko and Zeek, moving eastward through the Ukraine during the troubled years of 1917–19. To follow the story with ease, it is helpful to know some of the allusions to major events at the time in the Ukraine.

In Kiev, a group of Ukrainian nationalists declared a Republic soon after the February Revolution broke out in St. Petersburg. With the Bolshevik seizure of power in October, 1917, relations between the Ukrainians and the Bolsheviks grew strained. Among the Ukrainian leaders there figured the notorious anti-Semite Petlura. He and his colleagues favored the Whites. This led to war and the occupation of Kiev by the Bolsheviks on February 8, 1918. The Ukrainians then appealed to the Germans to help them and on March 2, 1918, Kiev fell to linked forces of the German army and the Petlura irregulars.

With the Armistice of November 11, 1918, defeated Germany abandoned her military occupation and Petlura became commander-in-chief of a new "Ukrainian Directorate." But the Bolsheviks, having regrouped their forces, took Kharkov on November 29, 1918, and entered Kiev in February, 1919. The Civil War had now begun in earnest. Petlura, in retreat, massacred Jews wherever he found them. Bergelson's story closes in late December, 1918, with allusions to the approaching massacres.

Civil War begins *in medias res*. Botchko and Zeek appear at a Jewish inn on the east side of the Dnieper River, somewhat north of Kiev. The time is late March, 1918, just after the first Bolshevik retreat from Kiev.

Chapter Two takes place in a nearby forest between March and late summer, 1918. However, there is a long flashback which takes us back to a year earlier, when Botchko is leading a regiment from the eastern front of World War I into the tiny southwestern Ukrainian town of Zvill. Here he falls in love with Frosia and spends autumn, 1917 with her. The unruly regiment begins to disintegrate, as does civil order in the Ukraine.

Now on their own, Botchko and Zeek go to join the Bolsheviks defending Kiev in February, 1918. At this point, the story returns to time present, and Chapter Two ends with Botchko, Zeek and their somewhat ambiguous "Comrade" Andreyuk leaving the forest in which they have been hiding and setting off for Kharkov.

The rainy autumn of 1918 dominates Chapter Three, which is set on an estate south of Kharkov. The German occupation and its retreat are counterpointed by aimless wanderings over the ravaged land by the leading characters in search of the Bolsheviks.

Chapter Four centers on a Jewish inn at the little southeastern Ukrainian town of Alexandrovka in winter, 1918. It is mainly inhabited by Jews caught in an impossible situation—they seem to be awaiting their destruction passively. The arrival of Botchko and his Bolshevik comrades seems to coincide with the new Red offensive of late November, 1918. Meanwhile, however, the Petlura bands are lurking in the area, as the story ends in an abrupt silence.

Bergelson has his narrator maintain a detached, ironic, if not ambivalent, view of the characters and events. Violent action is not shown, only anticipations of and reactions to it. Everything is muted yet ominous, fearful. Anthropomorphized descriptions of nature provide an equivalent to the psychological atmosphere. Plot is replaced by what Russian critics call *skaz*, the narrator's manner of telling his story through patterned repetitions.

—*S.L.W.*

I
Weary from Spring Plowing, the Horses Stand Listless

ON A DUNGHILL toward dusk an old lonely brood hen clucked and squawked in the warm manure and laid no eggs.

Halfway between a large swampy forest and a poor, backwoods village, a wizened inn warmed its curved roof—squatting in the glow of the setting sun—and could not get warm.

Towards evening, a rattling new horse and wagon brought by a sturdy fellow with a long narrow face wearing brand new boots.

Jumping off, he whirled on one heel and looked about not so much with his black eyes as with his smile, which ran back and forth over a thin, arched, split upper lip. Feeling quite at home, he looked into the kitchen.

"So where is Reyzel, Malke? Still in the village?"

For a moment, the old Jewish woman stopped pounding her fists into the sour leaven. Going to rake back her hair with the sleeve of her doughy hand, she only managed to wipe her running nose.

"The maid?" (as if she were spitting into the dough) "The maid grabbed the goose—ran to see how the Petluras will lead the Germans into the village . . . they even say with music—what do you think?"

She breathed heavily.

"And what's it like in the village? Did they round up the Bolsheviks?"

"Of course."

The young man didn't stop grinning. He rubbed the tip of his nose with a finger. His eyes seemed to wander and appeared distracted.

"Just a few minutes ago," he said, "the Germans were moving them out."

"Many?"

"About forty."

"Petrik too? That Bolshevik?"

"None other."

"There'll be no one to work for you in the woods."

"Don't worry . . . there's always someone."

Silence. A raspy throat spluttered in the next large room.

"Have the Germans taken over the village, Voli?"

"They've taken over, lock, stock, and barrel, Noah. . ."

The young man entered the dark nearby room.

On a little sofa the dozing owner sat—like an overblown slippery ball—his shoulders leaning against a warm heater, his feet tucked under and his head continually slipping down to his chest. For years he had done business in the village with the gentiles: in wintertime lending them money, in summertime taking back their grain. He spent every minute going over the accounts in his head: how much he was owed from each separately and from everyone together. The young man who had just sat down was alone at the table on the other side of the room, apparently waiting for the maid. He, too, seemed to nod off with the smile still glued to his thin, turned-up, nibbling lips.

"You know, Noah"—the young man blurted from his smiling doze—"I have to thank God for escaping by the skin of my teeth."

"How so?"

"Peyseh was killed, Peyseh who was blind in one eye! He had served, too, just like me, in the woods at the ten-mile marker."

"And so?"

"The day before yesterday he had to travel to Voloderka for woodcutters."

"So?"

"And I was supposed to go with him."

It became quiet. The old man in the corner seemed to have never stopped dozing, and his head once again began to slip, and once again he kept adding figures in his head. The young man was soon asleep too. In the kitchen the oven blazed. The kneading trough creaked loudly under the old woman's wrinkled hand. Outside in the dark, in front of the window, a pair of unfamiliar shadows quivered.

"Once again," the old woman croaked with a deathlike rattle, "just as I said; keep the door bolted, frogs are hopping about . . . ever since the Sabbath. We don't know them. Who knows where they're from . . ."

The young man snorted through his sleep:

"From Kiev. From the other side of the Dnieper. They're Bolsheviks. Since the Germans took over in just one night, they didn't even have time to grab a stitch of clothes. Those the river let past, as they say, survived. The others now roam about in twos and threes and avoid the houses. They're picked up one by one in the villages. If you're moving about the forest . . . suddenly you see one. They've been so badly beaten, no one's afraid of them. I'm going back to sleep, Malke."

Having traveled a long hard road, two men in filthy, mudsplattered overcoats came here, to the obscure inn, and knocked on the door. They hesitated: to enter or not?

A noose hung over each village—for "choking" Bolsheviks. All around were scattered larger and smaller units of the Ukrainian and German forces. From the other side of the distant field and muddy path, a sodden sky approached the village. Snug homes beckoned to them in the evening haze. But the peacefulness of the village lay concealed by the lurking danger.

One of the two was called Botchko.

The other, Zeek.

Finally they unbolted the door of the inn and went in—to have a drink, to ask questions, to eat something perhaps. The old woman answered them:

"We've nothing."

"No bread?"

"None to be had. They just rounded up the Bolsheviks in the village today. My maid went to see and is still not back."

Why did she suddenly need to mention the Bolsheviks? Was she frightened by two strange faces at nightfall and was she trying to warn that the countryside was not entirely lawless?

Botchko and Zeek seemed to pay no attention as they passed the ladle back and forth and glanced sidelong at the old woman. She was a lean, bony, wrinkled old thing. They could have knocked her down with just one blow. But there was no need for that. They went into the second large room, sat down, chewed dry bread, and waited for tea. They kept on chewing and looked with amazement at the run-down creature on the sofa—a curiosity. Even though it was now warm outside, it sat by the fiery-warm heater and was somewhat asleep and somewhat awake and one could not know if it heard what was going on around it or not.

"Kachoo!"

Zeek sneezed deliberately to see whether this creature would wake up or not.

Only the dozing young man at the head of the table woke up. He opened his dark eyes and quickly buttered his thin, cleft, nibbling lips with a slippery little smile.

"Are you perhaps coming from work, neighbors?"

"No," both stopped chewing at the same time.

"So you're looking for work?"

"Sure—looking."

"Perhaps here in our woods, neighbors?"

Botchko and Zeek stared at each other.

"We could, why not?"

"Chopping wood?"

Botchko and Zeek suddenly began to talk to each other, almost too softly. A crafty ray of light crept into the black eyes of the young man; his eyes soon met the fire in Zeek's and his own died out.

"The campsite, however, is far away. Four miles deep into the forest . . . and wet."

"We know," snuffled Botchko, looking down quietly. How often he had worked in wet lands!

That same evening Botchko and Zeek were bouncing along with the young man in the little wagon on the way to a strange forest. It was a cool night. In the late winter frost, many distant stars from the dark sky looked down upon the village and in all the houses the inhabitants were already fast asleep.

"Giddy-up," the young man said calmly.

It meant:

"Sleep, sleep—these are men we know."

They parked the wagon in the corner of the village, near the church. On both sides of the wagon were stains from geese brought to market. An old Ukrainian voice approached, sounding harsh and ill-disposed:

"Who goes there?"

The young man answered in a sullen voice:

"It's me. From the Marshener Forest District—my woodcutters."

And the wagon went on undisturbed.

The young man no longer made any noise. Drawing his neck deep into his shoulders, shrinking into a ball, he let his horse run on against the long sparkling icy road, prancing freely up against a hill and with a moon which was rising there just over the treetops of an angry forest. It appeared as if the young man were innocent, lost in his dreams and dozing away. He was glad that he had obtained a pair of woodcutters cheaply for his wet campsite. Suddenly he turned his pale face to them—to Zeek and Botchko and began to peer at them. He kept staring at them with a wet grin on his arched lips and, with a glint of fire in his pupils, unexpectedly shut one eye and with the second, gave a wink.

"From the Bolsheviks, perhaps? Just south of Kiev?"

Standing on his knees, Zeek looked around in the wagon for something with which to defend himself but the young man quickly blurted:

"It's all the same to me. The main thing is: stay calm, cut wood and don't leave the campsite. It's a bit wet, so take care ... the Germans are out patrolling all over the place ... but they won't go there."

II
Longing for the South, Bound for the North

High above the fir tops, over the tufty heads of hundred-year-old alders, kindling threads of gold, sewn through the green sash of pine needles, flamed the second half of a late summer day.

Below, starting from the late afternoon to the twilight hour, a chill passed over the swampy floor, around broken branches, wood tar and toppled tree trunks. Shadowy breezes drifted into a tranquil velvet darkness.

Botchko and Zeek, the only "team" here in the depths of the thick woods, put aside the ax, sluggishly drew up to the fire, shoved their feet in and dried their soaking sandals together with the rags on top of them—they had hardly worked that day.

Zeek, the taller of the two, with a scar shaped like a half moon near the left eye, on that same day put suspenders over his blue shirt (a souvenir from the time before the war when he was a worker in Chicago). In the early dawn he caught a young woman wandering deep in the dry part of the woods—a sort of widow who went about looking for work in a distant swampy hamlet. He engaged her in conversation and learned that her husband had been hanged shortly after their wedding because he had gone to Kiev along with the Bolsheviks during the winter.

He led the girl back to the isolated swampy campground and conferred with Botchko:

"Let her stay? What do you think, Vladimir?"

They spoke to each other for a while in guarded words and spat expertly between gritted teeth on the woodpile while both of them stared with icy bovine eyes at the young woman. Remaining at a proper distance, she glanced downward coyly and plucked the leaves one by one from a small shrub.

Zeek's long face with its uneasy angles seemed to elicit pity like the face of a victim:

"Could she stay, Vladimir? Could she stack wood?"

A momentary pause.

"Could she, Vladimir?"

Botchko finally nodded his head, his velvet black eyes bulging as if he had difficulty swallowing and, as usual, he stroked first his large left whisker and then his right—meaning:

"Yes!"

For the next four or five hours the sharp saw seemed more taut than ever in their muscular hands.

All around and beyond in the deep stillness of the forest there was no one to hear how sharp-toothed steel sneaked back and forth through thick humid logs and sawed with patient skill, with silent echoes, with the beat of well-measured breathing.

They never stopped casting lustful glances at the short red dress and the red colored feet. Zeek's restless pupils sparkled with pleasure.

"A pair of sexy little feet. . . . From God, eh?"

"Yes, yesiree," he kept on, happy with his flashy American words which set off a chorus of echoes in the stillness of the forest.

From a distance between the thick tree trunks, he was able to see all the while how the girl, with an old colored shawl enveloping her like a crucifix across her full breasts, awkwardly brought together the rough planks, held them close to her breast while she placed them in orderly rows, and bashfully glanced toward the men who were here with her alone, unobserved, in the depths of the woods.

"Get to work . . . no standing around."

The men, with unabated energy, worked the saw back and forth with their hands.

Only with the first slanting beams of the sun did lanky Zeek suddenly feel the urge to go and see how the girl was working.

From a distance, between the thick stumps of trees, Botchko saw how Zeek began a conversation, how he took her two hands and how suspiciously the woman, with young eyes like greenish grapes, swelled her doubled chin. She was embarrassed and kept her mouth at a proper distance from him. But bashfully she drew him to her, moving towards the half-soaked grasses beneath the freshly piled stacks of wood, moving backwards and disappearing behind them with him. It lasted a while.

The straining ear imagined it heard a struggle there between bodies.

"Yes, yesiree," Zeek's stentorian voice called out from behind the woodstack.

And it became still again. A frightened grayish-black bird, the color of twilight, which was still hiding in its nest somewhere in the woodpile, flew so low over Botchko's head that his spine felt the frightening flutter of its large wings.

Botchko bristled as if he were angry with someone. He drew to a side, rolled cheap tobacco into a cigar, and sat down next to a smoking fire with his back to the stacks of wood and to what was happening behind them.

Something made him take hold of the ax which was lying nearby. He checked its sharp edge, and soon threw it down, went into a three-cornered ragged hut sunk in mire, emerged from there with a photograph of a young girl, sat down at the edge of the fire and stared at it for a long time.

The girl in the photograph seemed special: a tall girl with a haughty little nose and with happy grey eyes always ready to wink.

Her upper lip was full and curved up so that her dark, passionate, little teeth appeared happy with a fresh nibbling lust.

"Don't be bashful, my little fool . . . so . . . faster . . . faster."

One glance was enough to break a real man's heart. Moreover she had a happy-sounding name: Frosia.

"Frosia . . . Frosia . . ."

Sitting by the fire, bent over, his feet akimbo, Botchko looked longingly into the face on the picture. He seemed to drift far off, pondering deeply within himself.

The more his pining gaze drank up the girl's eyes, her nose, her teeth, the more he felt a quivering in his breast. With each moment his heart yearned still more for the happy time of a year ago. His nose soon filled with the pleasant smell of bygone lust-sated autumn days, of yellow leaves which fell from the trees like musty pillow-down. And his memory was drawn back there ... when did it all take place? Last year? Yes, last year. ...

... Between two ditches alongside the unpaved road cutting through green clouds passed a regiment of soldiers. It spread terror in the region of Gorin, the long river and boundary line.

The regiment overpowered its officers, saying it no longer needed superiors.

On its own, it selected a former deserter, a thrice-decorated squadron leader who owned his own horse. That was none other than Vladimir Botchko.

"Botchko," they shouted from every side, "what are you waiting for? You have your own horse, so ride at the head of the regiment. Be the commander!"

And from that moment on, he always rode slowly at the head of the regiment on his light bay. He did not turn around to look at the thousand-man regiment. He had only to raise his hand as a signal and the entire regiment unleashed a joyous song—as open and un-bounded as the fading fields around, as life itself, for not quite seven months now without a tsar or gentry.

"Ulia, Ulia."

"Ulia, Ulia!" sang the regiment, and both bright and plain faces overflowed with red-hot enthusiasm. It showed in their Cossack curls, their oxen strength, their unfettered, virile shoulders.

Peasants passing in the opposite direction gaped with wide-open eyes as they approached this regiment, and Jews in their wagons clung to each other, shuddering at the soldiers' laughing teeth, fearful of hearing the words "filthy Jew" and yet somehow mistaken, somehow not able to understand.

It was good and fine this way.

Nobles were fleeing in all directions, and wherever the regiment went it found empty shuttered manors and delighted peasants who scratched their heads wisely.

"*Nimo Paniv*" (No more aristocrats), they told the soldiers, "*Pavtikali!*" (They ran away).

And the soldiers laughed.

All along its path the regiment announced that it was battling its way home—it no longer wished to fight on the front. Only here in

Zvill—the town in the South—it was detained for a month.

There, in a large white house on the main street, Frosia lived.

She was at most nineteen years old, but she had already managed to accomplish something: she served in the white house as wetnurse to a Jewish child.

Every èvening Botchko sat there in the enclosed veranda of the Jewish garden. He was enveloped in a tight-fitting officer's coat and his new black boots trod on the fallen yellow leaves as if on something forbidden and delicate.

When Frosia came out to him, he placed her on his knee in the pitch-dark and followed her breath up to her lips. She purposely blew on his nose, puffing the scent of mint candy laced with the fragrance of an unbridled autumn night. At times a stronger smell of onions emerged—she intentionally consumed heavy food to spite her Jewish mistress, who stuffed her with milk and eggs so that the Jewish bastard would become fat from her.

"And where is your own infant, Frosia?"

"Left behind somewhere near the noble's privy," and she did not even know if it were still alive or not. Filled with spite, she wanted the Jewish bastard whom she suckled to ache with stomach cramps. She purposely ate gassy foods—may the devil take him—for reluctantly, from day to day, she was falling more and more in love with him, this alien bastard. Wasn't she right? After all, her employers were only "filthy Jews."

"We ought to put a bullet in every last Jew in town. Right? Botchko? What do you say?"

"Say something," patting him on the chin, still moist from shaving, and pulling some long whiskers so that he would talk.

Botchko squinted for a second, breathed in deeply and quickly shook his head in order to free his whiskers. He pressed her between his knees—since she was already seated in his lap—and felt her thin soft legs under the light dress.

Right now it made no difference to him whether or not Jews were shot—he was in love with Frosia. As he drew her full breasts toward him, it bothered him that someone else was suckling them, such well-formed breasts! He wanted to bite them.

"The fact is," he said, "we should shoot everyone who's been suckled."

And both burst out laughing.

"Will they all be shot?"

Botchko, bending toward her, smiled: "Sure!"

Under a threatening autumnal sky the town grew steadily darker. A pack of dogs spent the day following a bitch in heat, and soldiers, guzzling and rowdy, stared with frenzied eyes at the copulating dogs.

On the road, it was cool and muddy. After each sneeze, a soldier thought he could smell an appealing woman in the air.

The best piece of luck had fallen to Botchko; he had Frosia.

On a Saturday night, he was seated in the enclosed Jewish veranda with Frosia on his lap when some soldiers from his regiment broke into a rich house on the other side of town, near the synagogue where penitential prayers were being intoned. Fleeing from the synagogue to their families, the Jews barred every door in their houses and waited in terror through the night, later emerging to ask repeatedly:

"Did they get anyone?"

"No one?"

Until the local druggist—a Jew who hated Jews—stopped a Jew in the street and slyly asked with needling chuckles:

"So, is there anyone here worth seizing? Is there?"

It happened on a vile Sunday dawn.

The water under the bridges looked cold and murky, like the dirty side of invading winter. Poking about idly in the market, the soldiers, wearing little scarves on their necks, with strange reddened faces and eyes that seemed brutish, sensual, and dull, passed the time like people on holiday.

At the edge of town, near the muddy bridges, the soldiers loitered among squatting beggars who kept blinking their dead eyes. Overheard: how they babbled nervously; witnessed: how a blind man's shaky hand on a scratchy bandura jarred the rhythm of his monkish song.

The blinking eyes of these dead eyes were like frightening reminders of Judgment Day, of the fire and brimstone of the world to come, of blood that will wash across a sinful, verminous world.

But the soldierly ear could make out in this babbling something

as real and familiar as the baying of dogs in the night. Loaded rifles
dangled from military shoulders, and suddenly shots were heard
from the market place. A hunt was on, a free-for-all. People fell dead
on the spot and shops were rifled:

"It's begun, begun!" voices running away, screamed in fright.

"And why? What's up?" At the smoke shop they wouldn't give
the soldiers a discount on tobacco.

The lady of the big white house meanwhile was standing outside
arguing with Frosia to go inside to the child.

"You've nothing on. You'll catch a cold, Frosia. The child will
get sick," as she tugged Frosia by the sleeve. But Frosia pushed her
aside violently. She had no intention of budging from the spot, and,
folding her arms across her breasts, she remained hunched over,
shivering from the cold and staring at the shop, watching how they
kept carrying off the goods, not caring what was stolen.

"Take it all, my darlings. Sin! You can sin," she murmured with
chattering teeth.

She sought out Botchko from a distance but could not find him.
In the town people were also looking for him. They hoped to buy
him off with cash.

"Let him go somewhere else with his regiment. The town's had
enough."

But when they started talking to him, it became clear that the
regiment was planning to leave anyway. The men wanted to go
home. But they couldn't. At the railroad station they were told there
were no cars.

"There aren't any."

"Really?"

"Just as I said."

The druggist, this Jew without pity, finally showed that a new
order had come into the world if the Jews approached him and asked
for favors. A good turn might be done even for worms—as long as
they knew who he was in the world.

The money the town had planned to give Botchko ended up
passing through the druggist's hands into those of two officials—the
key men at the station. Suddenly, out of nowhere, trains appeared
for the regiment. Suddenly employees of the depot began to move
the soldiers, pushing them and glibly wishing them all the best.

"All aboard, all aboard!"

"Grab a car, take a seat."

"Hurry, faster, faster—that means move!"

"If not, you'll be stuck here another six months. You'll have to go on foot. . . ."

They loaded the cars in haste. Everyone piled in, one on top of the other, bundles on top of people, people on top of bundles, everywhere sweaty wet hair, rapid breathing. Two large bells did not stop clanging for a second. They kept ringing in order to swell the growing, roaring confusion, inside and out, of voices shouting, "Farewell."

"Take care of yourself, Frosia!"

Botchko, the highest ranking figure in the regiment, dressed up with all sorts of weapons, stood for the last time facing Frosia and had no time to look deeply into her tear-filled eyes—so quickly did the train pull away and disappear.

The two locomotives, one in front, the other in back, were puffing heavily. After nineteen miles the first stations appeared and were passed breathlessly.

Towards evening, stopping at a large train depot, the locomotives, pretending to need water and take on coal, raced off never to return. Just disappeared as if they never were.

The men spent the whole cool night breaking boards for fires next to the cars, warming themselves like monkeys and speaking only about the two lost locomotives.

"They're black devils, ghosts of the dead. Silent, dumb. Speak to them and they don't answer. Clumsy, overheated, and can't say a word as if they don't see you. They're evil spirits, that's why it has become so quiet."

"If we could get hold of them now!"

And back in Zvill they quickly forgot everything, as if the regiment had not been there for a year.

Early in the morning, with loaded rifles, the men set off for the train depot to demand new locomotives. They went there with savage determination, never suspecting they would come upon a large station teeming with human creatures. The place was black with soot and grime as if it were a barrack. Spread over the floors were contorted and gnawing faces like unkempt patients in hospitals, caked with mud, snoring away, indifferent to everything. In an adjacent grimy room were gathered the main employees of the depot, who stared with indifference at the new arrivals pointing their guns down on them. They just blinked their eyes, hardly listening to what was asked of them. No answer was given, not even a word. They behaved as if they had already been shot a thousand times and once more would alter nothing.

Meanwhile several soldiers took it upon themselves to board the various trains which were passing through the depot. Some asked: "No brass around? Really none?"

The regiment was beginning to fall apart, run away, disappear. Botchko and Zeek took to loitering about the many troop transports which were kept on a side track. They stuck their noses into everything:

"Comrades, where are you off to?"

"Home."

"How long have you been here?"

"Five days."

"A week for us already."

"It's our second."

"And the brass? Nowhere around? Nowhere to be seen?"

Shunted far-off on a siding, near a disturbingly long and strange-looking troop transport which seemed abandoned, puffed an almost new, green, enormous locomotive acting as if it were just learning to run. All it needed was to be hooked up and it would be off. No eye would be able to keep up with it.

"So, where are you off to?" Botchko and Zeek inquired.

No answer.

"Nowhere," someone blurted out, a young fellow patching his overcoat.

But from inside the car eyes glared at him sternly, waiting to see if he would open his mouth again.

"They're off to somewhere, no?" Botchko?"

"That's clear!"

And both started to shuffle about, again slowly circling the troop train.

Towards evening one of them noticed a dark-haired fellow in a student's overcoat on the last car. He was sitting on the squalid floor among many who were sleeping. The visor of the student's hat was turned to one of his somewhat large wrinkled ears. Alone, he ate quickly, drawing his food with a wooden spoon directly from the large black pot placed between his feet.

His roving eyes responded to passing glances even while his mouth continued to eat rapidly.

"What are you hanging around here for?" he finally asked Botchko and Zeek.

"We want to go too," they answered unsteadily.

"Where?"

"Where you're going!"

"Where we go?"

The dark-haired fellow in the student's overcoat suddenly stopped eating. He jumped off the car and looked them straight in the eye.

"Kiev's burning," he said.

"And so?"

"Burning on all sides."

"For a long time?"

"It's the fifth day."

"Oh?"

"They want to put the old tsar back in again."

"So what should we do?"

"The Bolsheviks are coming to help!"

"We're Bolsheviks too!"

"Why didn't you say so?"

"Well, what can we do?"

"Climb aboard quickly, quickly! The locomotive's pulling out."

And so:

In the dark they met up with Andreyuk—a tricky, absent-minded chatterbox with a dirty, stubbly face, not lacking in cunning, whose deeply etched cheeks made it difficult for them to decide if he were young or old. In the night as the train was jolting about and everyone was sleeping, he pointed with his eyes to the dark-haired fellow in the student's overcoat and told them in secret that it was Petrun, a political agitator. "He's taking everyone to Kiev. He

already sent several transports ahead and now he is on the last one.
Everyone believes in him. He tells only the truth."

Botchko never saw Frosia again.

Petrun kept on swearing day and night that as he lived and
breathed:

"I expect the devil to pop out of you, Botchko. You hear what I
say, the devil! Can you read and write?"

"I can."

"Fine, you don't need any more."

Botchko desired but one more thing—that Frosia could have
stood there and heard such compliments. She had promised to wait
for him. If he did not come back soon she would go to him, wherever
he might be. She would seek and find him.

He wanted to go back to her but instead went with Petrun to
Kiev and then from there they fled elsewhere. He was drawn the
whole time to her in the South but together with Zeek they traveled
further North, hiding out deep in the quiet swampy dampness of
unfamiliar woods. But Frosia . . .

Frosia?

Was she still nursing that Jewish brat? Or did she go back to her
little prince? Or had she already looked for him in Kiev and now was
on her way North? Could she be coming, Frosia? Could she be
nearby? . . .

. . . Every evening Botchko sat by the fire, bent over her photo,
and let his imagination wander. The more his lowered gaze drank in
his lover's eyes, her nose and teeth, the more he felt a quivering in
his breast. His ears strained to hear the slightest rustle which might
be taken for a footfall in the deep, still forest night. Until one
evening the actual tread of unknown feet was heard heavy and
unsure. Even decaying branches seemed to hesitate whether or not
to snap under the footsteps.

Again a quiet summer evening, but also a late summer evening—
somewhat like an old father with his brightest and last born.

The vast forest was wrapped in a strange silence, a gift reserved
for itself: a late warming silence simmered slowly, sending up a
discomforting smell.

High over the bushy heads of trees, the day still burned brightly, while below, on the swampy cool floor of the forest, the cellar chill spread rapidly. Botchko and Zeek were sitting by the fire with drawn faces, as if catching their breath, and listening intently as heavy steps snapped the branches somewhere in the surrounding silence. Stepping stealthily, hesitating and then remaining still, pausing and then drawing nearer, coming forward, among the thick far-flung tree trunks, there emerged at last, as though a feint, something dark, of medium build and solid. It disappeared for a minute and again drew closer—a nobleman? a complete stranger? The new patent-leather boots captured an oblique ray of sunlight, producing a black-mirrored gleam that expired. From a distance it looked like a noble. He drew nearer, even closer, with an intelligent face, full of lines, so that one could not know if the face were young or old, but there was something very distinct about it—Andreyuk!

"Andreyuk? . . . Is it you? Andreyuk?"

The "noble" shut one eye and with the second gave a wink, meaning:

"Shhhhh . . . It's me!"

"Where are you coming from, Andreyuk?"

"From far away, even farther than Kharkov."

"And who sent you?"

"Petrun! He sent me and even paid for these clothes, what do you think? And ordered me to find you and not return empty-handed. He even gave me money for the trip. Can you imagine, even paid for the clothes?"

Andreyuk beamed with delight. The new black suit fitted him poorly and was much too baggy. The red necktie was shoved to a side and on his neck he wore a strange paper collar, so stark white that his thick, furrowed neck and wrinkled face appeared dark brown—as if smeared with tar.

"Nice clothes?" he beamed. "As I said, Petrun ordered all of this, told me to find them, you and many more . . . and not to return empty-handed."

"What's up, Andreyuk?"

"It's this way."

Andreyuk looked around, bent over:

"There's a revolutionary council," he whispered softly, "but it's in hiding."

"Where?"

"There, south of Kharkov."

"So?"

"We've got to go there," Petrun said. "We've got to have you."

Botchko stood a while looking at Andreyuk and whistled—he was pondering the new clothes on him, especially the dashing new patent-leather boots.

He stroked both his left and right whiskers. He had wanted to go South to Frosia. But now for sure he would go North with Andreyuk and Zeek to Petrun—but, it passed his mind, if he put on such clothes as Andreyuk's he could enter Zvill and go straight to Frosia . . .

"Listen," he said, "Andreyuk, ah, would you mind, I mean, just for a minute could I try on . . ."

And right there, he tried on Andreyuk's clothes. Andreyuk wanted to have them back immediately and began to flatter him.

" 'I expect the devil to pop out of you Botchko.' You hear what Petrun says about you! 'A devil,' he says. 'I need him here,' he says. 'I must have him here.' "

Soon after, they packed up, loaded everything, and in the early evening, set off on their journey.

Botchko led the way. He, who longed for the South, headed North.

III

A Fast-moving Hidden Storm

A heavy rain poured down from a late September sky. And below, in utter darkness, stood a large bulging wooden railroad station with its name rubbed off. A name lost forever.

It was raining hard.

Like a beleaguered prey, the steam engine was kept waiting by the hour for the moment to leave. The free hands and feet of the rain clutched the roofs and stairways and even washed the old locomotive which, exhausted from going to the front, had a sickly-hot smell of burnt-out oil. It smoked unbelievably:

"To drag on? Must I drag on?"

A drunkard staggered about by the wheels, a smiling creature with a red nose wearing the insignia of an engineer on his hat, and pointed to the locomotive with a stick.

"Worn out? Are you, good friend? A tough old age. Tell the truth, you didn't need all this work. How we hate machines."

"We, Russians—ha!"

At last the train stirred from the spot.

The man with the insignia on his hat squeezed into one of the packed cars where there was hardly any light. An indistinct group of faces, noisy and thirsty like happy-go-lucky people at a country fair, faded in the smoky, sticky air. And the man with the insignia sat crushed in a corner of his bench, smiling with his drunk-red nose and kept both hands on the pommel of his stick.

"A Russian," he said, "hates machines! The Russian earth is big and soft. And yet it's plowed with sticks because machine's a dirty word—the creation of the devil!"

He winked to his neighbor, an old peasant, and continued talking:

"They forced these trains on us Russians! They forced them."

And suddenly he began to recite:

" 'Straight the little road, past the little hills,/ rails and bridges and telegraph poles,/ and by the side, our Russian bones.' "

"Our Russian bones . . . ha?"

But no one listened to him. The peasants' bundles, which they sat on or placed beneath the benches, reeked throughout the train—the only talk was of Germans who had their own troubles at home and of aristocrats who fled in terror.

"They're leaving everything behind."

"Empty houses."

Someone drew on a cigarette, exhaled and spat:

"This time . . . in a corner you grab a noble . . . slit his throat as did the Butvinikers—their lord; if not, he'll be back again when it's over."

"With whom? With the Germans?"

"With them, with them, the whole poisonous lot."

"And Jews too! The Jews are on their side."

"No, wait a second, I know a Jew . . ."

"Shut up! Let someone else have a word."

A wry smile passed the lips of an old, tough gentile—hatless, with slightly grey trimmed hair, wearing a crucifix on his bright coat of coarse wool. He kept pushing his smiling face into the aisle and made grimaces, imitating a language he did not know: German.

"Ger, ger, ger, ger. . . !"

In his village, he complained, the Germans had whipped people for the lumber which they plundered from the noble's forest and gave ninety lashes to everyone for the "free" sacks of flour removed from the Jew's mill—and he grumbled angrily in the foreign tongue:

"Ger, ger, ger, ger, ger!"

And for the entire time, he kept his hands on the spot where they gave the entire village up to ninety licks.

"Even women"—said he—"even they were not spared. That's for certain! And three young girls who did not wish to submit, fled to Orshe—to the Bolsheviks."

Someone said randomly:

"Not only in Orshe are there Bolsheviks."

And soon the entire car began to "embroider."

"Much closer than that."

"Eighty miles south of Kharkov."

"The Cossacks are driving them from the South. They won't come here. Is that what you're saying?"

"They'll come, they'll come."

"I'm telling you, our's won't let them! Our power . . ."

"Who? You? Or them?"

And from all sides eyes fell on a pair with a Ukrainian coat-of-arms on their caps, who were sitting silently in a dark corner of the car. Botchko and Zeek. This was Botchko's disguise: to dress up as Ukrainian nationalists, the Petlurans who for the time had the upper hand in this area.

But no one looked at them for long because a young Jewish boy began to speak. It seemed he made a mistake—he wanted to climb up on a bench right in the middle of the car in order to deliver a speech. But the man with the engineer's insignia on his hat gave him a blow with his stick.

"Mind your own business, filthy Jew!"

And another: "Haven't found anyone to fawn on?"

And from all sides they began to push and punch him, knocking his hat off. He started to cry with a cowed beggarly face. His nose grew wet and red but his voice couldn't be heard. And it was rather odd: the blows that should have gone to them, Zeek and Botchko, went to him, this Jewish boy. Botchko smoothed first his right whisker and then his left. A troublesome eyelash signaled he was spoiling for a fight, but Zeek held him back.

"Stay where you are, Botchko, listen to me, just stay where you are!"

They remained sitting on the bundles, facing one another, smoking cheap tobacco and spitting. Each time he inhaled, Botchko's face lit up with a mean, savage hue. Where had Andreyuk disappeared to? Wasn't he in the corner where the Jewish student was taking a beating? Searching for Andreyuk, they found him in the middle of the car sitting next to the old Russian who just a little earlier had been recounting how the Germans whipped everyone and how the nobles were fleeing. He was lying through every wrinkle of his face and was continually asking the same question.

"Are the noblemen's estates still empty? Will they no longer come back?"

Zeek pulled him away from there and took him to task.

"What's going on, Andreyuk? What are you up to with the noblemen's estate?"

Andreyuk appeared confused. Glancing about and lying through every wrinkle on his face:

"Tomorrow," he whispered, "we'll arrive . . . tomorrow."

"And then what?"

Andreyuk took a second look around.

"He's in a nobleman's estate. . . ."

"Petrun?"

"Sh-h-h-h-h-hh! No one else!"

But as Andreyuk swore, it seemed he said more with his body.

Botchko's eyes lay in wait, watching for the slightest sign in the wrinkles on his dark, deceiving face. Andreyuk was capable of anything, and there in the longed-for "south of Kharkov" or even sooner, while traveling, he could have sold their souls—Botchko's and Zeek's—and cheaply too, as only Andreyuk could, a soul for a guilder.

"Listen, remember!"

"All right, all right."

"Are you telling the truth, Andreyuk?"
"Nothing less."
"Petrun's really waiting for us?"
"He's waiting, he's waiting.

Somewhere just "south of Kharkov," not far from a town, stood an empty shuttered estate, right in the middle of a field, with a large old-fashioned stable. The stable could not fail to delight with its many high little windows, ventilating the stalls below, in spite of the fact that no horses belonging to the nobleman were left to stamp their feet. Dead black ravens dangled from the dusty crossbeams as if in abject despair, unable to protect anyone from evil spirits: the stable was empty.

In a dark little earthen hut nearby, Andreyuk spent the whole first day after his arrival lying about on a high straw bed surrounded by many horse blankets which smelled sharply of stabled horses and of fleas. Flat on his back with flute in hand, he played in long, long breaths the one and only tune which had stretched across the whole sixteen years before the war when he had been employed as a coachman on this estate. No one could have accompanied the twists and turns of the melody, yet through this song Andreyuk delivered his stinging protests to the world, his insinuating reproaches.

"And where are the horses?" asked Botchko. He was a lover of horses. Their leftover smell tickled his nose more than all others.

"With the peasants in the villages," snorted Andreyuk, "Grigor's plowing with a dappled stallion."

"And where's the nobleman?"

"He's in the town. Not far from here, with the Jews. Milking the animals himself!"

In the space of Andreyuk's missing front teeth could be seen the darting red tip of his tongue. He was about to put the flute back to his lips when Botchko interrupted:

"Stop being so smart."

"Yea, so?"

"Answer when we talk to you. When's Petrun coming?"

"He'll come."

Around the manor house with its boarded shutters, a sparse young forest had recently been chopped down as if in spite, not for any use, but simply so that no forest would exist on the face of the earth—and to make someone forever sad that once there had been a forest here.

The young shoots were slashed a yard above the ground. In the dusk, their yellow remains against the setting sun reflected sickly pain, like unattended yellowish wounds making claims upon the world.

Andreyuk went looking there for kindling. And he watched, watched how an unknown bitch was playing with an unknown male. Suddenly he started chasing away the dogs just at the moment when they were beginning to take pleasure from one another.

Afterwards, all three, Andreyuk, Botchko and Zeek, standing by a fence at a corner of the ruined forest, stared at the nearby green fields which spread down to a valley. In the distance, their eyes stopped at the rough-finished barracks on a mountainside next to a trim little town which was at the foot of the mountain.

Red and green roofs glistened in the pure blue expanse facing the sun, while higher, in the golden rays, a host of silver crosses shimmered on a church.

A light breeze, spiced with green herbs arrived from the distant South and tantalized their noses with a hint of chlorine which, now, at sunset, would rise from the still warm wash—the smell of Frosia's neatly pressed white jacket.

The light breeze dissipated quickly, only the memory of the chlorine remained in Botchko's nose—Frosia's smell.

"What are you looking at?" he asked. "What do you see, Andreyuk, out there?"

"Sh, sh, sh," Andreyuk winked disturbingly, "he's there, he went to town."

"Petrun?"

"Himself, he's living with the priest."

"So?"

"So he's not here now. He's gone north. Eighty miles—to our side, he went to the Bolsheviks."

"Are you telling the truth?"

And they scrutinized him closely with their eyes. They quarreled with him and carried out a resolution. Zeek, in deadly earnest, came near to Andreyuk:

"Give us proof, speak up. You hear what we're saying? In plain
language, show us!"

In the pitch dark, Andreyuk pulled out a little candle and a ring
of keys from under his bed and went with Botchko and Zeek to the
estate. They pried open a small door on a balcony, lit a candle and
began wandering through the entire set of slowly moldering rooms,
with shattered window panes here and there behind the barred
shutters.

The hollow emptiness of the manor rang through the rotting
floors from each heavy step of three pairs of feet.

Three long shadows, feeling their way, groped and searched
along torn wallpapered halls which were splashed here and there
with ink and splattered with the blood of raped victims.

"Where are we heading? Andreyuk?"

"Just ahead, just ahead."

Still another set of ransacked rooms reeked of desolation, like
dungeons.

"Here, here we are."

He led them to a little door with keys on it and unlocked it. He
was the first to go in with a lit candle in hand, and then Botchko and
Zeek entered.

"What's this?"

Newspapers. Piles of bundled newspapers filled the lower part of
a long room and barely allowed a little passage for one person
through the middle. It was the same throughout: appeals, proclama-
tions. Zeek, an illiterate, picked one of them up in his hand and
peered deeply into it as if with near-sighted eyes.

"Take a look, Botchko, is it one of ours?"

"Yea, from the Bolsheviks."

And by the light of the candle both of them clambered after
Andreyuk, scouring all the packages and bundles of the manor and
noticing a cupboard with many, many leaden pellets in the drawers
and with something black—a cast-iron pot covered with cheap cloth.
Botchko looked under the covering with a knowledgeable air and
then stroked his right whisker and his left one.

"A small printing press," he said, "like those at the front."

"Ha!"

Andreyuk beamed with delight. He held the candle high above his head. His mouth gaped in wonder that Botchko and Zeek didn't see the main thing.

"Look up!" he winked.

"Oh!"

An old filthy student's coat splattered with mud was hanging on a hook high in a corner. The dirty cotton padding stuck out from between the worn green lining: it was wadding from Petrun's student days.

"So Petrun was working here, Andreyuk?"

"Yes, Petrun, Petrun, he and a friend of his, a Jew comrade, and me, I helped."

"And what did you do?"

"Turned the wheel."

"And where is he now, Petrun?"

"With the Bolsheviks. And maybe around here in the villages."

"What's he doing?"

"Recruiting regiments . . ."

For several days, day in, day out, Botchko was unable to stop dreaming of the sweet smell rising from the hot wash and from chlorine: Frosia's smell. At night, sleeping was easy. And shortly he would hear footsteps. Someone would knock on the door of the hut and silently they would go off into the night, and in silence they would hear in the nearby dark, thief-infested woods, tinkling little chains of military horses. They were waiting for him, Botchko. If Petrun could form a regiment, then he, Botchko, would be its commander. He had already shown his mettle: how to lead a regiment in hard-pressed battle—he had been drunk that night to boot, and yet he kept the regiment together, leading it here, to the South, right here, to Frosia.

Often by the light of a candle, while Andreyuk and Zeek were fast asleep, he would fumble through his bundle for the little photograph of Frosia and stare at it for hours, and each time he consumed her delicious haughty little nose, her rich upper lip— which was arched so that, below, her dark passionate little teeth appeared tempting and beckoning with lively, biting lust. And this creature loved to stand in the cold at a distance and watch how in the depths of the marketplace shops are being looted: and this creature's name is Frosia.

"You're just a slippery little snake, right? Frosia."

But one day followed the other and Petrun had yet to return or send a message or make clear that he was somewhere in the area.

Botchko began to wander about, looking for Petrun. He asked Zeek to join him and went off for a day or two from their "place," returned, and stayed the night. They took off again together.

Andreyuk didn't stop warning them:

"Don't go, you hear? . . . In those barracks there are three brigades—German ones!"

But Botchko and Zeek answered him bluntly:

"Stay home, keep guard!"

And they themselves risked their few remaining years and went off—so fascinating was this region and so potent its attraction.

Moving through a pleasant new district, their eyes were suddenly shocked and disturbed by what they saw about them. Botchko stood smoothing out his right whisker and his left one. So did Zeek.

"What do you see, Botchko?"

"Nothing. But someone's been ruling here with an iron hand."

"Who? Germans?"

And they walked on farther, past ruined, threatening houses, which could no longer ask for the passer-by's rank.

At a crossroads, the directions on the signboard were crossed out, but as they sought to decipher what was defaced, it seemed to say:

"Go where you desire and when you will. There are no more place-names here, or people either. Pass over the length and breadth of the land."

And they walked on, farther and farther, staring in bewilderment at half-empty, half-inhabited places which grimaced indignantly and darkly through burned-out gaping windows, dampened in the bronze autumn wind and remembering in anger, brooding unceasingly: the worst devastation had already occurred in the surrounding region.

Now the devastations occurred as small slippery bits and pieces, like sticky droplets of late autumn rain dripping down. Everything was sanctioned now in this vast innocent land, although something new was in store for its tired aching furrows: a devastation was in preparation there, something unique and, if a good deed, better than ever before.

Onward, trudging onward, Botchko and Zeek took side roads and byways until once, just as night was falling, they came upon a new unknown district and were intimidated by it as if a thousand fixed ears were eavesdropping. Every blade of grass and shrub listened intently. In the heart of the valley was a pair of pretty little towns, joined together by a tall drawbridge over a river. The valley prided itself on many little villages, concealed in its distant fading greenery—apparently it was from those settlements, as night drew near, that thousands of anxious voices now rose, made weak and indistinct by the distance. Did they again have to welcome, as in the past, those full-dress regiments on parade? Again have to shout, in order to please someone, those long drawn-out "hurrahs?"

Just past a dark forest, on a little hill beside a steep embankment, Botchko and Zeek stood staring out over the land.

From the distance, coming from the twin towns, wending its way along the roads—a long sandy diagonal—loomed a heavy-laden wagon, rattling about. It was harnessed with more than one pair of horses, that was quite clear: a strange wagon, a wide and unusually large one, jolting along with many gray jostled creatures, taut and strained, pushed and shoved about from one side to the next. They seemed to be Germans—young German soldiers.

Botchko and Zeek immediately sought to flee, turning back into the forest, moving along beneath the trees.

Botchko and Zeek moved to a side road and penetrated deeper into the forest. They came upon a narrow path which slinked between the trees, searching, groping and getting lost in the unknown wooded darkness.

A little breeze passed through the trees. A slight drizzle trickled down, barely moist and sticky. Having taken the narrow path, they became apprehensive. Where did it lead to: perhaps to a hidden sinful little place or perhaps to a saint, a holy recluse who would emerge before one's eyes to become the savior of the world?

Discomfited and late, they came back to Andreyuk. Exhausted from their foray, they snored away the remaining night, tucked in Andreyuk's horse blankets.

Early in the morning they were roused from sleep by the report of gunshots. Drowsily fleeing out of Andreyuk's hut, they went hunting for a safe place to hide. A wholly exposed setting. They began to run. But the surrounding countryside lay naked without any protective cover. They dragged themselves from place to place, sluggishly, foolishly, with each blast of the guns. What could it mean? A mass murder? A holiday? An unprecedented, or perhaps a resounding recoronation of an entire land—the return of a tsar?

A few miles away, having run from the hut through side fields and circled about, they stopped and pretended to be calm. They began to look back to the town.

The yellow, red and black colors of the German troops were fluttering on tall telegraph poles, on the many-gabled barracks and on rooftop chimneys. From various sides, the tired guns were growing still, and between one volley and the next, they could clearly hear many voices, mixed together with the blowing wind and with the heightened playing of orchestras. Zeek wanted to guess.

"Religious holidays, maybe? A celebration?"

But Andreyuk shook his head: no.

"They're not ringing," he said, "all the churches are silent."

Finally they separated: Andreyuk went off to find out what had occurred, and Botchko remained here in the field next to a young forest—he always felt safe when a forest lay close by. Here he remained with mounting impatience for a long time. Andreyuk, however, enjoyed poking into strangers' celebrations and did not return until twilight. This time he did not lie through even one crease in his wrinkled face—for once, Andreyuk spoke "the honest truth" which he summed up in few words:

"The Germans have gone crazy."

The Germans had become either mad or divinely inspired. They sought a truce, carousing for three days on end with Bolsheviks—and ended up depressed and stupefied.

"So, the end has come," whimpered the merchants, "farewell to the Germans."

Slowly, with a precision only they understood, the Germans withdrew their columns little by little from all around and quietly stole away on a dark September night, as they made their long mournful trek home.

And nights that came were moribund, dumb. . . .

By the light of red torches which sent up smoke high above their heads, small bedraggled groups of horsemen, silent as corpses, pressed on, lifeless columns in meaningless order.

They carried within themselves something mute, sad, and languishing, like their own distant, restless homeland.

And because of them, from all around, from sleepy villages which blur the night, strained wide-open mouths, wailing, wailing in terror, following constantly behind, sending them off with desperate lamenting yelps.

Night after night Botchko listened to these terrible howls and stayed awake in the dark until the breaking dawn. Standing all alone in a corner of the battered forest, by the fence, he looked off to the distant blind darkness where the broad highway yields to a forest, to a valley and to a little bridge. He waited while the smoking red spots moved away slowly.

And as always, when the fiery spots showed themselves, not a brain in his head could think, but his heart went limp every time and coveted a rifle, a large one, and powerful, so that from that spot he could fire on those red spots and smash one skull after the other.

"Bang, bang, bang"—his ear didn't fail to keep on imagining the whistling crackle of the bullets.

Until one night he really did hear a blast in the distance near the regiment. A shiver went through the ranks and remained suspended through the night in the red smoke rising round the regiment. And something stammered far off. The torpid Germans were firing a deadly machine gun.

Botchko quickly awakened Zeek and Andreyuk. Half dazed still with sleep, they made their way to the fence and listened. Botchko pulled at his whiskers. He was drawn here as if in chains. In daylight all three went off to look at the spot, where, according to their calculations, the shooting, the night before, should have taken place. But after clambering about for some time, they were unable to find any evidence.

They began to tramp about on the byways, remaining overnight in a pleasant forest which they reached—being near a highway—by crawling on all fours, and hid out in deep trenches, until in early morning all at once everything became clear.

Somewhere within the little forest deep in the sands were entire villages waiting to overwhelm the multitude of German horsemen, to beat them, to tear their flesh apart as if they were carcasses, and to rob their horses, their small arms and rifles.

Within such a forest were also Botchko, Andreyuk and Zeek—who emerged once to be included unwillingly with such a village, and like everyone else, received their portion of the spoils.

The fight was easy in the gray light of day—like any battle with a corpse. After the first shot from the few worn-out rifles, the Germans hoisted a white flag and asked what they wanted. Botchko, who had led almost everyone, answered:

"Everything. We went everything you've got!"

The others let him choose for himself and for his own the best rifles. He pondered over each rifle, smoothed his right whisker and his left one, and tested with his sharp eye the accuracy of its aim. Then he left the villagers in peace.

Now they were alone, a threesome, a small well-armed band, each bearing two rifles and girded with clips of bullets around the hips and across the breasts on a diagonal.

Well armed, they began to ramble about each day on the roads and frightened lonely passers-by from a distance—death's three terrible envoys!

But in the surrounding district almost everyone else was also a small armed band—messenger of death.

Wars threatened every night in dreams—wars without end and without a goal; they were liable to break out at any moment—as many as there were people in the land.

Meanwhile, everyone swallowed up the filthy days of the year, increased the troubles on the roads, and destroyed the bridges.

Slapped by savage winds into sharp slanting storms, and sliced down as if by knotted whips, the late October rains brought floods by day and by night upon the tender body of the land. The rains spread gloom over the earth and kept the peasant in a tear-reddened cottage while under a truly well-stocked village roof . . .

In Andreyuk's little earthen hut, they divided their spoils: Zeek demanded that all three should head north: why remain here? We should go up there, to our own, to the Bolsheviks. Andreyuk, enjoying his new life on the estate, lied through every wrinkle on his face.

"Wait for Petrun," he said, "one has to listen and follow."

And Botchko became mean, and deadly silent, saying he couldn't give a damn about anyone. He was taking his two rifles and was going off by himself, back to Frosia.

Zeek was angry with him, challenged him, glowered at him with spiteful eyes and refused to speak with him. He wandered about all alone outside and noticed how the strong, week-long rains continued to pour down endlessly. But once on a wet, gray, Sunday-like dawn when Botchko had put together his bundle, placed both rifles by his feet and tore up a pair of rags into firm strips and bound his feet with them and pushed them down through the long narrow boot—Zeek began to get upset.

"Listen, Botchko," he said, "wait up, perhaps I'll go with you."

Botchko didn't answer, he was entirely absorbed with his new bindings, which did not slip into the boot.

Silently, they armed themselves. With bundles on their backs, they left the house. But when they had gone on a bit, they heard Andreyuk calling behind them. They could not understand what he wanted over the heavy downpour. They looked back and saw: Andreyuk was weighed down with a pack on his back and shouldering both rifles. He quickly locked the door of the small earthen hut and ran after them.

IV
Alexandrovka

Alexandrovka had seen better days—a little old town, at the foot of sandy Mount Mariopol, whose few hundred bald roofs wearily lay in wait in an open field without even a river nearby. And it seemed from a distance that the townspeople consumed their lives in gloom, recollecting:

"Once there were shingles . . . once there was a flood . . . and holy patriarchs too—the patriarchs of the Book . . ."

Leyzerke hailed from Alexandrovka—the late bonesetter's brat—tough, dark, a locksmith, who worked for Nikolayev in the factory. And the girls said: "What a fellow . . . and so good-looking." All Alexandrovka knew that he had already seen the inside of a jail:

Leyzerke had been shackled to far-off Siberia. He was nineteen years old then. During the war, a townsman from Alexandrovka thought he recognized him in his brigade—far off, on the front lines. All Alexandrovka understood what that meant: well, so "he took a 'new' name" which no doubt his superiors ordered him to use among the troops—"may the devil take him."

Had it not been a fact that three months later in the middle of the war he had joined a band of young Gentiles from a large village surrounding the Bobrover sugar factory and afterwards hid out in the attics of Alexandrovka, would anyone have dared ask: "Tell me, Leyzerke, are they expensive? I mean those two gold teeth of yours which you earned on the front lines . . ."

And had it not been a fact that, in the days of Kerensky, he was one of the labor deputies in the Parliament, would any questions have been raised later, about why he had joined the Bolsheviks flying over Kiev in an airplane? Once again, for a rather long time, he hid out in the attics of Alexandrovka and no one knew where he disappeared to. If, as the legend states, a blemish on an ox once destroyed Betar, then, on account of Leyzerke, all Alexandrovka would be annihilated.°

One night, six of Petlura's men rode into Alexandrovka from off the highway looking for Leyzerke at his sister's house and did not find him. Then they broke into Soyvel the seamstress' house on the new square. There they spent the whole night becoming dead drunk. Aiming at the storm lamp, they shot three times at the ceiling and, choking with laughter, made fun of the Bolsheviks hiding in the woods and of the peasants who were going about stirring up trouble

---

° According to a Talmudic legend, Jerusalem was destroyed because a disgruntled man denounced the Judeans as rebels to the Romans. To test this assertion, the Emperor sent a calf to the temple for sacrifice. On the way, the disgruntled man made a blemish on the calf's tongue which rendered the animal unfit according to Jewish law. The fearful Rabbis, unwilling to sacrifice the calf, thought of killing the man in order to prevent further betrayal, but were prevailed upon to let him go. The Emperor now convinced of *lèse-majesté*, ordered the destruction of Jerusalem.

Bergelson confused this tale about Jerusalem with the legend of Betar's destruction—on account of a broken shaft of a royal litter—which is narrated in the same folio with more blood and gore. Or by substituting obscure Betar for Jerusalem, did he hope to avoid a dangerous confrontation with the Soviet censor over ideologically unacceptable allusions: first, to a religious text, the Talmud, and second to Jerusalem with its national and religious connotations?—*Trans.*

around the Bobrover sugar factory. They promised to return soon and shoot the entire town.

Very early the next morning the tongues of Alexandrovka were wagging about nothing else.

"Zilpah, the servant girl, the one with the big mouth, was raped at Soyvel the seamstress' house."

"Zilpah? . . . with the swollen lips?"

And night itself recalled more than anything the previous one—that long, evil, eternal night. Vacant eyes stared numbly at the perennial dawn and watched a bright speck burn like rusty iron against a buckwheat black sky. A forgotten lamp in the house of the seamstress also burnt on throughout the day like a candle lit in memory of the dead . . . The wet roofs, in cold-blooded horror, let misfortune trickle down drop by drop, while begging for mercy from the world . . . a wasted effort—the world was mute and cold. The district was deserted all around. The moveable holocaust—Petlura's divisions—traveled the highway and beyond the highway, cutting down Jews and exterminating towns.

In Alexandrovka, anyhow, they made a fire at the appropriate time in the middle of the day, but the smoke from the chimneys did not rise straight up, it curled slowly as usual. The seamstress, too, continued to stammer slowly, very slowly, fearful that people would take a dim view of her. She swore to herself that they took no more from her than the brass samovar, some money, and a Passover jug with preserves—so did she swear, as if frightened that she would lose her reputation in town. What else?

"Where is your Bolshevik?" all of them cried out—"You're hiding him, we know, he's been stirring all the villages around Bobrovitz against us."

"So, this is your Leyzerke!"

"You think we didn't know?"

"These Bolsheviks of ours will do us all in."

Drop by drop, misfortune trickled down the roofs in cold-blooded horror. Misshapen windows looked up at the mountain and stared down at the marketplace where hotheaded townsmen hurled bloodcurdling curses at the echoing winds:

"Even to his father's father!"

The late bonesetter's brat Leyzerke was fuming at what he heard, and Elik the butcher received his share too:

"A socialist!"

"He knew what Leyzerke was up to in Bobrovitz."

"Didn't say a word."

Finally Leyzerke could no longer stand listening to the curses.

But Leyzerke had parents buried here in the cemetery and Alexandrovka wanted the earth to cast out his dead father and swallow up the son.

The smoke from the chimneys of Alexandrovka did not rise straight up then, but curled slowly as usual. And crooked windows peered out on a mountain and upon a group of babbling idlers— forever starving babblers trapped in poverty-stricken streets of the unsettled region around them—who prattled on about everything related to their lives in Alexandrovka.

"Trouble, trouble."

"Bobrovitz is up to something—the entire village!"

"They want to pull down the bridges."

"Let them shoot up Bobrovitz, let them shoot it up! . . ."

From then on, Alexandrovka no longer lit lamps at night. And peasants from the surrounding neighborhood laughed heartily, but in the end grew afraid to come near. From the very first night they could hear from the highway how terror drove leprous voices to shout in the night as a cry of distress from an entire town. The desperate town sought someone in the cold skies and found nothing, just a vast emptiness. The darker the night, the more fearful the voices—Alexandrovka was locked in combat with darkness and repelled every newly imagined assault by those who dug trenches alongside the highway. Alexandrovka repudiated Leyzerke and let it be known in the strongest terms that Leyzerke was no longer one of them.

At night in little spaces between the crooked mud houses, among heavy bald roofs which appeared ancient and blind, impoverished, unfortunate, dragged here as from a distant foreign home, Alexandrovka gave up sleeping. A stumbling funeral procession went its way night after night on the pitted earth through mute narrow streets and around meat markets and the synagogue. Was there ever such a watch—a frightful night congregation, girded as if for prayer, and laden with dreadful stakes, wash-paddles, and charred baker's poles?

Someone's strong, somewhat hunched shoulder came up and hovered about. The watch was kept by Hayml Bashevis—Hayml the innkeeper, a squat little man—an important person once who served a murdered noble, and Kiveh the wagon driver—Kiveh, who smelled of old crushed kernels of millet like his old blind horse, and whose lips were thick, swollen and a little crooked as were Zilpah's, his raped younger sister. His crooked left foot, everyone knew, had been further crippled by himself when, just before he was conscripted, he intentionally placed his foot between the wheels of his old wagon, gave one piercing scream, and then dragged out a quivering foot bent all out of shape.

Kiveh savagely banged each stake of the fence, clanging an old brass tray, rattling a large tinny alms box, rusted and bent without a cover. He could not bear that Elik the socialist did not join the watch—why should Elik sleep? He banged loudly around the house where Elik lived, and if someone was napping in the house or if someone in the middle of the night was tossing and turning in his sleep, he would think that the knocking went on for years, drawn from far and wide. Kiveh the cripple was indomitable—forever wild, irascible, stubborn, bitter. He suffered in the middle of the night from his old fear of all types of weapons and of guns. He threatened the armed world, placing it against his crooked ever-quivering foot.

In those dark days Alexandrovka felt the destructive force in the surrounding district creeping forward on its belly like a living reality.

They thought of everything.

"The Bolsheviks are driving off the Petluras."

"Petlura's fleeing."

In those days Botchko and a group of insurgents came out of the thick forest for the first time, made off with machine guns and rifles and killed a small corps of Petluras who were digging trenches on both sides of the main road.

Petlura's troops moved away from the highway and took to crawling quickly up a mountain to a large village, when suddenly the flying column crumbled and withdrew, shaken. The resisting village had encountered the scattered remnants and had flung the stragglers off to a side—the village was called Bobrovitz.

Botchko was unaware of his supporters there in the large village on the mountainside. He began to emerge each time from another corner of the woods, driving off the Petlura detachments to the large village and watching how the village repulsed them each evening, casting them off with hardly any weapons. After that, they fired through the night and did not allow anyone to collect the abandoned weapons.

The district around Alexandrovka slept easily that night, like an invalid. A light breeze died off for a while and then picked up again with volleys of gunfire which chattered with the whispering night. In blunt, rushing spasms the streams of gunshots awakened the little nested birds in the surrounding plots of forest, driving their scattered bands down, below the level of the town roofs, and they pursued the hunt deep into the dark land.

Once, on a pale damp dawn a breeze over Alexandrovka was full of light, fresh, fluttering cries of just those sleeping birds, and after that it suddenly became still and fearful—just as if a toothache had suddenly stopped bothering the district and the district had laid down and had fallen asleep in full daylight.

People came to the young, lean Elik, both ritual slaughterer and socialist, and asked him what it meant. Elik's eyes suddenly began to hurt him. They were very red and quite bloodshot. He was annoyed and offended:

"Why come and ask me? Why am I supposed to know everything?"

In those days Botchko and a small squad passed close to Alexandrovka.

For two nights he attempted to come closer. He set up machine guns on both sides of town and fired into the air—just a short spurt—as if to test them. It meant:

"Is anybody in town? Is Petlura gone? . . . Can we come in?"

And both times, in the middle of the night, it was Kiveh the cripple, on his watch, who answered him—the reply consisting of many repeated fierce blows on the brass tray and on the misshapen tin alms box. To each volley from the foot of the mountain a raucous crude din from the village responded: a stubborn banging on the fences which for a while seemed to die off only to return, shortly after, renewed and forceful.

Botchko listened closely and did not know what the unpleasant banging in the village meant. Finally he sent ahead a lively pair of horsemen.

This happened on Thursday night.

On Thursday night—when all Alexandrovka still slept—Hayml Bashevis, a squat little man with a little yellowish pointed beard came out of his inn at the end of the street.

He breathed deeply and smelled the air; a thought passed through his mind . . . it takes time and perhaps in enough time God will help—it will yet become peaceful: he coughed fully, as only Hayml Bashevis could, with spittle. Packed tightly into his large overcoat, he suddenly heard:

On the edge of the village in the frosty air, someone was swearing in all directions with biting Russian curses. Ambling about, he riddled everything in sight with the foulest tongue like whip lashes on a naked body. Hayml Bashevis entered the courtyard of his sizeable inn and beheld a strange-looking rider in a leather jacket and leather pants—a blond man with an arrogant Cossack curl. He was armed with a sawed-off shotgun, a large rifle, a sword and two grenades hanging off the long clips of bullets wound about him. He sat jauntily on his large gray horse, which had a hungry, drawn-up belly. He was hurling curses at Tekli, a washerwoman's husband, who was standing near him with an ax hanging from his belt and a stolen batch of wood on his shoulders:

"Speak up! Say something! Up your . . ."

And difficult to believe!

He cursed him not for the stolen wood but for his Ukrainian which he, the speaker, did not understand.

Hayml Bashevis went into the house and watched through the window:

The horseman went riding about the village—and not alone. A second was riding abreast with him, a rather small figure in a perforated blocked hat with a scarf on his neck. They stood still a few times peering into side streets and then rode off quickly out of town.

They left town as riders who had never slackened their pace and as they waved their hands about to someone in the distance, it seemed quite clear: they were conveying a message.

On that early morning, Botchko and his squad entered Alexandrovka.

It was a typically dark, tingling cold Friday. The arrival of Sabbath seemed certain but then demurred; it vacillated and time dragged on with a kind of feverish monotony. A low flame in the oven soothed the *tsholent*.° The chimneys of the houses were smoking, rather unevenly, without certainty; smoldering greasy rags were sending up fumes which poisoned the air.

And candles were lit at dusk.

Beneath the old bald roofs, crooked windows with early-lit Sabbath candles shined brightly upon the people who passed by Hayml Bashevis's inn. They looked at the two cannon which had been hauled here from some swampy place. They stared at the plank marked in crooked red letters, "STAFF," and at the blond fellow with his Cossack curl who, every once in a while, jumped upon his exhausted horse, hid a letter under his hat and rode quickly out of the village. They chattered:

"Still more rebels will come."

"Many, many more have still to come."

"Chinese as well—one of them said."

"And Leyzerke the bonesetter's son is here. He's here."

"He's here. There's Leyzerke now."

And what did it mean?

That Leyzerke did not go very far from Alexandrovka. . . . He was concealed by his gentile friends in Bobrovitz and spurred them on.

Perhaps he told the group of Bolsheviks in the forest that they could come here; or perhaps together with his Bobrovitz friends he faced the sporadic firing of Petlura's scattered troops who were fleeing from the highway; or perhaps he remained hidden in an attic after all—as if in a prison cell. He was made of iron and steel, that Leyzerke!

"Look, look, he's already wearing a gray overcoat that hangs down to his feet and he has a pistol in his belt—where did he get hold of one so quickly?"

This time he did not have a minute to stop and talk with anyone—moving at a steady pace with the intense concern of a busy man who sees no one but the person towards whom he strides.

Their eyes continued to follow him:

° *tsholent*—a stew, usually prepared for the Sabbath.

"He's helping the Bolsheviks."

"He's bringing in new people."

"He's helping to put two to three in a room."

He went off quickly with Botchko somewhere. Came back and then went off elsewhere—both of them in long gray overcoats. Then, for a short moment, they slowed down.

"Who is really the top man—Botchko or him?"

In the middle of the street, he suddenly began to fulminate at someone like an artist—he summoned his wrath, his great wrath—here was a brand new Leyzerke:

"A commandant, a commandant!"

Through the chinks in the door at Hayml Bashevis's, they observed how Leyzerke entered and met with Botchko for the first time in his room.

"I come from Bobrovitz," he said, "from the noble and revolutionary town of Bobrovitz." And after that he went off with someone else on horseback.

By candle-lighting time, the people noticed how he rode back to the inn and how Andreyuk, who, with rifle in hand, stood guard at the door, recognized him already and let him enter at will.

It meant that nothing could be accomplished by the village elders in summoning Leyzerke's sister to the rabbi who solemnly warned her that Leyzerke should not become involved—on account of Leyzerke the entire town could be exterminated!

Shortly after this, individual elders privately went to Leyzerke for favors. Even Hayml Bashevis, in his own inn, lay in wait for him and stood before him bareheaded as though in the presence of an aristocrat. And with a weeping face and much grimacing as if a dear one lay dead in his house:

"Leyzerke," he said trembling, "take them away from me, Leyzerke. Please, I beg you, they're eating me out of house and home, Leyzerke ... hold them off a bit ... do me just one little favor, Leyzerke!"

But Leyzerke only looked at Hayml Bashevis for a moment—and then somewhat absent-mindedly, but calmly, quietly, said to him:

"Hayml Bashevis, I hate your guts!"

Translated by Seth L. Wolitz

≈ *Zelmenyaner*

BY MOSHE KULBAK

THIS IS Reb Zelmele's courtyard.

An old wall: bricks held by crumbling plaster. Two rows of houses full of his descendants, the Zelmenyaner. Also, stables, cellars, garrets—it all looks like a narrow street. Summer, when day was breaking, tiny Reb Zelmele would go into the yard dressed in nothing but his underdrawers. He would move a brick or, with all his might, carry a shovelful of dung.

Where does Reb Zelmele come from?

There is a family tradition that he's from the deep Ukraine. At any rate, it was here that he married Grandma Boshe, and here that she began to bear children.

Grandma Boshe, it is related, bore them without premeditation, one after the other, in a sort of frenzy. The children grew up quickly. They were dark-haired, with broad little shoulders. True Zelmenyaner. They would soon pass into Reb Zelmele's jurisdiction. He did not spoil them. He would wait a little—then have them learn a trade.

One of these, Folye, became a tanner when he was only ten. It was because of some incident about a horse.

No one noticed, but these children began to breed. Daughters-in-law of varying fertility were gathered into the fold; also a complement of sons-in-law. All of the houses were overrun by lively and swarthy little Zelmenyaner. Only a few blondes were visible. This, too—only among the girls. In general, it was a thin strain: it left no great impression. A few yellow youngsters have been added lately. How they crept into the family is still unexplained.

Zelmenyaner are dark, big-boned, with low, broad foreheads. A Zelmenyaner has a fleshy nose. A Zelmenyaner has dimples in his cheek. As a rule, he is calm and quiet; he looks at things obliquely. There are mighty speakers, both male and female, especially among the young. A few are brazen. But, at bottom, even these are shy Zelmenyaner. Because they fell under a modern influence, they make believe they're different. Zelmenyaner are patient; they are not angry people. They are silent when melancholy, silent when glad; although there is a kind of Zelmenyaner who can glow like iron.

In the course of generations, they have worked out a smell that is their own—a soft kind of smell, as of newly gathered hay and some other ingredient.

It will sometimes happen: a coach is packed, people are yawning into the cold morning; suddenly a passenger rubs his eyes and says:

"Aren't you from N.?"

"Yes."

"Aren't you Reb Zelmele's grandson?"

"Yes. His grandson."

The other folds his arms back into his sleeves and continues his journey. In his sleep, he had become aware of Reb Zelmele's odor—although, surely, no one in our town has thought about this matter. It has not occurred to any one that a Zelmenyaner has a distinct odor.

There is another family peculiarity—it is the men who have it. A Zelmenyaner is fond of sighing. He does it for no particular reason. He holds his breath, then lets escape from between his lips a kind of happy tender whinny that otherwise you would hear only in a stall where horses are munching their oats.

Which goes to prove that Reb Zelmele was raised in a community of farmers. It also shows that a Zelmenyaner is plain, like a piece of bread.

There are no barren women in the family. No one dies before her time. (Except for Aunt Hessye.)

If one has a blemish—he is not a sprout of Reb Zelmele's seed. Even if he smells of hay . . .

When he began to see blossoms of the fourth generation, Reb Zelmele started to prepare for his journey. He wrote his will on the inside cover of a religious Book; he lingered for a while without any purpose—and then he died.

He was a simple man. He wrote the will in Yiddish—with the proper Hebrew phrases. Since the Book has been mislaid (God knows where), it may be useful to reconstruct his will from memory:

Monday, the year . . . (erased).

I propose, while I am still alive, to divide it among my children, the way it's going to be after my hundred years. I propose that it should be this way. My children will continue to live in my yard. The piece of cemetery lot I own, let it be sold, getting for it about four hundred rubles. The pew in the synagogue, let them also sell it, taking for it about one hundred fifty rubles. Also, I have about a thousand rubles. They are under the sixth brick in the oven to the right. Let it be divided this way. To my son Itche—one hundred fifty rubles, seeing that my son Itche has already taken one hundred fifty rubles as advance on his inheritance while I was still alive. To my zon Zishe— two hundred rubles; and to my son Yude also—two hundred rubles; to my son Folye also—two hundred rubles; to my daughter Haye-Mashe—one hundred rubles; to my daughter Motle also—one hundred rubles; and to my daughter Roshe also—one hundred rubles; and give back to Hurewitz the one hundred sixty I took from him to give to my son Itche as advance on the inheritance while I was still alive; it should be returned. Fifteen rubles should be given to charity and what is left used for my funeral expenses to take me to the Everlasting World. The house articles belong to Sarah-Boshe my wife. After her one hundred years, let my daughters, the three of them, divide—only two pillows should be given to Hayke, Itche's unmarried daughter, and that is how my daughters should divide it. Only my clothing should go to the sons. The lambskin coat to whoever needs it; otherwise the way it falls by lot, only there should be no quarreling about it, let it be in a pleasant manner and the way that I have divided it myself, let no strangers do it. You are welcome to it, enjoy the things with pleasure. That is what I wish with all my heart. And then, after my hundred years, let them not forget me, as far as possible, even if it's only to say Kaddish.

From me—Zalman-Elye, son of Reb Leib Chvust

Grandma Boshe outlived her husband by a good number of years and it is possible to say that she still is living. True, she does not see, she does not walk, does not hear, the way she ought to—yet she is alive. She resembles an old hen more than a human being, and she does not even know that our world has changed.

Grandma Boshe is concerned only with herself. If she still has thoughts, they must be strange, made from quite a different material than the usual thoughts.

Sometimes, in the evening, as she wanders in the dark, she will suddenly speak to a red necktie.

"Motele, why haven't you gone to the synagogue?"

Dark Motele—he has begun to smell faintly of hay—walks over, rolls her shawl away from grandma's ear and shouts:

"Grandma, I am a Pioneer!" °

She nods her head.

"Aye, aye! He has prayed already. What *shul* did you go to?"

That is how she'll leave the world, in a calm old-fashioned way. The wall of the courtyard is solid where Reb Zelmele had built it; and, every year, she is able to make out a new addition of silent little creatures.

In the summer, when she goes into the yard, she sits on the steps and beams because she sees how, from every door, little versions of Reb Zelmele pour like black poppy seeds.

The big sun is shining on this rebirth.

That is Grandma Boshe.

The second generation has branched off into three mighty streams and several tributaries. The pillars of the family were—and are to this day—Uncle Itche, Uncle Zishe, and Uncle Yude.

Uncle Folye is apart. He walks through life in his own detached and hard-working way. He is not concerned with what happens here because he believes that he has been insulted. He is a gorger, particularly fond of baked potato pudding. The thoughts that he conceives are things that no one knows, because he does not tell them.

The others seem more commonplace; in them, the root is difficult to make out—though they were also formed under Reb Zelmele's supervision and move around the world carrying his odor with them.

Uncle Zishe has a special niche in the family. He is considered a man of standing. A chubby watchmaker, with a rectangular brow and a square beard. He is a swooner; or perhaps this is something he pretends.

In the old days, people would bring him papers to decipher. He

° Pioneer—the Communist children's organization.

would take the jeweller's loupe out of his eye, ask you to sit; then patiently would read it word by word. But even if he couldn't read it, he had this virtue: he could tell you by heart what was in the paper.

He had a nice understanding.

The chief merit of his reading was that, then and there, he could give you his advice about the undertaking.

It is said that a rare power lay concealed within him.

His wife, Aunt Gitte, brought two daughters into the world with a lot more trouble than is proper in this family. One is Tunke; a pure Zelmenyaner. The second has a touch of sweet melancholy that Aunt Gitte, with all respect, has smuggled into the family. We should forgive Aunt Gitte. Everybody feels she is not to blame—she stems from a rabbinical family.

Uncle Itche is a prince of paupers. It is he who couldn't wait and while Reb Zelmele was still alive took an advance on his inheritance. He is a tailor, a sewer-on of patches. His tall sewing machine, skinny and clumsy, clatters day and night.

It deafens the courtyard.

Uncle Itche produces the true Zelmenyaner. His are the highest proof. It is thought that in this regard he has outdone even Reb Zelmele himself.

Besides all the habits common to our family, Uncle Itche has worked up a habit of his own. He sneezes with a loud cry.

Once, when she heard him sneeze, a neighbor fainted.

In the tense times of the Civil War, the people in the courtyard were upset by his sneezing. Uncle Zishe even found it necessary to visit Uncle Itche in order to discuss this subject.

"Itche, do you know that because of your sneezing we stand in mortal peril?"

What could Itche answer? It was undeniable. Sneezes—and cries—would keep erupting!

They kept thinking of ways to deal with the situation. It was Aunt Malkele herself who found the right solution. When it was about to happen, Uncle Itche would grab his nose and fall into bed. Then Aunt Malkele would cover him with a pillow, and throw herself upon him. If she was busy, she put one of the children on top of him. There, beneath the bed clothes, he would finish his sneezing, shake off the feathers and go back to work.

In times of peace, it was no threat. The opposite, in fact.

Summer, early in the morning, half the courtyard still in shadow. A neat Uncle Itche is already by his open window, banging on the machine. Suddenly he sneezes: the dark wailing cry of a man in agony. The courtyard starts to waken, people rub their eyes, many leap out of their beds.

"What is it?"

"Nothing! Uncle Itche is sneezing."

"Nothing, nothing!"

Meanwhile, everywhere windows and casements open, ejecting a variety of black and shaggy Zelmenyaner heads. Shouts from every side.

"Uncle, your health!"

"Uncle, to life!"

"To health, to life, to your many years!"

Uncle Yude, now, is another kind of man. Another and a strange one. A carpenter, a skinny fellow, with a glossy little beard. He wore his spectacles on the tip of his nose; he would always be looking over them. That is why he always seemed so angry. No doubt, he wore them for reasons of beauty and a sense of personal dignity. He would work in spectacles, he would eat in spectacles. Sleep in his spectacles? Well, I think not.

Uncle Yude was a philosopher and widower.

His wife, Aunt Hessye, died in the German advance, together with a *shochet*. It was not a pretty death.

When it happened, Uncle Yude went to the synagogue to observe his seven days of mourning, sat behind the stove and didn't want to rise. He had decided to give up his worldly concerns and to occupy himself only with serious thoughts. An honorable occupation, it must be admitted. But the town insisted, so that, finally, he went back to his workshop.

What happened to Aunt Hessye?

Our town lay in the line of artillery fire. The housewives in the street locked up their homes and went into Reb Zelmele's cellar. Suddenly, Aunt Hessye had a yearning for chicken broth. Why? Because in the stifling air of the cellar, she had looked so long at Reb Ezekiel the *shochet* that she felt a desire for chicken. So she caught a hen, he took his ritual knife, and they went out to slaughter the chicken.

A thud: every pane in the yard was shattered.

Later, a neighbor rapped on the cellar door and told them to come out. Aunt Hessye lay serene and pale, as if nothing had occurred. Near her, his beard pointing up, lay the *shochet's* head. He, the *shochet* proper, lay on a fallen fence, the knife in his hand.

Nearby stood the hen, philosophizing.

Uncle Yude keeps a gloomy silence; other Zelmenyaner are cheerfully silent. Except for this minor deviation, he has been true to the traditions of Reb Zelmele.

In him, the love of nature which is active in the family found its strongest expression. Uncle Yude used to raise geese in the entry to his house. There had been words about one of his hens. If it rained, he would put out a bucket for water; and, in the spring, he felt it necessary to rise before dawn to go picking sorrel. His love of beams and boards is probably also due to this reaching out to nature. He would plane a board with love, even fervor. In short, Uncle Yude loved carpentry. Add that he had a weak spot for the fiddle, for singing, and, in general, the making of music.

Before I finish, it may be worth while to pay more attention to one of the younger members. This is Berre Chvust, Uncle Itche's oldest.

There is a youth—a hero! He is a silent tanner. During the Civil War, in the battles around the city of Kazan, he won the Order of the Red Flag because of his cool Zelmenyaner valor.

He was with the Red Army in the attack on Warsaw.

It was there he almost got killed, falling into Polish hands. But, with the help of a few miracles, he contrived to change his clothes and get home on foot.

When he came into the house, there was much shrieking. The whole courtyard gathered, even Uncle Zishe deigned to join the others. Berre sat down, began slowly to take off his boots, and announced to Aunt Malkele:

"Mama, give me some food!"

With bitter energy, he began to dig into the feast while staring out at the balcony. Uncle Yude spat and left; the others sidled out. Berre finished eating, put his boots on, and once more went off to wage war.

A World, Eh?

The courtyard is quiet.

War and revolutions have finally passed through it. They have done it peacefully enough; save for the misfortune Aunt Hessye innocently suffered, all for a foolish bit of soup.

The Zelmenyaner returned from various fronts in stiff tunics and unravelling winter caps. At first they prowled around the courtyard like wolves, devouring whatever they found at hand, but gradually they were lured into the houses. You addressed them softly—until, somehow, you evoked their former appearance. In the winter, the tunics were nailed into the doors for insulation, and even to this day unravelled caps are lying somewhere behind the stove. Sometimes, in a heavy frost, Uncle Itche may dig up one of these caps, pull it down below his beard and go out to get a load of wood for Aunt Malkele.

This is what the war has left.

Uncle Folye is the least wordy of the Zelmenyaner. He never says a word because, when he was small, he had been insulted in this very courtyard. However, no one is eager to make Folye speak.

After him in this respect comes Uncle Itche's Berre, another rare character, at present a member of the Second District Militia. You may never see him because he gets here only to catch some sleep on his father's hard workbench. He is no problem either.

Should it happen that one of the young folks starts to spout the current foolishness, there is a homely remedy. For those who chatter, a louder word is still enough to stop them; and, if it gets more serious, a slap is helpful.

"High time the rubbish was knocked out of your head." This from Uncle Zishe.

"Time to be a grownup." This from Uncle Itche.

"And above all"—this from Uncle Yude—"will there ever be a stop to that babbling?"

Uncle Yude, we imagine, has his daughter Hayele in mind. He would like to see her married to a decent human being. Recently, he has put aside his plane and wanders all day through the houses of study looking for a solid fellow. He prefers a *shochet*.

The other day, he arranged a meeting with that kind of suitor. On this occasion, there would be a blizzard! Nonetheless, Hayele went there, took a post in the secluded corner her father had designated, and began to wait. In the drifts, it was impossible to make out the shape of any living creature—let alone a bridegroom. Still, she apparently wanted to get married so badly that she snuggled against a wall, determined to wait for her intended as long as necessary.

Late at night, Uncle Yude in his bed remembered his daughter; so he ran out and brought her home, more dead than alive.

In the courtyard they have an explanation of why the fellow failed to appear. "It's clear he did not want to get married in a frost!"

There is a Zelmenyaner who would marry Hayele. Yes, even in a frost! He is an elderly bachelor; thirty-eight, maybe more. A man of iron silence! As we have noticed, he comes every night to his father's house to sleep on the hard workbench. It is thought they suit each other; but the love between them still has to develop.

Her father, Uncle Yude, is sure to be against it. For the following reasons:

1) A Zelmenyaner dislikes a Zelmenyaner.
2) The groom (Berre) isn't our kind.
3) He is too bossy in the courtyard.

Just at this time, as if for spite, he has played a trick at his mother's expense—one that has shaken the older Zelmenyaner down to their marrow.

What happened?

Aunt Malkele decided to see Berre in the militia.

"Berre, how is it we never see you smile? One might imagine . . ."

As she tells it, Berre did manage a smile. Maybe he did, maybe he didn't. But he sat there a long time, looking up at his mother who stood bundled in her shawl—while he snorted through his nose. Finally, he asked:

"Ma, do you have enough to live on?"

Uncle Itche is a cheerful fellow. Therefore, it follows that he cannot make a living.

Berre gave a sigh. From between his lips, he let out a delicate whinny (see Chapter One) and said:

"Ma, are you aware that you aren't literate?"

She was not aware! Berre explained and advised her that she should take steps to liquidate her ignorance.

Then he got up and phoned the Institute of Teachers.

It was January. Aunt Malkele walked home—freezing. She thought:

"That Berre! It is better if you see him more seldom."

In the courtyard, pandemonium broke loose.

In the morning, a teacher did appear, a young one with a forelock creeping from beneath his visor.

Seeing this, Aunt Malkele began to have palpitations. She washed herself quickly, took off her apron and sat, shyly, by the edge of the table. Aunt Malkele was frightened. She had no idea what was going to happen and, in despair, looked in the teacher's eyes. Since he wasn't certain either what he was supposed to do, he also turned red under the visor of his cap.

Com-Youth ° (those chatterboxes) has its writing material under lock and key; and it turned out that Malkele's own bottle held flies instead of ink. She kept blowing into its neck. But as her teacher told her, it was too late. A pen was drawn from behind the mirror; its cobwebs were wiped away; the teacher pressed the point against his fingernail. It became apparent that it really was an ancient pen— from even before the Revolution.

From that day on, Aunt Malkele kept the habit. If you take a pen in hand, you test it on your fingernail to see if it works. That is the sign of a cultured person.

Uncle Itche was equally upset. Still, he offered his notebook. Out of the box in his sewing machine, he took a twisted copybook to which a pen had been tied with string. Uncle Itche straightened the book on his knee and, his elbows trembling, gave it to the teacher.

An audience had gathered. The place was crowded. They marvelled; they shrugged their shoulders.

Finally, Uncle Itche could contain himself no longer:

° Com-Youth—the Communist youth organization.

"A world, eh?"

Uncle Yude looked at him crossly—from beneath his spectacles—and answered:

"Wouldn't it be better to be lying in the ground?"

A reference to Aunt Hessye who already has been liberated from the bonds of education.

Only Uncle Zishe took the matter calmly. Standing to a side, he pulled a hair in his beard, and with a benevolent smile, he said:

"Nice children!"

But they got used to the idea. They knew that the teacher would come each evening. Aunt Malkele, one must admit, had achieved a lot; the ability was there. Yet one must also concede that, when it came to learning, she was a little lazy.

"My mind isn't with it," Aunt Malkele would argue—like a little schoolgirl; which was hard to fathom in a woman of such understanding.

Once, the teacher, when he didn't find her home, took it on himself to complain to her husband, Uncle Itche:

"Your wife," he said, "has enough ability, but she doesn't treat the subject with the proper interest."

"Really?" Uncle Itche was astonished.

And later, he reproached Aunt Malkele:

"How can you be that way?" Uncle Itche was angry. "It probably will cost us money?"

At first, she became flustered; even turned red, but in a moment came up with an excuse.

"I have no book . . ."

This was something he just couldn't accept.

"Aren't there enough books in the house? Have you already studied what is in all those books?"

Aunt Malkele saw her answer would not do. So she came up with another excuse:

"But I can't see. . . . A lens fell out of my glasses."

Do not think that Uncle Itche is always so severe. It wouldn't hurt to remember that we are dealing with a case of old-fashioned love: forty-two years old. He felt for his wife.

In fact, the following once happened:

The teacher is expected, so Aunt Malkele intends to rush off to the city, when, suddenly, dark Motele runs in with a shout:

"Auntie, the teacher's coming!"

They say Aunt Malkele became so rattled that she crawled into the bed in her overcoat, felt boots and with the market basket. Uncle Itche tucked her in. After which, he clasped his hands, tilted his head a little to the side (Oh, these Zelmenyaner!) and—with a show of unmistakable melancholy—said to the teacher:

"My old lady, doesn't feel entirely.... Mark it as a lesson, Comrade Teacher, and you'll give us back the hour."

Nonetheless, Aunt Malkele has accomplished a good deal.

Deep winter. Windows overgrown with snow. Com-Youth is in its clubs. Auntie sits up nights; spotted with ink, she sits and works with the pen. On the table, an eight-hour lamp—which all tailors have. Wind whistles through the chimney. Uncle Itche is on one side of the table: he rips and mends. She sits on the other—buried in her papers. Her pen scratches. Then, her face shining, she slides a sheet of paper to him. Uncle Itche holds her note near the lamp, he can read only at a distance.

Aunt Malkele has written in this fashion:

"I am healthy, you are sewing, go to the stove, take out the pot, we will drink tea. From me your highly esteemed wife Malkele Chvust."

Uncle Itche smiles, pleased. Later, when they're having tea, he engages her in an instructive chat. He doesn't bother with trifles, but goes to the heart of the matter.

"This is not the way to write. When one speaks it doesn't matter, but writing has to be refined."

Aunt Malkele becomes uneasy. He says:

"For example, you wrote 'I am healthy.' This is not a refined way of expressing the thought. It is not permissible to put it like that."

"Really? How then?"

"One ought to write . . ." He closes his eyes. "One ought to write 'I discover myself to be in the best, most perfect health.' "

Aunt Malkele sees that her husband is correct. He goes on to say:

"Copy the examples in a book of letters. These new methods are entirely without taste. You should also read some books. They will

make you wise. There was a writer, Shomer.° One could learn
something from him. Today's are useless—all about the sun and
moon."

Outside, the winter lay in darkness—a cold, silver bowl.

A frightful frost persisted—always zero weather. The white roofs
crept down to the ground. In the evening, the drift would glitter;
and the air above stung like a bluish brandy.

Night has just fallen, but the streets are empty.

Who are these two who allow themselves to go strolling in such a
night? Uncle Itche's Berre and Uncle Yude's Hayele have come
down from the ice in the courtyard and turned into the street.

High time, if something is to be accomplished! Berre isn't
affected by the cold. Hayele, however, was shrinking into her collar.
Her high boots were tapping as if she were marching to the gallows.

They were saying in the courtyard:

"What can you do with a girl who does her courting only in a
frost or blizzard?"

Berre and Hayele were silent. He ran a little in front, getting up
his courage. When he was in battle near Kazan, it was much simpler.

"Hayele," he asked, "do I please you somewhat?"

Uncle Yude's Hayele had been waiting a long time for such an
approach to the subject. She answered with a smile:

"This is not the way to ask . . ."

"Why?"

By this time, he was also smiling. Suddenly, the winter leaped
within her like a silver fish—Zelmenyaner women have a feeling for
nature—and she asked him roguishly:

"Do I please you?"

Berre smiled and smiled.

Now, what happened next?

Hayele suddenly enclosed his head in her stout, perpetually
frozen arms and began to kiss his lips, his nose, and the hard dimples
of his cheek.

° Shomer—a Yiddish writer of high-flown popular romances. Kulbak's use here is
ironic.

The situation was certainly clarified. It merely seemed strange for them to be standing in a savage frost kissing without end or limit. Moreover, later an elderly man happened to go through that street and, on this very place, his foot got frozen.

Then they walked on, and it was cold. They came to an intersection where a light was burning. In the circle of an electric lamp, frozen coachmen warmed themselves in the hot breath of their horses. All was quiet, as in the middle of a field.

Berre looked at the clock and called a sleigh.

"There is still time to go to the registry office."

This was a little too much for Uncle Yude's Hayele. The evening had been full. She had thought of going home, where, in the silence, on the warm couch that smelled of her father's shavings, she would try to think it over. Love was beating in her brain. Her heavy Zelmenyaner blood was scarcely able to digest it.

But the sleigh was near them. Berre seated his bride and arranged the corners of the frozen blanket. The sleigh shot off; as it slid across the width of the street, she snuggled up to Berre with Zelmenyaner energy until she felt his cold wide shoulders and the sense they always gave her of the restfulness of oak.

Hayele went home in the wintry night. All around the frost was green, like a piece of ill-made glass. Her lonely steps were resounding in her ears. She came to the courtyard and paused by the house, but didn't go in to her father. She went a little further—to Aunt Malkele's.

Uncle Itche was swallowing big gulps of tea; he was still conducting his educational chat:

"One should study in a book of penmanship. Many letters like it if you add a flourish. Very pretty is the way that the letter *tess* will lend itself to a flourish—and the final letter *fay*. You can also do something with a *lamed*. Malkele, remember the notes I sent before we were married. Did they show you my handwriting, at least? A pity," he sighed. "A bunch of years already that I haven't used a pen."

Uproar

Next morning there was an uproar. The yard looked like an anthill. In their bare slippers, they ran through the frost of one household to the next. And in each place—long deliberations.

"How could this happen? Such a disgrace in Reb Zelmele's yard!"

"Without proper rites!"

"Hope it doesn't happen to us!"

The old Zelmenyaner prowled with their beards thrust out before them—they moaned and heaved their shoulders. The young chatterboxes, smelling that the air was loaded, followed what was happening from beneath their caps. Uncle Yude was beside himself. A sign—he stood in the middle of the house, chewing on his little beard. Hayele lay in the other room, red with humiliation. And he, Uncle Yude, kept blowing into his plane, working in a fever and directing his complaints into the board so that she would hear it on the other side of the wall.

"Goat, where are you running? Why so eager for the oats?"

Uncle Yude was a strange person. He was a philosopher—a widower, too. Suddenly he laid the plane on the worktable and stood motionless a while, showing his angry face to the universe. He thought, there is a saying of Reb Zelmele: A wedding should be celebrated with music.

His fiddle was on the wall; he took it down and walked to the wooden partition—on the other side lay his Hayele. He made preparations, rolled away his shiny beard, closed his eyes, and began to play!

This was supposed to signify: musicians are playing at Hayele's wedding.

At first, the tune was really like that of a musician at the veiling of a bride. But even then you could smell in it an aroma of death, as of a song in a graveyard. It plucked at the heart. Then he began a God-Full-of-Mercy, a tune about Hessye leaving the world too soon, without the honor of being at her daughter's wedding. Tears poured from his eyes; his wet lashes blinked against his glasses. He did not see what was before him, he was merely listening to a gloomy rhapsody that came pouring from within him about the unlovely death of his wife, Aunt Hessye.

Then he also played a tune about the hen.

Who knows how long he would have stood by the small partition if, suddenly, he had not heard a sobbing from the other side—a cry that was muffled yet kept growing louder. One could tell that Hayele, in a fit of tears, was tossing and turning on her pillow.

He seized a dipper of water and went into her room. Hayele was wailing. She raised herself weakly, took a sip of water, and sagged back into the pillow. Uncle Yude gave her a pat on the head, a mark that he was pleased with the bride's tears; then, quietly, went back to his workroom.

Back to his labor with the ax and plane. He puttered all day without complaint. One might imagine he had stopped brooding about the unfortunate alliance. Only in the evening did it come to his notice that, somehow, the cabinet he had begun that morning had turned into a bench—an ordinary little bench.

The next day was a day off for Berre.

How do we know this? There is an indication: If he removes his boots, it is a sign he's resting. That is when he becomes a strong, untroubled man. Barefoot, in parade trousers, he roams around the house, stealing from the pots, grabbing a fritter from Aunt Malkele's skillet, dipping it in something, then popping it—by way of his mouth—into his stomach. He reads the papers while he is standing, then sits on the workbench, his feet underneath him, and tunes the balalaika.

Berre knows a few clumsy songs he has brought with him from the front. They are buried in him as in a cellar, but it sometimes happens that he lets them out. He uses a deep belly-voice, and, when he loses himself, his eyes creep out in bliss over his forehead.

He sings a trifle strangely.

But you shouldn't think Berre is so involved with music that he forgets about daily life. He will suddenly break off his deep ecstatic song in order to announce:

"Mama, it's the day for butter in the Tserokop." °

° Tserokop—cooperative store

After which he resumes his song with even greater rapture: he drools with enthusiasm, accompanied by the jingle of his poor balalaika.

Oh, let us celebrate the way that the Zelmenyaner act out their role in world history!

Berre has been sitting for hours on the workbench, his bare feet beneath him, playing his balalaika. Which tells us that the bridegroom is enjoying the traditional days of feasting. His shirt is unbuttoned, his lips are protruding, and the oaklike voice keeps pouring out of his belly:

> Riding to Rostov-on-Don,
> I took a loaf of bread.
> Riding to Rostov-on-Don,
> I knocked the bourgeois on the head.

One heard comments in the courtyard:

"Wives they need, these chatterboxes? What they need is the plague!"

"The donkeys! What have they to do with wives?"

While Uncle Yude went into Hayele's room:

"Why are you lying here? Your husband is throned in a companionship of rabbis and is gushing hunks of Torah!"

When Berre had enough of booming like a drum, he got up and left. He didn't find it necessary to mention that he was married.

Later that evening, after heated deliberations, Aunt Malkele went to Berre in the militia. We know of old that she always has happy inspirations. Once again, it was her idea to invite him to cake and brandy.

"All right, so one isn't religious, still, one is a human being . . ."

She went through cold dark corridors before she found his room. There, having moved the tables, the bridegroom stood between them, red-faced and out of breath, and was mopping the floor.

Aunt Malkele was ashamed. She became angry.

"It's not fitting for you to do this. You could get someone."

Wiping his moustaches Berre answered that it's no trouble; he knew the trick himself. He put away the brush and welcomed his mother with Zelmenyaner warmth.

Aunt Malkele sat down and made herself at ease. No reason to hurry. She took the pen from the table and tried it on her nail.

"Nu," he asked her, "what's doing with you?"

"You know," she answered. "One studies a bit of Yiddish . . . a bit of Russian . . ."

Thus they talked round and round the subject.

Do not think Aunt Malkele has forgotten the reason for coming this evening. She has not forgotten. Yet a person has to know how to approach another person; it wasn't without reason that clever Aunt Malkele has been sent on this errand; though Uncle Yude had been fuming all day long, promising that, when he got there, he would make mincemeat of that pretty son-in-law of his. No, Aunt Malkele had forgotten nothing! She even managed to sneak in an observation that inscribing names in a register is without substance. It isn't to one's taste.

Berre smiled.

It was then she invited him to cake and brandy. And Aunt Malkele conceded:

"It is understood, no ceremony, of course. After all, we are sort of modern."

In the courtyard, they made preparations for a quiet wedding.

Odors hovered round the chimneys. *Hallehs* were braided as in the olden days. Aunt Gitte knows the secret of a special confection of dough cooked in honey, which her distant blue rabbis found delight in. Odors of cinnamon and saffron were floating round the courtyard.

Only Uncle Yude was still looking rebellious; yet without anger. He had some kind of garment the color of sand; it had a brown silken collar, like a thong. He was shaking it over the snow.

We should also approach and take a peek in Uncle Zishe's window. If a rectangular beard makes its appearance, if a hand is on it, if it holds it firmly and this beard is being combed from the bottom up—that is a sign there will be great festivities in the courtyard.

The beard is here!

Tsalke brought a bottle of wine. Things are happening. Since sunrise, Uncle Itche has been circulating. Like a dove—silence in a human form—Uncle Itche merely listens to what others are saying. Meanwhile, he is trying to avoid Aunt Malkele's glances.

Why?

He likes to take a drop of whiskey on these occasions; then he starts to kiss the women. It is thought he isn't very intelligent.

The day sidled off, without any sunset. In Uncle Yude's house, they lit the big lacquered iron lamp, which hung down like a mechanical contraption. The house was spotless. It smelled of fresh pine boards. Only in the entry there remained the nasty odor of the geese he had raised there.

Uncle Yude's little beard glittered with cold water. In his stiff old-fashioned suit he looked something like a little village priest who had strayed among the Zelmenyaner. They brought Aunt Boshe, wearing the garments of an ancient queen, irradiated by a little stole sewn with black beads of a thousand different shades. On her head— a whole flower garden. Uncle Itche edged his way into the room, hair washed and beard trimmed with a little scissors. After this, Uncle Zishe and Aunt Gitte. Uncle Folye did not come. This was expected; he had been insulted when young. Last of all came Tsalke, Uncle Yude's bungler. He is educated, always engrossed in books, one of the new scholars. Soon as someone says a word, he leaps up in amazement:

"What? What did you say?"

And puts it down in a little notebook. He is most intimate with Grandma Boshe; this isn't customary among young people. He has another habit. From time to time, he attempts to take his life. But, at the moment, that isn't to the point.

With Zelmenyaner calm, they took places at the table and began to wait for the bridegroom.

As soon as Berre appeared on the threshold, the relatives were overwhelmed with a deep silence; not the sort of thing you expect at a wedding. There were surreptitious glances, with a quivering of lashes. Even so, he found this festive gathering suspect. That is why he quickly made a pronouncement.

"It appears clear, according to certain indications, that you are preparing to have a beautiful affair." He was looking at the dressed-up bride, sitting on a cushion in the place of honor, higher than the others. "Am I right or wrong?"

"Of course," said Uncle Yude sharply. "An occasion, isn't it?"

He answered crossly because he doesn't know how to play up to people.

At this point Berre took out his newspapers and began to read them. That is how the Zelmenyaner came to surmise things would not go off smoothly. Only the overheated Uncle Itche, a string holding his collar, sat there ready for another cup. Suddenly, he felt a pinch on his knee. Aunt Malkele, under the table, was letting him know her despair. At this, he, too, started to look round him with suspicion.

When Berre finished the papers, he released the famous whinny and began to look at the lamp. They were familiar with this procedure. He was setting himself to outsilence the wedding.

Not a great achievement, yet it requires a certain amount of knowledge. Berre went about it in approximately such a fashion:

He sat quietly, the way one sits in a railroad station waiting for a train. He looked at the lamp; and, by doing this, created stones of silence which weighed on the spirit of his relatives. After ten minutes of this, everybody was depressed.

The first who could not stand it was Uncle Yude. He bent forward in his chair. Black, sharp little eyes crept out over his glasses:

"Maybe you will say a word, my pretty son-in-law?"

To his help came Uncle Itche:

"A word, I tell you . . . it is your wedding!"

"Who has harmed you?" Aunt Malkele began to plead.

Berre answered slowly:

"Don't bother me. I'm sitting and thinking about something else."

"You might let us know, for example, what a man is thinking?" Uncle Yude kept at Berre.

"I am sitting and thinking how one would go about electrifying the courtyard."

The Zelmenyaner looked at one another. They knew of no troubles. As far as they were concerned, there was no reason to worry about the courtyard. And if one granted that there were such reasons, this was not the moment in which to reveal them. Uncle Yude explained the decencies: in a delicate manner, he let Berre have it. He isn't one of those who swallow an affront.

Berre stood up, asked Hayele to get her coat, and bride and groom departed.

A deep disgrace. The Zelmenyaner sat around the table with long faces, looking at the cloth. Suddenly—a frenzy took hold of Uncle Yude. He seized the bottle and smashed it to the floor, then he grabbed his own beard, as if to tear it from its bed.

An uproar. People began to edge towards the door. Only Uncle Zishe stood there calmly, full of smiles which spread from beneath his lashes. He pulled on a hair of his beard:

"Nice children! . . ."

Uncle Yude turned and began to wag his index finger.

"Just you wait, Zishe. You have not yet had your chicken pox and measles. You still have daughters! . . ."

Uncle Zishe's nose was pale: but he answered coolly and succinctly:

"Let everybody know. Zishe the watchmaker's daughters will definitely get married according to the rites of Israel and Moses!"

After midnight Uncle Zishe raised his sleepy, cubical head from his pillow and began to wake his wife:

"Is Sarah here yet? I'm asking you, is Sarah here yet?"

He meant his older daughter, Sonia—the one who works in the Folkomfin.°

Electricity

Berre appeared in the courtyard. From the heavens fell a warmish and unwintry glow that sprinkled the double windows with an intimation of spring. Berre slowly walked along the black path that led through the yard. After him—a worker. They looked at roofs, tapped walls, and made drawings with their fingers against the sky.

° Folkomfin—Department of Finance.

If that is the case . . . the people in the courtyard again became uneasy:

"A new evil decree!"

"What has he thought of now? This philosopher!"

Aunt Malkele perceived that it was a proper time for her to spread the books on the table.

Berre went inside. He studied rafters and walls, then went out. The implication was that he didn't find it necessary to say a single word.

In the evening, a rumor spread that Berre is about to electrify the courtyard. He will take away their lamps and, instead, will give them electricity.

At first, they didn't know what to make of it all or how to measure the damage. A few even thought it might be a benefit. By and large, the members of the family, grabbing a warm garment, hurried to Uncle Zishe to hear what he would say. There they found the change was going to be bad because of two reasons:

1) No one knew how to go about it, and
2) electricity is not for common people.

"I like electricity when rich people have it." This from Uncle Yude.

"You have my word. He will run us into the grave." Uncle Zishe, pacing back and forth, was speaking to his beard.

Only Uncle Itche, blinking his eyes, was puzzled.

"I don't understand. Why is there a problem? Don't they have electricity in the synagogue?"

Uncle Zishe stopped his pacing: he was riveted to the spot.

"Listen to our sage," he addressed the women, "In the synagogue there's a podium. Does that mean we need one here?"

It made a bad impression on Grandma Boshe. At first she gathered that Berre was going to dig a well in the courtyard. She remembered sadly that Reb Zelmele had always dreamed of having his own well; though this was not to be, for all his life he drank alien water. He never realized his dream. Finally, she caught on to what was being discussed. She could barely speak—but it was to the point.

"As long as I live, I will not allow you to chop down the walls."

That night, the sky was composed of tiny stars. The senior Zelmenyaner stood in the dark courtyard waiting to see Berre. They were wrapped in shawls, with the collars up: they were sniffling. Later, near midnight, he came in from the street. They surrounded him, blocking his way:

"Bandit—why are you picking on us?"

"Let us finish out our years with the old lamps!"

"Spare us your electricity!"

"Brother, stop torturing the poor."

In the morning a workman knocked on Uncle Itche's door and asked for a ladder. It had begun! Tools and rolls of wire lay in the middle of the courtyard. The workmen were treating the Zelmenyaner domain without a touch of pity.

The Zelmenyaner themselves went about their business quietly, without animation, as if someone in the courtyard were on his deathbed.

They watched what was happening, but with averted eyes.

Uncle Zishe seated himself at his watchmaker's table—he wouldn't deign to go out. He thought this a way of putting them down. By contrast, Uncle Itche kept roaming around, even where he didn't belong, so that the workmen had to yell at him from their ladders.

Old men with gray beards gathered in the courtyard to observe the work and discuss reflectively what electricity might do. They saw the yard being pierced with wire for no reason they could fathom. And in this they detected a finger of persecution. They stood about in circles all of that day.

In the evening a man with a sealskin object on his head—it resembled a cap—explained the virtues and rationale of electricity; but he did it so profoundly that no living human being was able to understand it.

You might say he lacked the power of elucidation.

Suddenly, Uncle Yude sprang up, as if from nowhere, and, being a divinely inspired philosopher, began, from his post behind the crowd, to explain to them the secret of electricity.   /

"Foolish people! Why can't you understand? You have seen the brick building, the one with the chimney—by the edge of the river.

Yes? Well, this building pumps water into itself. So it boils over into electricity. Then it sends it out over the wires."

They did not understand.

"Foolish people! Why don't you understand?" Uncle Yude was getting excited. "If a kettle boils, there is steam. Isn't there?"

"There is."

"What is steam? Don't you know? Steam is almost smoke. Smoke is almost fire."

"From this, you soon get electricity," interposed the fellow with the sealskin object on his head.

At this, Uncle Yude glared at the circle of people from behind his glasses. He laid his hands on his backside and he walked off. He left because it isn't in his nature to argue with creatures who don't know anything.

A few days later—it was evening—the electricity was turned on. A thin, foreign gleam flowed into the houses and burst out of the windows into the courtyard. One could only sit, at a loss, speechless.

Thousands of little shadows that, for generations, had spent their lives on these walls, were suddenly swept away as with a broom and disappeared. Rooms became more spacious, less confining.

Oh, it isn't a small thing for a person in his later years to get used to these new shadows, longer and thinner, now creeping along the walls.

Uncle Itche's shadow, for example, lay there all winter with its feet to the machine, its head on the cookstove. Now the stove looks brand new and white, as if it had been plastered; the shadow has disappeared. A strange kind of heartache! Uncle Itche sought his shadow, carefully, slowly, till he managed to find it, abandoned and concealed, somewhere under his workbench.

Aunt Malkele stood in the middle of the room a long time. Hands crossed upon her heart, she contemplated the cold rays of the new lamp. Then said with a sigh:

"For this electricity, it would not hurt to be a few years younger."

Uncle Itche didn't answer. He was still occupied with shadows. He moved his machine and arranged the benches. Suddenly he took the lamp, put it on the dresser, and covered it with paper. What is there to say? He was distraught. He grabbed his jacket and rushed into the courtyard. It was full of light. All the Zelmenyaner were in their homes. So, being a devoted son, he ran to grandma's house. He did this just in time, because the electricity had startled Grandma Boshe like a clap of thunder. She sat there, buttoned for the winter, looking at the bulb with unfocussed eyes; and, when she noticed a living human being, said:

"There is nothing more for me to do here. Better I should go and join your father!"

Uncle Itche was so flustered, he started to dissuade her:

"Where will you go in the night?"

One has to admit it: since then, Grandma Boshe is not all here. Maybe they are right, all those who argue that she had lingered a little too long.

Uncle Yude was a different sort of person. He was both a philosopher and widower. He pretended that he didn't notice how bright it had become in the houses. He was devious. Electricity burned and he puttered at the bench. But when his work was finished, he made a point of lighting the old lamp and sitting down to look in a religious book.

Don't worry. Uncle Yude won't let anybody cram electricity down his throat!

Uncle Yude's Hayele, watching this performance from her bedroom, wondered why her father suddenly had felt a need to look into a book. She was seething. However, Uncle Yude sat calmly and serenely, making strange faces—the picture of a man who has forgotten the world and is completely involved in spiritual matters.

When she could stand it no longer, she tore out of her room in a frenzy and blew out the light.

"Lunatic, don't you see the electricity is burning?"

Uncle Yude closed his book, put it on the dresser—then began to stroll around the house, to the music of a tune he was humming, a Hasidic tune.

Thus was the electrical revolution consummated.

In the varying light that came remotely from all sorts of

windows, the courtyard lost its customary nighttime visage. Swatches of bluish snow glistened in the dark and distant corners. As if with outspread fingers, electricity caught the walls, groping into the most secret hiding places.

Uncle Itche left the house, checked that nobody was watching, then passed a quiet spot between Uncle Yude's and the stable. It had been very dark there. Now, when going by, he saw that another comfort of his life had vanished; it was full of light—as in midday. Uncle Itche turned away, angry at the world and its new contraptions.

Muddy rivulets, like those of spring, trickled from beneath the ice, running downhill into the street with a cool tinkle. Standing in shadows, Uncle Itche noticed how Uncle Zishe, too, had come out of his house; and that, near the stable, a third person—it would seem—had coughed.

It was a quiet night; so quiet you could hear the scraping of electric wires on the pavement. Bright bars of light lay in fat darkness: knife blades resting in a black sheath.

The three Zelmenyaner were wandering about the courtyard, trying not to step on the wires which lay on the ground like bandages on Reb Zelmele's legacy. They blew their noses in fury and from time to time uttered that delicate whinny which is the property of this family alone.

They met near Reb Zishe's stoop, and stood for a long time stroking their beards in silence.

Uncle Itche could contain himself no longer.

"A world, eh?"

Uncle Yude looked at him with anger from beneath his glasses:

"Wouldn't it be better to be lying in the ground?"

He was thinking of Aunt Hessye, who was already there.

Only Uncle Zishe stood without anger, pulling on a hair of his beard. Even now, he gave a gloomy smile and said:

"Nice children!"

It was precisely then that Uncle Folye, dressed only in his shorts, jumped out of his bed, drank three dippers of water and went back to sleep.

More About Electricity

Electricity had conquered. If Reb Zelmele had been granted leave to return, he would have passed the courtyard and gone further for he certainly would have supposed an official lived here. These long narrow houses fill up every evening with a cool fire and lie in darkness, with their golden, sickly windows, like invalids drawing air through a little tube.

There was a rumor that the suburbs were getting inferior electricity—whatever is left over at the bottom of the barrel. When they heard this, the Zelmenyaner were mightily upset. If the report was true, their response was justified. It is only fair. If you give us electricity, give us good quality! They even came to an agreement that Aunt Malkele should go and tell her son Berre that injustice has been done. For once, however, she became stubborn and on no account would she accept this errand. The reason she gave is hard to understand:

"Wherefore must I always be the scapegoat?"

There began a bout of electrical fever. The young Zelmenyaner, who were much impressed with what Berre had achieved, drew the "Ilyich lamps" into their rooms. They crawled over the damp walls, across the roofs, and rolled out the wires. They hammered as one used to—once upon a time—when erecting a tabernacle before Succoth. The courtyard was electrified down to its foundation. Every Zelmenyaner ran with a hammer in hand, screws in his pockets, and pieces of wire. Uncle Itche's Falke gave each his instructions. Electricity was sparkling out of their eyes!

In those dark suburban nights, when the oil-lit homes were bathing in anticipation of spring, the Zelmenyaner courtyard lit up like a railway station.

Neighbors hurried to the windows and with round eyes marvelled:

"Look, my dear ones! See to what heights human beings may reach!"

The old wall is full to the brim with electricity. No wonder. A demon has been at work, Uncle Itche's Falke—of whom they say that, with electricity and a piece of bread, he could be content to pass his whole life.

He lived in the courtyard, in a little apartment, with Uncle Yude's Tsalke and, by reason of this, the yard was electrified from top to bottom—with superior electricity.

Who is Uncle Itche's Falke? He is a student in a vocational school. Long pig bristles creep from beneath his cap. He's a good boy. He gave notice of himself the moment he was born—entering the world with a loud cry. At the age of six months, he tore his navel. When five years old, he was scalded by a samovar. He was thirteen when someone split his lip. He is running around in a worn-out windbreaker of Berre's, a booklet beneath his arm—and swallows the world! He has enough hustle for all the Zelmenyaner. He keeps a work box full of ironware, hammers, screws and chisels. He repairs his own shoes. He paves the yard with cobblestones. He roofs the house and puts in panes. He has begun to gather cut-down beer bottles that he fills with bluish liquid in which he marinates pieces of copper, iron or coal.

Who is Uncle Yude's Tsalke?

He is a scholar, always in his books. A forelock is combed to one side: looks like a broad sideburn. Glasses on his nose . . .

Tsalke has a bad habit. From time to time, he tries to take his life. People rack their brains. Where did he get it? Zelmenyaner live a hundred years or more. Reb Zelmele himself lingered a long while without anything to do. This did not make him die.

No one knows where Tsalke got the habit!

As for Uncle Folye, the situation is as follows:

At first he thought the electricity in the courtyard was introduced by the Bolsheviks. He was pleased that, at long last, someone was giving orders to the Zelmenyaner. It was clear this was public business because the electricity came down from porcelain pots on the tall poles. The little pots and poles have always suggested governmental affairs.

Uncle Folye issued a pronouncement that when he's away at work, electricity isn't to be used in the house. His wife is never allowed to go near it—it is beyond a woman's understanding. Only dark Motele occasionally has permission to touch the switch. (In his father's presence.) He believes the boy has turned out well. Uncle Folye likes him.

At work, the wily Folye said to Trukhim the Lame:

"If you come to my house, we will light the electricity and have a pleasant time."

"You don't say!," the other was amazed. "Who gave you electricity?"

"What do you mean? You know who—the government!"

That day, at the stables, Uncle Folye was disabused. When he came home, his countenance was black. He immediately put his wife on the stand—and it turned out that the electricity had been introduced by Berre.

He finished his meal by the light of an old lamp.

For several days he went around in silence and thought of angry schemes. He looked out of his window down into the courtyard.

"The Zelmenyaner won't live to see the day when Folye has to be grateful for a favor." The hairs of his moustache twitched like the whiskers of a famished tomcat.

Sunday, the first day of rest with springlike weather, while the Zelmenyaner were lolling around the courtyard, he put a ladder up against his window and began to cut the wires. He also broke the porcelain insulators. The Zelmenyaner started a loud wailing. But they didn't want to get entangled with this assassin. Then Uncle Itche's Falke ran up with a revolver:

"Saboteur! Get down! I'm going to shoot!"

He didn't get down. Falke didn't shoot.

"I will see to it that you rot in prison," Uncle Itche shouted to the ladder.

Uncle Folye did not look around him. He sat on his perch, his back to the courtyard, and cold-bloodedly removed the fixtures. He was going to demolish this Zelmenyaner gift down to the very roots. Here Uncle Zishe came out of his house. Banging on a window, he called a Zelmenyaner and said:

"Why are we doing nothing? Someone should call Berre."

"But if it starts a brawl? We should think of that!"

In truth, this made Uncle Zishe pause. But he answered that it didn't matter, so they ran for Berre.

The women quietly went around the courtyard, removing sticks and stones. After all, as they say, it's one's flesh and blood. Also, out of curiosity, some ran into the street to see if any neighbors have surmised what is about to happen.

Only Uncle Folye seemed to be indifferent. He looked around him with a watery glance, as if he had no personal involvement. (A casual bystander!) When he had ripped everything off the walls, he descended slowly, looked up to see if he had finished the job to his satisfaction and then, like the others, began to wait for Berre.

Berre came into the yard, hard head thrust forward; he took slow and wide steps, moving his feet as if he were dragging them in a swamp. They had never seen Berre walk in such a fashion.

Uncle Folye apparently understood what this gait portended. He languidly unbuttoned his jacket and threw it down beside him. He stood quietly by the wall and waited. Berre, not uttering a word, approached him without hurry. As of their own volition, heads tilted forward. Red necks grew taut, testing their powers. Suddenly—a crack of foreheads.

"Stop it!" the women wept.

It was too late. They stood skull to skull and grabbed each other's shoulders with such force that it twisted their bones.

Uncle Folye sighed, then they both rolled on the ground. No blows had been seen, though one of Berre's ears had begun to bleed. Berre lay on top, like a rafter. His hands were flailing underneath—so you could not see what he was doing to his uncle.

It took a long time. Uncle Folye's back slowly came into view. His whole shirt was bloody.

Then Berre got to his feet. Uncle Folye too, with a scraped face. One eye swollen like a fist. In deliberate fashion, he walked to his jacket, threw it over his shoulder, then he pointed a warning finger to Berre.

"You scoundrel! Don't put any more electricity into my house!"

Satisfied, he walked away.

Aunt Malkele ran out with a broom and swept the spot where these Zelmenyaner had been murdering each other. That is how the matter ended.

Early in the Spring

Early in the spring, an incident occurred.

Uncle Zishe's Sonia, from the Folkomfin, came into the courtyard with a tall, wide fellow who walked heavily with White Russian steps. He could barely get through Uncle Zishe's low door. He uttered a hearty *dzien dobry* and immediately followed Sonia into the second room.

Uncle Zishe took off his jeweller's loupe, slowly wheeled to Aunt Gitte, and with furious surprise began to look in her eyes. She was buttoned up, sitting by the window, hands near her heart. She was engaged in her after-dinner silence. In a dumb show the two of them went through the following conversation:

"Gitte, your daughter doesn't please me!"

Aunt Gitte is silent. But, in her case, that is the same as speaking.

"You know, my wife, it's all your fault!"

Aunt Gitte says nothing. But, in her case . . .

"Tell me, how can a mother fail to see what is going on under her nose?"

That is how he abused her.

Then he went out to inspect the property. Does a glass need putty—especially in the window that looks into Sonia's room? A good proprietor, he tapped the shutters and to prove his concern, he looked through the glass.

Sonia was rather ashamed of her father's behavior, but she and her friend were apparently on good terms. All that they did was make witty remarks about the habits of this petty bourgeois and his limitless curiosity.

Uncle Zishe returned to his large loupe, sticking his eye into the innards of a dusty clock, breathing through his nose, silent and bitter with the whole world.

No secrets in the courtyard. Aunt Malkele bent a finger into her mouth, closing one eye, staring with the other in Uncle Itche's direction—who stopped his banging on the sewing machine. He was afraid that Tsalke (Heaven preserve us) had again taken his life.

He went into the yard.

Zelmenyaner daughters-in-law, new Reb Zelmeles beneath their hearts, were standing at the threshold, whispering to one another, pretending to be sighing:

"No doubt about it. He's a real *goy!*"

Barefoot Uncle Itche, a joker with the ladies, asked them:

"How do you know he is a *goy?*"

He put his needle in the pouch, hitched up his pants and went past the window. The crowd was growing. Dark Motele climbed a window frame and with roguish eye began to wink at Sonia to show her he understands why she brought this large man into the house.

They waited for the couple to reappear on the threshold.

It was then that Uncle Zishe came out on the stoop. His hands unsteady, in a tearful voice:

"Vulgar insects that you are—a respectable person won't be able to show his face in the courtyard."

Alas, it was an act. He had enough weighing on his heart.

That night, he didn't go to sleep. He sat half dressed on the bed and waited—waited for his precious daughter. As soon as Sonia came stealing into the house—it was after midnight—he rose:

"Listen, you wretch. Don't bring any *goyim* into my house. You hear me?"

He was warming up:

"You—chatterbox!"

Then he felt an unexpected tightening around the heart. He sat on the bed—rigid and green, with a lifeless nose.

Lanky Aunt Gitte stood up from beneath the blanket, like a scarecrow in a field. In her fright, she took on a mannish voice. She began to heat water and get hot towels. Sonia ran for a doctor.

Uncle Zishe lay spread out like a wedding guest, his four-cornered beard on his bare yellow chest. Slowly, he raised a big, heavy eyebrow—and soon he thought:

"As if they know how to revive a person!"

In the morning, the customary birds were singing.

It was truly spring. Days were hot and dear, as if hammered in a forge. The sun, standing in the courtyard, is like glowing iron.

Wherever there's a pane—it sparkles with dark beams. Silence. If you want, you may even hear how nettles grow by the wall. (Alas, nobody wants to hear!) The yard is hotter than any other place. The sun bakes audibly.

How is Uncle Zishe doing after yesterday's infirmity?

As you know, one is not allowed to ask about Uncle Zishe's health. But looking through the pane is a universal right. It is quiet around Uncle Zishe's window. The curtain is drawn. This is the only mute and opaque window in the yard—the only one that has nothing to say.

Hayele now has to have a place in which to raise a new family of Zelmenyaner. She has bought a bed, a samovar, and a brush for scrubbing the floor.

Uncle Yude's Tsalke and his roommate Falke were asked to, please, tidy up the quarters they had had for nothing. They moved to her old room, downstairs in Uncle Yude's.

More About Tsalke

(Tsalke is in love with Sonia's sister Tunke.

In the previous chapter, he spent the afternoon with Tunke, who teased him. . . .)

Tsalke has been drifting around the courtyard. He is distraught—his tie twisted to a side.

Uncle Itche who, from his window, is able to survey all that is happening has for many days kept a suspicious eye on Tsalke's behavior.

At midnight, they heard somber, wild cries. (This was Uncle Itche shouting.) The yard was paralyzed with fear. People ran out of the houses; long feminine nightgowns and dishevelled masculine nightshirts pale in the darkness. The shouts came from somewhere up above: one would think, from Uncle Yude's garret.

That was when Uncle Folye's mournful little wife began to jab his ribs.

"Get up—they're killing people in the yard."

Folye turned on his other side and began to growl into his moustache.

"Let them! It is their business. I have to get up early for work."

"Folye, have mercy!" She wouldn't let him rest, pulling the pillows from beneath his head. So he went out. Though he was sleepy, he flew up the ladder to Uncle Yude's attic, taking several rungs at a time.

The shouting stopped.

The Zelmenyaner were huddled, sniffling, head tilted, looking at the opening to Uncle Yude's attic.

"Someone has to run for Berre." Their teeth were chattering. "Without Berre we can do nothing."

Falke came out with appropriate weapons—a flashlight on his breast, a revolver in his hand—and also ran up into the attic.

"Robbers! Answer! What's the trouble here?"

Soon the thin electric glow spread once again from the attic trapdoor. You could hear his gulping voice.

"It's nothing. Nothing. Tsalke has committed suicide."

"Really?"

"For good?"

"No. Like always. It's just like always."

Uncle Itche had been sitting by his threshold, watching to see if anything might happen. Late at night, he noticed how Tsalke came running out of the house without any jacket; grabbing the ladder that stood near the stable, lifting it with more than his usual strength, he put it against the roof and, like one possessed, ran into the attic.

Should Uncle Itche have followed?

He should. That's what everybody says. As it happened, he caught him at the proper moment.

Tsalke, however, was so embittered that he managed to lift one of his feet and use it, like a stick, on Uncle Itche's head. Uncle Itche was overwhelmed with a great fear. If he himself is supporting Tsalke, whose foot is banging on his head?

That is when he began to give the alarm.

Uncle Folye draped Tsalke around his neck and carried him down into the house, carefully, like a piece of china. They made a new bed and undressed Tsalke. In their curiosity, they stood around him, watching how he drew breath, slowly opened his cold eyes— and slowly closed them.

"We ought to have jam!"

"Look, he's faint. We need a bit of jam."

Tsalke turned to the wall. Aunt Malkele had been waiting for this opportunity. She grabbed his clothing, emptying his pockets, feeling the seams, for some deep secret. In a trouser pocket they found an object which, according to all signs, had been a pocket handkerchief, two bone buttons, and, in the vest pocket—a small wrinkled paper.

Uncle Itche ran to get Aunt Malkele's glasses.

In the other room, the older Zelmenyaner gathered quietly around her. She read the note with toil and trouble. There were a few strange words and their meanings. Then, at the very bottom, she unexpectedly came on a few perplexing lines.

"Is it better to say, 'I love Tunke' or 'I care for Tunke'?"

Tunke, *Tunke* . . .

They looked at one another. Soon Uncle Zishe got the note in his possession; then they quietly went back to the hanged man's room.

After he had the jam, the critically ill man felt a bit better. He even smiled to the others, as if to say, "Here I was behaving myself, when I suddenly go and do this terrible thing!"

Uncle Yude, moving among the others, was quiet, easygoing, soft and comfortable, as if in stocking feet. He was evidently pleased that his boy had survived, though you couldn't tell it by his face. His pale little eyes were casting furious glances the way they always did.

The others calmed down. If they were worried now, it was because of Hayele who, according to Aunt Malkele's calculations, has long been at a point where she should not get excited. However, Hayele remarked:

"Do not eat your heart out. I won't get scared. My child is dearer to me than he is."

Late at night, Berre came home from the militia. He was walking with slow self-satisfaction: like a proprietor, he was chewing polly seeds and spitting toward the sky.

All the lamps were burning in the courtyard. Odd. The doors were open in Uncle Yude's house. He went in and, immediately, understood the nature of the celebration.

The Zelmenyaner lowered their heads—as if they were responsible for Tsalke's crazy ways.

Berre leaned on the foot of the bed. For a long time, he reflectively peeled the seeds, meanwhile looking at the guest of honor. Finally, he let the soft Zelmenyaner whinny come up from deep in his heart.

He muttered, "Shmintellectual!"

Aunt Malkele nodded sadly—a sign that she agrees.

The yard was sound asleep. Since Falke hollers when he dreams, he was sent to spend the night with his father, Uncle Itche, lest he disturb the invalid, Tsalke.

The moon silently wandered over Uncle Yude's roof. Tsalke lay with open eyes. He felt as if he were in the sea a thousand miles from shore. He was twice depressed—mentally and physically in distress. He could even hear the moonlight as it trembled on the shutters.

He heard how someone slowly pushes the door.

Uncle Yude's voice:

"Tsollie, are you sleeping?"

"No—not yet."

Uncle Yude came in sideways, then he sat silently upon the bed: sat a long time, plucking his beard, getting ready to say something that, apparently, was of great importance to him. Finally, after a tiny cough, he began in a sermonizing voice.

"Tsollie, take a lesson from the others. Our old world is too narrow for 'em. Why are you still sitting at your books? You can be a Bolshevik, too, like them. . . . Look, you silly fellow, think it over and become a Bolshevik. . . . And to tell you the truth, a father should get a bit of compassion. One doesn't live forever. One wants to have a son to say Kaddish for him, like all other people. Is that wrong? . . . I understand it if one sometimes tries to commit suicide—why not? I understand it—once or twice. But you do it every minute. And it's clear (the Lord have mercy!) that you are not fated to succeed. So there is a question. Tsollie, why should you go against the wishes of both God and man?"

Uncle Yude stopped. He watched the thread of moonlight that worked its way through the shutter, then began again, this time a little softer, as if entrusting a secret.

"Don't think that I'm not on their side. No I really am. . . . They should have gotten rid of the tsar, very necessary. He was a nothing, not truly a ruler. . . . But when they pick on our bit of religion—no, that isn't right . . . not the least bit . . . simply isn't nice. . . . A wedding ought to be a wedding, a *brith* ought to be a *brith* and it's sometimes right to say a prayer—why not? . . . What is this wonderful achievement? So you didn't pray! Whom are you hurting? . . . Listen, Tsollie, if they only let me get to them and talk it over, things would be different. . . . They may be modern people, speak a lot of languages, but one has to have something up here too. . . . No, eh? . . . And this—the way they pick on rich people: between you and me, that is silly too. . . . The rich, after all, used to help you make a living. . . . You got nothing from a shoemaker or tailor. . . . So, you see, if they only had a bit of common sense, they would make peace: especially with the bosses—after all, they're refined. You might need advice or may want 'em to give you a recommendation. . . . No, eh? . . . Tsollie, are you sleeping?"

"No—not yet."

"You see, a young man should never separate himself from the community. . . . When you become a Bolshevik, you carry their flag, say what one has to say . . . and, sometimes, if you have a chance to do a Jew a favor, that is appreciated; you will be admired by our people too! . . . You're a person (God be praised) who can use a pen. So you might write, give them to understand—why not show 'em that they have made a mistake?"

Uncle Yude sighed.

"Listen, sometimes I look at the electricity, how it's burning, and I think: there is no God—there is electricity. . . . How does it hit you? This lamp is God? This lamp punishes the sinners and rewards the saints? . . . Did it give the Commandments to Moses, this little lamp? . . . I ask you, what do these people use instead of a brain? . . . What if I break this lamp—does it mean that there is no more God in the world? . . . Only chaos? . . . Tsollie, are you sleeping?"

"No—not yet."

"So, forgive me." Uncle Yude is warming up to the subject.

"You're an educated man. Help me understand—satisfy my curiosity. What is at the bottom of all this? Don't they see or don't they hear? . . . Help me understand. How can men with beards, people full of years, publicly profane the Sabbath? . . . What's at the bottom of all this? . . . What are they thinking? . . . Comrade Lenin is a great man. Certainly—a great man. Yet what does he know when it comes to matters of faith? . . . Let us even assume that he is touched by grace—so what? . . . Does it mean that Moses has become a nothing? . . . King David a nothing? . . . The Vilna Gaon is nobody at all? . . . You know, Tsollie. Sometimes one gets a fire in one's head: so one desires to escape to the House of Study, behind the big stove, and think the matter through. Tsollie, are you sleeping?"

"Yes, I'm sleeping a little bit already."

Uncle Yude sat, hunched up on the bed. At this time, he looked like a little Orthodox priest who had lost his way. A few drops of moonlight sprinkled one of his lenses and a small area of hollow cheek. He got up, stood a good while with his back to Tsalke, lost in his thoughts; then he turned his head.

"Maybe I should play a little on my fiddle. It's a long time since I have held it in my hand."

"Whatever you please."

In the dark, he stood over the bed and played as if he wanted to draw out Tsalke's soul—not by means of hanging, but through sweet and old-fashioned lamentation. There was a scent of singing in a graveyard. Melancholy blossomed, opened, like a plant in water. The tune stumbled, gasping for breath, strangely broken, dead, like a blind eye—furiously blinking, struggling to see.

It was dark.

Then he played about the hen! A different kind of tears—about the Fates, who go their own way, indifferent to us all.

Radio

(Uncle Itche's Falke has decided to install a radio system in the courtyard . . .)

He will harness the airwaves with antennas and fill the houses with concerts, fiddles, voices. But he has no money.

So he put together a list of progressive elements. Then he went around the Zelmenyaner houses to agitate for his proposal.

There was a hubbub. This is understandable: when you use electricity, then—at least—you save some kerosene. But this is music, singing to no obvious purpose. And, to make it worse, Falke swallowed his words; you could not understand what he was after.

Aunt Gitte—at first—gathered that he would climb up on the roof, sit there and sing and they, below, would give him money.

"An easy way," she said, "to make a living."

But Falke persisted. He did not care that Uncle Zishe was glaring as he would at a spider. Falke kept repeating:

"Electricity is the basis of industry. Radio—of brains."

In a couple of days, he had about twenty-five rubles and sat down to the job.

They began—the first, thin and slanting rains. Behind them, the silenced summer, with a million muddy colors, was extinguished in the autumn gardens. The cheerless green of beet tops, with their raised veins of lilac, lay—trampled—between the garden beds. Dirty yellow, dirty orange, dirty bronze, all drifted underfoot, without any sound.

In those days (when they still had no antennas), they could hear only faint and pitiful voices.

A dirty shower was dripping when Falke asked his father to help him raise the strongest possible antenna. Uncle Itche put on a torn coat, one that is good only for climbing housetops. Then, going through the attic, they crawled on the roof.

Uncle Itche had been there two-and-forty years before. He could not believe the hundred tenements and structures that he now saw, through the dull mesh of autumn trees, to be the same city that had once been there. Falke, however, didn't let him stand there, with his beard in hand, gaping at the town. Falke was dragging a long wire; and his pockets were stuffed with nails and wires which weighed his pants down.

He was running his father from one end of the roof to the other. I won't say that Uncle Itche did not like this game. In fact—he did like it. Because, by nature, Uncle Itche is not really a tailor. And, truly, when does a person have the opportunity of strolling around a roof without having to justify it to anyone?

A dirty shower drizzling: they lay there, twisting, on the wet roof by the chimney, hammering the last nails into the antenna.

Falke asked: "Do you believe in the Soviet power, or don't you?"

"Of course! What a question!"

"So why don't you shave your beard off? Look, it's dripping."

"I will tell you the truth. If I took my beard off, I would look a bit younger, too. But it wouldn't look right to people."

"A petty bourgeois remains a petty bourgeois!" said Falke to the chimney.

"I will tell you the truth. I trim it a little. Sometimes here—or there. You can't do it all at once!"

Days passed. All that could be heard in the earphones were hoarse, distant winds. They heard the autumn weather of the European lands.

During these days, Falke was in despair.

Uncle Zishe said at mealtime that Falke may stand on his head; he will not succeed in installing a system. Because, in addition to everything he's done, it must have a pendulum.

"I am a watchmaker," he said. "You cannot tell me anything about these objects. You may think a clock runs all by itself. Oh, no—in addition to everything, you must install a pendulum."

He said no more. But Uncle Zishe's words go a long way. People began to urge Falke to use it.

"Hang up a pendulum," they pleaded. "Don't be stubborn."

"How can it hurt? Sometimes you should listen to an older person too."

Falke was out of his mind. He hurled the hammer to the ground and began shouting: "Where should I hang it? Up in the sky? The old tinker is gonna teach me how to install a radio! Let him first learn a little bit of physics—our new Marconi!"

All hung in the balance. In general, the yard began to doubt Soviet achievements. It was only then, one time late at night, that dark Motele—Folye's son—ran into the courtyard, hollering that, in his box, he had begun to hear the sound of balalaikas.

The courtyard exploded; they leaped from the windows—all to

Uncle Folye's house. It was so. There, in Motele's radio, a tinkling of balalaikas. Then, from somewhere far, someone with a human voice: "Hello! Hello! Hello!"

They sat, bunched, round the radio boxes. Eyes popping like a bird's, they heard—in amazement—a speech about "bread futures" in the U.S.S.R. The earphones were passed from one to another and the busy Falke ran through the homes giving lessons in the art of listening.

In his own house, Uncle Yude fell to his with a frenzy. He lit all the electric lights and, with closed eyes, he sat and listened. No one could get near his radio. And when Tsalke saw the tears in his eyes, he went to Uncle Zishe's in order to discover what his father was hearing.

A violincello was being played in Moscow.

At this time, all were gathered in Uncle Zishe's. Apparently they were waiting to hear his opinion.

Hayele came down and asked if she could hear the radio or might it harm the unborn child. Falke got angry and began to explain that according to the laws of music, the music wouldn't get to her belly. Here Aunt Gitte interrupted her own rabbinical silence and advised her not to worry, she could postpone the radio till after childbirth.

In the morning, Grandma Boshe noticed a pole on the roof. She crept around the houses to make an investigation. She suspected Falke—that he was handling pigeons. Tunke, who likes to spend time with grandma, brought her to a radio and put earphones on her. Grandma, more's the pity, was able to hear nothing and understand nothing.

She thought the radio dials were part of a clock.

Falke has perfected the radio: now you can hear almost all of Europe. He is learning Morse code and getting ready to be a master of shortwave.

Sonia

What of Uncle Zishe's Sonia, she who has a job in the Folkomfin—is she a person?

It is said she is.

Why is Sonia always cold? Why is she on the sofa, wrapped up in a shawl, hugging her shoulders? This is what Sonia has inherited from Aunt Gitte, who has smuggled frozen rabbinical blood into the family.

Sonia's skin is too fair for a Zelmenyaner. Furthermore, her eyes are a shiny blue. They seem to give off light—especially at night. This creates a great impression at the Folkomfin.

People thirty-five or over are very fond of Sonia.

Sometimes when she leaves the office, she is followed by as many as five officials. Hugging her shoulders, she gives a smile to this one, another smile to that one. Then they separate and all eat their lunch.

It is possible that she is also loved by everybody in the courtyard; but not enough for anyone to make a fuss. She has habits alien to the Zelmenyaner—that is sufficient reason. She is a stranger even to her sister Tunke who sleeps in the same bed. Of course, they don't really have a chance to exchange a couple of words, they keep different hours. It is only late at night that one occasionally hears a sleepy voice:

"*Oy-oy.* Take away those cold feet!"

In the morning, Sonia sits down to her toilette, spreading all sorts of soaps, brushes and powders on the bench near the pail of water. She is in no hurry, tidying herself for exactly an hour.

Uncle Zishe looks askance at the frivolous little jars. But since he knows that one has to be in step with the modern world, he will not make a direct complaint. He merely wonders where such behavior may lead.

Sonia (perish the thought) is not going to waste a word.

Quiet

As

A dove.

On her days off, she sits on the sofa and cleans her nails. After this, she wraps herself in her mother's shawl, wraps herself and reads.

In the evening, there is the tall and broad White Russian. He sits near the sofa. In the bluish darkness, they may utter a brief phrase: they laugh softly—though, sometimes, there isn't even that.

They speak in Russian:

"Reading Turgenev?" he says with sweet reproach. "Why don't you stop?"

"He writes excellently," says Uncle Zishe's Sonia. "What a sensibility! What harmony of colors!"

Sonia turns over on her back; she clasps her hands behind her head. Though the windowpanes are a solid blue, and the pieces of furniture stand like heavy shadows around the walls, what she sees before her eyes is a hot restless dream. It touches the skin of her body. Sonia is yearning; her heart is pounding. Nearby is Pavel Olshevsky with an indistinct and unlively face, like a slice of the White Russian landscape. His head is resting on the back of his chair. He feels he, too, is losing his equanimity.

He lights a cigaret and attempts to calm himself.

He loves Sonia because of her Jewish quietness. In general, he loves Jewish quietness; that is the way he once expressed himself to a friend, the chairman of his village Soviet. He likes the Jewish quietness that flows so spaciously from Aunt Gitte's presence and that, in this greenish evening, through the medium of Aunt Gitte's daughter, speaks with such passionate language in his peasant heart.

That is how they sit.

The impoverished White Russian evening sings as on a wooden whistle. Through the panes, a blue-lilac glow—the sort that is duplicated only in the peasant cloth of White Russian villages. Here, in this room, there are the thinnest shadows; and—nearer—on the sofa, a pair of clasped hands and a sheen of eyes that, at the present time, glitter with their owner's restlessness.

Almost always, at such moments, the door suddenly opens. Uncle Zishe steps across the threshold, saying—in Russian:

"Why don't you light the lamp? Here is the electric bulb."

And with an uncharacteristic smile on his solemnly composed face, he adds—in Yiddish:

"How many times have I told you not to bring any more *goyim* into the house?" Then he finishes with a sentence in Ukrainian:

"Comrade, my wife will put up the samovar, if you please."

After such devotion and hospitality on the part of Uncle Zishe, they get out as soon as they can. Sonia comes back late at night, quietly crawls under the blanket beside her sister Tunke and lies with open eyes.

"*Oy-oy.* Take away those cold feet!"

She lies with open eyes till day begins to break—thinking, weighing an important matter. In the deep night, she wrestles with her decision.

One time, when the thing was finally settled, Sonia closed her eyes and immediately fell into peaceful sleep.

Oh, praise the Zelmenyaner who can make a critical decision— then, having made it, immediately fall asleep!

A few wet days later, Uncle Zishe came flying out of the courtyard. He was limping badly—like a crow with broken wings. His overcoat unbuttoned, he began running to the city.

A watery wind tumbled into the house. For once, Aunt Gitte did not find it necessary to get up and close the door.

The courtyard suddenly teemed with people.

"What has happened this time?"

"What a family it is!"

It became quiet. Zelmenyaner were wearied by a new disaster— one you shouldn't mention, one you can't ignore.

"How is this possible? How could it happen to us?"

Falke came to his brother Berre with the proposal that they should explain to the older generation the meaning of Sonia's act— provide the proper indoctrination.

"What do you want? A meeting?"

"This is what I want."

He received no answer.

Berre, with an abstracted air, looked through the misty little window into the autumnal courtyard. He thought, ponderously, about the genteel Sonia who, although she sleeps with a peasant, has no true relationship with the proletariat. And, by contrast, the authentic gold—for example, Uncle Folye who, at that moment, was coming home from work. An empty pot (it had held potatoes which he had finished for lunch) was beneath his arm. Uncle Folye is a lot nearer to his heart.

In the early evening, Uncle Zishe came back. He was pale and quiet. Silently, he went into his house: with his foot, he turned rightside-up a bench that was near the stove, then he sat down and, with a finger, indicated to Aunt Gitte that she should take his shoes off and sit down near him.

A sob came from deep in her throat, a dry one without tears; then she removed his shoes and seated her long, skinny body near him. They sat, in silence, by the unlit stove.

One by one, the Zelmenyaner came stealing into the house—preoccupied Zelmenyaner, looking as if they had come here only to warm themselves.

Uncle Zishe sat, short and compact, like a butcher's block. He stared around him, yet it would seem that he saw no one. The disgrace was big. He sat, thinking that perhaps these other Zelmenyaner were to blame for everything—these vulgar insects who do not understand him or his daughters.

Uncle Yude came in late, stood at the threshold, his eyes, above his glasses, glaring at the dark oven where his defeated brother sat with a frozen face asking the world for justice. Uncle Yude's sharp little eyes whipped like iron rods. Zishe couldn't stand them. He suddenly covered his face and began to whimper. This is when Uncle Yude said quietly:

"You haughty fellow, why are you covering your face?"

The Zelmenyaner sat with open mouths—showing all their teeth. Uncle Zishe was so badly beaten that he answered nothing and did not take his hands from his face. His shoulders twitched. Suddenly, he turned his head; his cap fell into Aunt Gitte's lap and he, Zishe himself, toppled—like a pole—in a faint so deep and sound, it was difficult to revive him.

That is the way Uncle Zishe always behaves. As a last resort, he throws a faint and becomes the one who has been treated badly.

What of Uncle Yude?
While the Zelmenyaner were going home to sleep—there on the

stoop lit with autumn silver—he moved his glasses up his nose and said to the others:

"So what—you savages! What if she took a *goy?* A *goy* is frequently better than a Jew. So you're afraid of God!" Uncle Yude looked at the high, starry sky. "This for your God!"

And he showed the sky a big carpenter's fig.

Uncle Yude is a strange man.

A Demonstration

There are rumors that detachments of the Red Army on maneuvers will march through the city.

In the evening, Uncle Itche came from the craftsman's club with new tidings. He would tell his wife the meaning of current events. Though Aunt Malkele read the paper every day, when it came to purely political questions, he was more knowing than she. This time, he gave her to understand that world imperialism is planning to attack the U.S.S.R. We, for our part, must increase the defensive ability of our country and for that reason, we the craftsmen, are going to demonstrate in honor of the Red Army.

He added, "Malkele, look, get ready for me a pair of woolen stockings, so I shouldn't catch cold in the damp."

A red flag fluttered on top of the courtyard. They were getting dressed.

Uncle Folye, in a pair of glittering boots, came down from the courtyard, expansively wiping his moustache after eating. Little groups of tardy workmen were streaming from all corners to join their associations. Folye looked with scorn at this muck of craftsmen. As far as he was concerned, they ought not be admitted to this day's holiday for the proletariat.

"What do these milksops understand about the Red Army?" He smiled to himself. "If it were a question of a cantor singing—this they would understand!"

Uncle Folye's arrogance was a bit excessive. Uncle Itche had already put on two pairs of woolen stockings, and, for this occasion, had taken another snip at his beard: which, by the way, has recently begun to shrink, so that older people have started to shrug their shoulders.

What is more surprising is the case of Uncle Itche—he who aged so badly in the last couple of days, he who was silently hugging the walls. He, too, suddenly put on his coat, took his thick stick, saying to Aunt Gitte:

"I ought to go there too. I suppose I've got a bigger stake in this than others."

Only three women were left in the courtyard: Uncle Folye's wife, Aunt Gitte, Grandma Boshe. Grandma isn't doing badly. In the last months, she has regained some youthful vigor. She stands by the window, like a bird in a cage, and keeps chewing bread.

Noisy bands were booming somewhere in the distant streets. The staid metalworkers were already at the railroad station, the gloomy, thickset tanners, the cheerful tailors. Now came the miscellaneous groups. On a side street, the Vocational School began to sing. Forelocks protruded from beneath their caps; red shawls rocked between them like colored lights.

Among them is Itche's Falke, with his long strides, reading a technical manual.

The brass hats of the firemen were shining.

Then the craftsmen, with beards, long faces and round shoulders. In front of them dragged their old shabby band, with a patched-up drum, a huge, unpolished horn which—inarticulately—bellowed to the world.

Uncle Itche was right behind the band. His head on a side, a vase under his arm—a gift for the Red Army. He looked a bit like Berre.

The craftsmen walked slowly, lifting prudent feet—the way they lift their hammers in the workshop. They were talking politics, having a good time. In the middle of the column, yet apart from others, there was the sorrowful Uncle Zishe. He held his patrician stick in front of him; then he unbuttoned the coat near his neck, to make it easier to breathe. He is not used to walking in the footsteps of the proletariat.

Suddenly, the mended drum gave a giant's cough. Then, from the distance, a sound of hoofs. The street became a whirl of red blurs, eyes, laughter, brass trumpets.

Uncle Zishe had never heard such a storm of voices.

He was carried away like all the others; he too began to shout and suddenly thought to himself that he's a Bolshevik, that he's following the flag. He was frightened and pleased. Then, somehow, he found himself on the sidewalk; he straightened his dishevelled beard and—abashed—turned into a side street.

Uncle Zishe looked around, to see if decent people had observed his loss of dignity. Rather bent, he went away, up this empty little street, leaning on his respectable stick.

Recently, Uncle Zishe has become much older.

By contrast, let us praise a second uncle—Itche! He didn't lose himself in those heated moments. In chorus with the rest he enthusiastically sang the Russian songs. More, he waved his hands in time to the tune and even taught the less gifted craftsmen how a revolutionary song should be sung with expression. He went into a trance. He imposed order around himself. He was the heart of the demonstration.

Then he pushed his way, the vase above his head, and with a flourish gave it to a mounted, laughing commander in the name of all individual craftsmen. "Long live Soviet might!"

For a change, Uncle Itche is excited.

The commander leaped from his horse, plucked a flower from the vase and hastily began to look in Uncle Itche's lapel for a worthy place.

At this, the tears almost sprang from Itche's eyes. But he stood up, straight like a soldier, and, with a trembling voice, said:

"My son Berre is a Bolshevik too!"

The commander slapped his back, leaped up on his horse and— even from afar—waved to him, the representative of all individual craftsmen, in the name of "A" Division, which was riding through on its foaming horses, with a smell of steppes, rye bread and warm little shacks.

Uncle Zishe is seldom in the house. He is occupied with his disaster. Others have become involved, especially a kinsman of Aunt Gitte's, a dealer in flour. It is said that negotiations are in progress: a divorce is pending. Uncle Zishe is seen walking with this dealer in quiet little streets—suddenly they stop. Belly to belly, biting nails, stroking beards, they review the steps they have been contemplating.

There are rumors the son-in-law has agreed to let her go. Only he wants a little money. Others have the opposite idea. They say Olshevsky really is a decent fellow; he will let her go for nothing. The impediment is Zishe. He wants compensation for his aggravation—to be specific, a couple of hundred rubles.

No one in the courtyard knows about these rumors—least of all, Aunt Gitte. She sits alone in the house and contains her silence by the gray autumnal window.

Tunke has the needed credits. Any day now, she will get an assignment to—we gather—no less than Vladivostok. The young folks are envious. Eight of us are on the old sofa in Uncle Zishe's home.

Though it's dark we won't light the electricity. What for? What we want to do is to give her a few warm, sincere words before her journey.

"Tunke—I repeat. To Stepanov, quality is a subjective category."

"If Devorin recognizes the objectivity of the abstract, is that any better?"

"You damned metaphysician! I tell you you're not allowed to isolate the abstract from the concrete. . . ."

Peace

No one knows precisely how Sonia happened to make peace with her father. There are varying reports. One, from Aunt Gitte, says that Olshevsky, after a lot of wrangling with her kinsman the flour dealer, has promised in front of witnesses that, as soon as he has time away from his job, he is going to become a Jew.

A different story may be nearer the truth—that Uncle Zishe wrote a long letter on the subject to a certain rabbi in Moscow. To which the other answered: for the time being, one must remain silent and accept the present punishment or what may happen later—without any resentment. The law is explicit. Yet the rabbi consoled him, adding in a tiny script that the same thing happened in the Babylonian Exile, in the days of Ezra and Nehemiah ... *no new thing under the sun* ... nonetheless he advised him that he should observe the seven days of mourning.

Uncle Zishe, who has little respect for other Zelmenyaner, first spread his story about a Hebrew postcard from Moscow in the synagogue where—since Sonia's unfortunate wedding—he has become a frequent visitor. It was only later that this marvelous account arrived in the courtyard.

Uncle Yude at once decided the story was a lie. In order to convince himself—once when Uncle Zishe came out for some air, he opened his own window to the courtyard and shouted:

"Maybe you can show me the card you got from Moscow?"

Zishe answered coldly. "The card is in Hebrew.... You will understand as much as a chicken about human beings."

"A peek from a distance ..."

"A card like any postcard," Uncle Zishe answered calmly.

Maybe he got this Hebrew card from Moscow. Maybe; maybe not. But this is definite: that from then on, Sonia kept coming to her father's house—though, a few times, she left it in tears.

No one could understand what was going on in that snobbish household.

Uncle Itche would watch from his window. Or he often dropped into Uncle Zishe's house to see what time it is. It was always gloomy, silent, except for several clocks that were ticking on the walls.

But you cannot hide a thing from Uncle Itche. One evening, he noticed that the shutters were closed before the usual hour. He drifted around the wet courtyard, trying to make up his mind—till he went and looked through the gap in the shutters and saw a curious thing: in the big room, around the well-lit table, there sat Uncle Zishe, his son-in-law and daughter. They were drinking tea. In a short while, he was able to deduce that Uncle Zishe had declared peace.

At first, the courtyard watched the events with detachment; but the inhabitants soon began to mutter. It was because of a triviality. And—we must admit—Uncle Zishe was guilty.

It is known that a Zelmenyaner is plain, like a piece of bread. He takes things as they come and continues as he did. That is the way they accepted the marriage. In fact, the peasant Pavel Olshevsky made a good impression. He seemed to show a willingness to be a good relative to the family without exception. Uncle Zishe put his foot down. He would not allow others to enjoy his son-in-law.

He wanted a monopoly.

Then they learned that, not too long ago, Pavel Olshevsky had expressed the intention of taking all the Zelmenyaner to the moving pictures. He had learned that among the old people there were certain elements who had never seen a performance in their life.

One would think that Uncle Zishe would be pleased by such a considerate thought; but he became stubborn and told Olshevsky firmly that, if he wanted to stay on good terms with his new in-laws, he must not fraternize with those in the courtyard.

"They are a type of people—it does not hurt if you hold them at a little distance."

By this, he gave Pavliuk to understand that he is related only to a single household, and to no others. And to establish this, immediately issued a command to Aunt Gitte to get into her holiday garments. So it was only Zishe's seed who went to the movies—without the rest of the courtyard.

A slap in the face. Since Reb Zelmele had founded this family seat, such an indignity had never been visited upon them.

"It is not the movies. It's a matter of honor!"

Affronted, Aunt Malkele took Uncle Itche's arm and set out to the cinema. Uncle Folye collected his five–six children and went to the cinema. What is more important, Uncle Itche's Falke let it be known that if they were willing to put up some money, he could install a movie house in the stable. He began to bite his nails because he had too many creative thoughts. However, just then, Tunke—Zishe's other daughter—came to him with a proposal.

"If you want, you can ride with me to Vladivostok."

He stopped biting his nails and, in due course, flew off with Tunke.

No matter that Uncle Zishe has shamed a courtyard full of people—that a movie in the stable is a vital necessity. What do you expect? A young chatterbox, a ne'er-do-well!

It is reported that, for several weeks after the evening at the movies, Aunt Gitte was silent. Finally, when the time was right, she said, with bitter irony, apropos of this modern world:

"They make the place dark, so you shouldn't see the swindle."

She won't go again—not even if you paid her!

Others in the courtyard had a different opinion. There were even comments that the movies are superior to everything: this includes radio and electricity. As for Uncle Itche—it goes without saying. Once, when Aunt Malkele upset their supper in the oven, he tried to take advantage of what, he hoped, would be a yielding mood.

"Malkele," he said. "It might be a smart thing to pay another visit tonight to see the movies."

Alas, he wasn't able to prevail. He had to be content with reviewing in his mind all the ocean waters and white polar bears that had appeared before him that magical evening. His brain teeming with fantastic visions, he walked dreamily, trying to overhear if anyone said a word about moving pictures.

"This is a thing I never expected," he said to Aunt Malkele.

At night, stitching a pair of quilted pants, he thought with aching heart about white bears and frozen travelers on icebergs—people for whom such pants would be a Godsend. He has forgiven Zishe for his insult. He has even gone there to have a reconciliation.

"According to my understanding," he told Uncle Zishe, "it would seem that movies are a higher order than radio or electricity."

Uncle Zishe could not resist a dig.

"What a lot of understanding you have!"

Uncle Zishe isn't open. In addition to the usual human infirmities, he suffers from vanity. We suspect he's trying to put a nice face on his affairs. The story about a postcard from Moscow is surely a lie. He is spreading lies—but is eating his heart out. It turns out that he still can't come to terms with his daughter's marriage. One time, while they were going to sleep, he suddenly addressed his wife:

"What does it all amount to; now that we have married off our older daughter Sonia?"

"Yes!" Aunt Gitte answered. "In an auspicious hour!"

"Nu, and what do you think about the alliance?"

Before she could think of a consoling answer, he put out the light and said to her in the darkness:

"After all, it's a terrible thing for both of us."
Outside, it was beginning to freeze.

Marat

A deep snow had fallen. The yard had sunk so far beneath it that one could barely see pieces of the walls with their snowy little windows. The white roofs slid nearer to the ground. The corners of the houses stood wet and downy, painted as with plaster.

About midnight, Berre came out of his apartment, sleepy, wearing rubbers over his bare feet. He made his way carefully to Uncle Itche's and knocked on the window. The little curtain was raised, and Aunt Malkele's frightened face swam up, as from a dark pool, and was pasted to the glass. Berre could not think of how he ought to put it; he murmured in his moustache and pointed to his apartment.

Aunt Malkele caught on. "Something with Hayele?"

Berre nodded.

Berre experienced a long, difficult night. First of all, Aunt Malkele sent him for a sled. When he got the sled, both women insisted that he should ride with them to the clinic. You may take it for granted that he refused to do it. Also, that Hayele—overcoat and all—threw herself into the bed and, between one labor pain and the next, cried that it was better to have a child with a stone than with a Bolshevik! She came close to refusing to have the child at all.

Out of the earth—up grew Uncle Itche and, with characteristic violence, threatened to hit him.

"Is it your child or isn't it? You coarse creature!"

"Why are you so excited?" Berre answered smiling. "When I was born, you didn't take mother to a clinic either."

"Savage! How do you compare yourself to me?" He became even more angry. "I was a poor tailor. You are a Bolshevik. It is your clinic!"

Berre was wrong for still another reason, because it happened in different circumstances entirely. Aunt Malkele, we are told, went to the river to wash dirty linen. Without her wanting to, she had him by the laundry. She was carried home on a peasant's sled together with the baby; so, you see, after this happened, it didn't make sense to ask Uncle Itche to take her to the clinic.

This night, unbelievable as it may seem, they broke Berre down. He came along to the clinic.

On the way, Aunt Malkele kept lording it over Berre. Any time they passed a drugstore, she would send him out to buy various remedies about whose value she was the only authority.

The sled became crowded with assorted herbs, ointments and salves. He was silent, something like a fish. During the trip, he turned to his wife only once:

"Hayele, where did you put the key to the closet?"

Hayele grabbed her spine and, in bitter pain, began to complain to her mother-in-law that—even now—Berre does not understand her condition. He thinks only of his keys.

Berre answered that this having of a child is not his province: he does not have to mix in feminine affairs.

"What about a *brith?*" Aunt Malkele suddenly came out with one of her own concerns.

"Enough!" he answered. "You will have no occasion for such remnants of the past."

At precisely six in the morning, during a blizzard, a new Zelmenyaner was born. (The doctor even gave him a slap on his behind.) This little creature had a mop of black hair, broad shoulders and a faint odor of hay and something else. (See Chapter One.)

Berre sat drowsing in the dark corridor and, when Aunt Malkele woke him with her tidings, he gave a sigh of spiritual satisfaction. "If that is the case," he said, "I suppose it's all right to leave."

Berre went home, put up the samovar and had fifteen glasses of tea and preserves.

Later that morning, Aunt Malkele appeared in the courtyard with the happy news. Hearty kisses were exchanged with all Zelmenyaner, as well as any others she met on the way. They knew a *brith* was out of the question. There are some things that one cannot manage. All they wanted was to preserve the name.

Uncle Yude and Uncle Itche went upstairs to Berre and told him, very firmly, that they insisted the baby have the name of Zalman. Having said their say, they stood—like poor relations—waiting for his answer.

He replied, "I have to decide about the name. But, at any rate, it will not be Zalman. Grandpa Reb Zelmele, according to all indications, was a reactionary. And, besides, I am not entirely clear where grandpa got the money to build a courtyard."

"Do you mean to suggest that our father was a pickpocket?" They began to move in on Berre.

He did not find it necessary to answer.

In the morning, there came from the clinic Hayele's famous decision that her child is going to be called Zelmele. There was a smell of gunpowder. Berre kept a grim silence. But his cheekbones jutted—a sign that he accepted the challenge.

Com-Youth (the chatterboxes) were getting ready to make a demonstration.

It has been peaceful much too long in the courtyard!

The older people, hiding in their houses, pretended to be unaware of what was going on. Yet, with a corner of the eye, they scanned the field of battle. The sewing machine stitched; the plane planed; Uncle Zishe's old clocks ticked.

When Uncle Itche saw there were no changes, he began a tailor's song:

"I sew quilted pants ..." while he winked, slyly, to Aunt Malkele. "Our daughter-in-law (the Lord be praised) was a lucky find."

Evening. Aunt Malkele was going to the clinic when Berre called her; he asked her to tell Hayele that his son is called Marat.

Uncle Itche lifted his trousers. "Bring him here, the buffalo. I'll grind him to pieces."

Uncle Yude yelled up to Berre's window. "Who are you, you jackass, who intends to shame my father?"

Uncle Zishe stepped out too. He said to the women—(it's curious: why is he always speaking to women?)—"I have considered the matter. I see this question of a name will be a blot on our family for generations."

Even now, Uncle Yude's eyes climbed above his spectacles. "Your son-in-law, Zishke—isn't *he* a blot on the family?"

Uncle Zishe answered coldly: "One, I'm not speaking to you. Two, I have permission from a Moscow rabbi; and, three, if you weren't such an ignoramus, you would also have known that this already happened in the days of Ezra and Nehemiah ... *no new thing under the sun.*"

We are lucky Uncle Zishe did not throw a faint.

It was not a pleasant thing. Aunt Malkele just managed to get all of the combatants into her house. She was uneasy. We may surmise that it was she who incited the uncles in their struggle for Reb Zelmele's memory. Furthermore, she was not entirely innocent when it came to Hayele's announcement.

This uneasiness may be the reason why, later, coming from the clinic, she felt an obligation to go through the family house, saying: "What do you think? The clinic is abuzz about Berre's Marat!"

After that, she found an excuse to call Falke into Uncle Zishe's house, where the uncles were sitting around a glass of tea. He was asked to tell them about Marat, not Berre's, but the other, the one they didn't know. Was he an honest man? Did he like Jews?

Falke assured them that about his honesty there was no question. He explained Marat's role in the French Revolution, touched on the battle between the Jacobins and Girondists; he paused at the Paris Commune, criticizing the great mistakes which had then been made and ended with a eulogy of the October Revolution.

That night, the uncles added to their knowledge.

The Death of Uncle Zishe

Uncle Zishe smiled.

Everyone reports that he was feeling good that last winter evening. He was even joking with Falke and Aunt Malkele about the pretty grandchildren one has nowadays. (You still weren't allowed to mention sons-in-law.)

Who would have thought that, twenty-four hours later, Uncle Zishe would no longer be among the living?

Knowing this, we know that the softness which comes before death was what was speaking in him. For a long time, his big, yellowish eyes had been turning to the Zelmenyaner; and they had been too naive to realize that he was saying goodbye.

There is no doubt he had a premonition of death; like all old watchmakers who—to some degree—have to do with living toys. If they want, they slowly put the elements together: the thing works. And if they want, they put on the loupe, remove the little wheels and the little hairs: it is no more.

In the morning, he got up at daybreak. There was a sharp frost. He kindled the samovar and in the snowy blue that seeped through the windows, he began his prayers. Later, in his *tallith*, he took a hot glass of tea to Aunt Gitte in bed.

Aunt Gitte was filled with cold horror. Seeing a white *tallith* in the shadows, she felt that it was coming for her. In her haste, she was barely able to get a shawl upon her head when she first heard Uncle Zishe's loving voice:

"Drink, Gitte, drink. All of your life you made tea for me, and I don't know if I deserved it."

In amazement, Aunt Gitte didn't answer. All she understood was that something is wrong with her husband.

All morning, she stood by the stove, looking sideways at him as he was bent over the accounts, till she noticed that his shoulders and the nape of his neck were not entirely of this world. When it comes to the circumstances and intimations of death, there is no one as well versed as she.

Uncle Zishe died a few hours later—and for a somewhat foolish reason.

A peasant's frozen sled drove up to the courtyard. It carried a whiff of night-cold from the fields. A peasant and his wife crawled from beneath the straw—muffled, cloddish, with hard potato-noses. They asked for Zishe the watchmaker.

At first he thought they were bringing a clock from the village to be fixed. But it turned out (this was the trouble!) that they weren't the usual peasants from the village, but Zishe's close relations, no less than Sonia's in-laws. Now—they told him—when they come to market, they will have a place to leave the horse and wagon.

As you may imagine, Uncle Zishe broke into a cold sweat. He felt a sudden urge to put his arms around Aunt Gitte and sit down and cry. His kinsmen kept talking. Zishe somehow managed to answer; but the little peasant, as if for spite, kept repeating with enthusiasm:

"Are you really Zishe the watchmaker?"

Uncle Zishe snorted through his pale nose, looking through the window to see if the others knew of this misfortune. Of course, Uncle Itche was already drifting around the stoop, full of suspicion. There was a danger that the scoundrel was about to enter and ask for the time.

Uncle Zishe got up, dragged himself to the door and opened it to the yard. "Itche," he said faintly. "I suppose that you want to know the time?"

"Yes," Uncle Itche discovered. "I'm curious to know."

"It's a quarter to twelve." He turned awkwardly, sighed, and fell on the stoop, face down into the black snow.

The courtyard was calm. They waited, thinking that he was producing his usual swoon. They knew the reason—to send the uninvited guests on their way.

How surprised everybody was when it turned out that, this one time, he had really died! How bitter it became!

He had been deceiving the world a whole lifetime with his make-believe; and, even now, people think he has engineered his dying with a little twist—the yard should have to argue whether he is living or not.

What a strange way for a human being to act!

Uncle Zishe was dead. He was lying on the disordered bed in a deep corner of the house, with a puffed-out paunch and his cold beard pointing up to the ceiling. He lay as if to spite the others, and, near his head, Aunt Gitte with bony hands like drooping wings. She sat and watched how those who came in were moving around the house.

The peasants were sent away as soon as possible because, among other things, Uncle Itche was going to hit them.

Uncle Itche shouldn't be censured either, because this loyal brother took it to heart more than anyone else; he stood in the middle of the house, a big handkerchief for his fat tears, and yelled out loud like a kid who has been spanked. People asked for mercy. His voice shattered their ear drums.

On the other hand, Uncle Yude didn't appear. There are rumors that the madman is dissatisfied. He has some complaint about Uncle Zishe's death.

He came late that evening, when the dead body had been lowered to the floor. The children had already come from work. Grandma Boshe was sitting by the bed. Uncle Folye was standing, rather drowsily, near the stove. Uncle Yude raised his glasses like a doctor, bent down to the body and uncovered the face. They waited for his word. He stood a long time, shook his head and finally addressed the corpse.

"Zishke, you lived like a fool and an arrogant man; and now you've died . . . like a fool and an arrogant man!"

And he straightened up.

They let the matter go.

The family had not been together a long time. They felt a breath of Zelmenyaner restfulness and quiet, a raw smell of the White Russian earth. They all wanted the companionable evening to last. Even Uncle Folye.

Grandma was chewing something, swallowed it before she finished; after this, she said:

"To die in such a frost—that is no treat!"

She was speaking to herself. She meant that, for an older person, it is more seemly to die in milder weather.

They threw a glance at the old lady. The same ugly thought went through each head.

The young ones began to choke in their fists. Even Sonia who was sitting, depressed, in her hat and linen gloves, and was sniffing various bottles Pavel Olshevsky gave her—even Sonia smiled. It was on the verge of desecration of the dead.

Uncle Itche flared. "Chatterboxes—is this the theater, or a movie where they show you white bears?"

When things became still, they were first able to hear Uncle

Folye's bony laughter, just like rolling stones, from behind the stove. They could tell that he was tightening his belt. Maybe he might succeed in containing his laughter.

He was ashamed and went out of the house.

Indignant, Uncle Itche started to recite the Psalms. The young ones thought it was advisable to sidle out of the house as quickly as they could. Even Tunke—Uncle Zishe's—had to run off to a meeting. (Absence is forbidden.) Would they, please, delay the funeral? She will certainly be here in the morning. Falke flew away with Tunke. Since they've decided on Vladivostok, you cannot tear them apart.

The door was open, to let out the odor of the corpse.

Descending from the courtyard, Pavel Olshevsky—with a covert eagerness—asked his huddled wife why the uncles hadn't worn their prayer shawls and phylacteries and didn't blow the ram's horn. She replied that the older generation, apparently, isn't what it was; as for the ram's horn, he is mistaken, because they blow it only on Shavuoth in order to commemorate that Father Abraham had led the Jews from Egypt.

Only Aunt Gitte and Uncle Itche were left. They were able to catch their breath, then they lit the brass candlesticks by Uncle Zishe's head, turned the pictures upside down, covered the mirrors and clocks and began to prepare a funeral the way it ought to be.

Aunt Gitte even went over to the corpse, and announced in her bass voice:

"Zishe, you may be at ease. We will take you to the cemetery like a proper Jew."

Uncle Zishe didn't answer.

Uncle Yude came in at midnight. He had had some sleep. Without looking at the others, he started to recite the Psalms in a dry, early morning voice.

The young people came early in the morning. To them, this was a secular affair. The funeral was rushed.

"Women, enough of your bawling," they shouted. "It is enough."

Berre brought a black casket from who knows where. Before the women could get into their wrappings, the hearse flew off, so they had to chase it. You may understand that nobody had any great pleasure from this funeral. The scene at the cemetery was close to farce. It was then Aunt Malkele spoke to Berre severely.

"You'll let us finish our crying, you ruffian—won't you?"

"Good!" he answered. "But make it quicker!"

They were allowed to complete their weeping. The loudest lamentations came from Uncle Itche. In a teary voice, he said to Uncle Yude:

"A world—eh?"

Uncle Yude looked at him irately from beneath his glasses.

"Isn't it better to be lying in the earth?"

He meant Uncle Zishe, as well as Aunt Hessye.

Uncle Zishe was not standing calmly—not drawing a hair in his beard—not smiling benignly.

"Nice children!"

They came back late. Gray evening had crept over the courtyard. It was in shadows. No electricity. No warm stoves. It was bare, like their own mortification.

All of his life, Uncle Zishe had falsely been suspected of pretending to be a swooner—that he invented his infirmities to feed his self-importance. Now it turns out that Zishe was an honest man. He had honest diseases—and died before it was time. (Not like a certain older person in the courtyard!)

Miscellaneous Zelmenyaner

1.   Uncle Yude went to the stable for a board. He found a fragment of a postcard behind a rafter. On one side, it had a Moscow postmark. On the other—something in Hebrew. He took it to the house, where he deciphered this:

> The twenty-second of Elul. Good fortune to the maiden. To the honor of the worthy Reb Zissel, son of the late Reb Zalman. Peace to the near relations, the far, and also you—from . . .

The handwriting was rabbinical and tiny. A saddened Uncle

Yude stood there—card in hand—with his furious eyes upon the stove.

"Can it be that Zishke wasn't lying?"

After this, they learned that the story with the postcard lay heavily on Yude's conscience. He even went to Zishe's grave, to beg his forgiveness. You might say it was unimportant. But, in his mortification, he began to look haggard—and this may be the reason for his flight. One night, Uncle Yude vanished from the courtyard. For a long time, no one knew where he had gone. Though it is thought that he left the courtyard for a different reason.

This is the one they give:

After Uncle Zishe's death, Uncle Yude went around, looking gray and angry, without any word. When in such a mood, he loves to be contrary. One day—out of the clear blue sky—he went to Berre's and gloomily stood by the door.

"Good morning!"

"Good morning," answers Berre.

"I've come to ask you. How is my Zelmele?"

Berre answered calmly. "You are mistaken. I have no Reb Zelmele."

Uncle Yude drew his beard into his mouth. He was silent. Then, a little later.

"What is the name of your lovely son?"

"My lovely son is called Marat."

This finished the conversation.

As Hayele told it, Uncle Yude stood by the door a half hour or more. He left silently, carefully turning the knob, as you do when an invalid is in the house. He went down below and didn't go out.

2.   The streetcar left.

A curious thing. It left the station and ran over the streets. New cars, sparkling windows, nickel fittings, brand-new straps. The windows were full of people—and the whole contraption was either sliding down or flying up the hills, hastening, until it came to the suburb.

The Zelmenyaner heard a new kind of ringing near the courtyard. Of course, Uncle Itche was the first to hurry out. He was ready for a new experience. He came home late that night and, since he was ashamed to tell Aunt Malkele, he made the excuse that he was visiting a friend.

"Which friend?"

"A friend."

It was hard to believe. After he was married Uncle Itche could be found only near Aunt Malkele. He had had a friend when he was single—Orre the tailor; but that one has been dead a long time.

In the morning, he advised Aunt Malkele that she ought to try the tram—it's a special kind of pleasure.

"How do you know all this?"

"I understand . . ."

He didn't tell her that he had been riding all day around the city and, in doing this, had wasted lots of money.

After that, the Zelmenyaner took the tram more often. They rode to the depot and came back on foot. It was good; not so much the riding, but that you sit with people and are learning about the world. Aunt Malkele used to sit down, smiling and showing strangers (those who were not local) how one should behave when in a streetcar. She would also help them make change. In general, she felt related to people, just as she did in the courtyard itself.

3.   Tunke and Falke rode off to Vladivostok.

4.   Uncle Folye and Berre finally became friends.

They drank a lot of tea but they didn't speak. Uncle Folye looked at the floor dully. They drank more tea and remained silent. Suddenly, the sullen Folye leaned both elbows on the table and asked Berre simply, without any trimmings:

"Listen, Berrke, you are a true Communist—no?"

"Apropos of what?"

"I'm about to speak to you, one man to another."

"Well?"

Uncle Folye's eyes grew moist with cordiality.

"Listen, dear fellow. Sometimes, one feels like making a speech. What do you think of that? One is an old worker. So there is nothing wrong in getting up before a meeting and saying this and that. The people listen. . . . Do you ever speak?"

"It's heavy on the tongue. But if you start—you continue speaking."

"Listen, I have a different trouble. I can speak. But I haven't got what to say."

Hayele brought a nice potato pudding to the table.

5.   Uncle Itche finally removed his beard.

6.   Marat had indigestion. But it was not serious.

Uncle Yude

Three o'clock in the morning, he lit the little stove that he kept in the entry for the geese. A gray beshrouding night lay on the windowpanes. He performed the ritual washing of his hands; then he took an ancient little bag from above the stove and began to pack: the *tallith* and phylacteries, the fiddle, a pound of bread, a couple of onions—all that is needed by a living man for his travels.

It was too still. A sign of frost. As a precaution, Uncle Yude covered his ears with a little shawl and shoved his tiny beard into his collar. He lifted the bag on his shoulders. His rheumy eyes gave the place a final glare above his spectacles—as if he was looking for somebody to butt. Quietly, he left.

A turbid night lay heavy on the dark snow; from top to bottom, without any sky. Uncle Yude knew the way—he curved to the right and swam over little streets of pressed snow.

His eyes grew accustomed to it. A more vivid black—houses, poles and planks—peeled out of the encircling night. Then there came, pouring before his eyes, the snowy blue distance of the fields. Uncle Yude suddenly felt a sweet quieting of passions, a cooling of his fevered brain.

We are speaking of a winter night in the fields, when a man is fortunate to be in it alone, with a small bag, standing, waiting for a message from the world. So a bird, without an articulate thought or explicit feeling, sometimes is on a twig—staring, gaping, with its little eye.

We are saying that an ordinary Zelmenyaner may experience from time to time such enraptured moments—something like a crow.

The way creaked beneath his feet, over the hills, as far as the fixed pine-clad horizon.

Suddenly, it was even darker. Immediately after that, day began to break on the right. The pale snow grew more intensely white, the first fire pushed up from the snow—as if work had begun in a foundry.

The walker was growing tired.

He went up a hill. He knew that below there was a clearing—it was a landowner's estate where he had worked as a carpenter one summer. (Uncle Yude had been a world traveler when young.) Soon he could see the snowy orchards he remembered. A path lined with birches was on the left. It took you to the former landowner's house.

Its red roof was seen through the poplars.

It was still.

He entered a neglected courtyard, smelling of warm manure and horses. A bull bellowed from a distant stall. He shrugged off the snow; then he went to the two-story house.

It was "Red Acre"—a Jewish collective.

In the house, a big stove flickered, cooking pots on top. It was dark in corners. Half-sleeping wives were fussing—swinging chickens, peeling potatoes, or scrubbing pots.

They met him with curiosity.

He dropped his pack, sat down on the edge of a bench and threw irascible glances at the strange women. Since this wasn't the Zelmenyaner courtyard, they didn't understand the nature of this person and, to feel safe, they sent for a man.

From the yard there came a compact man with high boots and a small tangled beard like a splash of ink. Though it was midwinter, he smelled of apples.

He lit his pipe in the stove and asked:

"Where do you come from?"

In time, it became clear that here's a hungry person who would like to eat.

After he ate, Uncle Yude drifted around the yard and inspected the establishment. He liked the idea of a collective.

In one of their stalls, he saw a disconsolate hen. Uncle Yude is an expert when it comes to chickens; so he did some palping and decided that she had broken a leg. He took her into the house, asked them for a knife and worked all day. In the evening, the hen was walking around on a wooden leg, broad on top, narrow below, like the leg of a bench. They gathered they had to do with a carpenter. The "Red Acre" has need of a carpenter.

That night, the full collective gathered in the big house—men around the big table, women on the beds that stood near the walls—and began to probe. In the case of Uncle Yude, this isn't very easy. (He wouldn't let them feel his pulse.)

"Maybe you know your way around cattle?"

"Maybe you know your way around chickens?"

Of course, as you may imagine, Uncle Yude knows everything. If it is desired, he will even teach the kids a chapter in the Bible—sort of surreptitiously. It is not desired? All right—doesn't matter. In addition to everything else, he's a bit of atheist.

What he really wants is access to the chickens. Therefore—in the summer—he'll dig for horseradish, pick sorrel and mushrooms. About being a carpenter—not a single word.

Suddenly, he thought of a new vocation.

"Maybe you want someone to play the fiddle?"

As it turned out, they had an ear for music. Uncle Yude played and they were delighted. In this enthusiasm, Uncle Yude played his tune about the hen. The philosophical hen.

So, in midwinter, Uncle Yude became a member of the collective, a scarf around his neck, a straw in his beard. He knew his business. He hustled more than others, always moving around the courtyard with an axe and club. He would make a wooden bolt for a door. Or, if not, he would bathe a goose or prepare a lotion to smear on the calf of one of the perpetually pregnant women.

He became an intimate of the chickens. They say that he sat and spoke to them. They also say that, every now and then, he would play music for them on the fiddle. There is even a strange rumor they liked it and wanted more.

Occasionally Uncle Yude wanders to the village. They know he is the new man in the collective, the one who plays the fiddle. He strolls through the village, hands on his rump, and he squints—in a comfortable fashion—at the peasant enclosures. He is accepted. Uncle Yude has even managed to make a friend in the village, a little old potter.

They sit in his warm hut—by the bluish windows—chatting of world affairs.

"In Moscow," Uncle Yude tells him, "they're already making chickens of cotton batting."

"Untrue," says the potter.

"There is such a machine," Uncle Yude tells him.

"And their souls are made from what material?"

"Electricity," answers Uncle Yude.

"I would not let such chickens into my house . . ."

Uncle Yude and the potter are like two winter radishes under snow. They have an amazing love for each other. When the potter pays a return visit, they sit in the coop and feel if the hens are laying. Restful . . .

One time, when the potter came, Uncle Yude gave him a broad smile. It was a remarkable sight. Eyes closed; wrinkles ran over his entire face; a single dirty tooth jutted in the middle of his gum.

This smile is a sign that our Uncle Yude has finally acquired peace.

Grandma Boshe

Frost. The days are polished, like a moonlit night. The ground is like cold porcelain china. Muffled Zelmenyaner whisper in the courtyard. Wherefore? Grandma Boshe has finally taken to bed. They think it is final: she cannot hold her food.

Aunt Gitte came out of Grandma's house with a silent rabbinical face—threw a well-informed look around the courtyard and, in that pose, remained on the threshold. She is an expert in such matters; so she was surrounded.

Aunt Gitte tried to sound like her father the Rabbi. "As I understand it, the departure of her soul will undoubtedly take place some time after midnight . . ."

"Why must it take so long?"

She gave a flick of the shoulders, as if to say: this is not my responsibility.

The pillars of the family are missing. Gone the uncles, the two able leaders who, for many years, had turned the wheel of Zelmenyaner history. Missing the great Zelmenyaner who, with a look, showed you where your place was. Now you fumble in the dark. Grandma Boshe lies, like a plucked goose, on the other side of the stove; but nobody knows how to take charge, or even when to cry.

"Oh, we are desolate—we are desolate like stones!"

This from a person with the appearance of Uncle Itche. But without a beard! Two fat tears tumble from his gloomy eyes.

They came to Aunt Gitte. "How do you explain it?"

Not only is Grandma Boshe living, she is actually feeling better.

They went to Grandma's house and gathered around her bed. Aunt Gitte looked at her a long time, probing with her medicine-woman eyes. Finally she said, "She is from Lithuania. Such people die hard; but it won't take long."

Grandma Boshe lay—a small heap of bones that were gnawed by time.

In the evening Berre and Uncle Folye arrived. Nowadays, they travel together, to the clubs, the sessions and meetings. Berre told them to fix a bed in the big room. They transported Grandma to the new-made bed. This helped to revive her. She moaned and opened the little cracks of her eyes. Full of bitter insight, they roamed around the house and inspected everything.

The women first realized how efficient Berre could be. To oblige him, they said:

"We ought to have jam!"

"A bit of jam since she is feeling faint."

Grandma heard everything. They could see her gathering her last breath because she wants to speak. Immediately Uncle Itche was standing by her bed. Having gathered the required breath, she asked a favor—that they turn off the electricity. She cannot die beside such a fire.

Uncle Itche looked around him in despair—electricity was a

matter of principle—but Berre made a sign. "Don't start up with her. Turn off the light."

They lit an old-fashioned lamp. Silently, the Zelmenyaner sat around the bed in order to observe the departure of her soul. It would seem that there was nothing to hold it. Sure enough, the last moments began. The little feet straightened beneath the quilt: the little face grew ashen.

"She was a decent woman. She did not take what belongs to others. Not even one hair!"

The tiny lamp smoked. A thin faint light fell only on the bed and the surrounding bony Zelmenyaner faces. The house lay in darkness. Suddenly she gave a convulsive shudder—her head fell to one side. Everybody sighed. Is she alive? Then she opened her eyes and said, quite distinctly:

"I am dying for a bit of food."

Grandma wanted at least one meal before her last breath.

At this, Uncle Folye, that fastidious man, stood up in outrage, spat, and went out, banging the door. A quarrel seemed imminent.

But the shrewd Aunt Malkele knew what should be done. She grabbed a knife, cut a hunk of bread and brought it to Grandma. The dead woman opened her mouth a bit too widely. She even tried to chew but couldn't swallow.

She was too late with her last meal.

After a while, she actually died.

Aunt Gitte gave her what was owing. She closed her eyes and—so nobody might laugh—she quickly took the piece of bread from between her gums. They did everything one ought to do. After that, when Berre went to bed, the women took the opportunity to cry, so as not to shame the corpse. They shed a few sedate tears, without heartache—the way that moisture runs off a windowpane.

That is the way that Zelmenyaner cry.

Translated by Nathan Halper

≈ Under a Fence: A Revue

BY DER NISTER

Introductory Note

When this story first appeared in the Soviet Yiddish periodical, *Di royte velt*, in 1929, its editor, perhaps anticipating that it would evoke a storm of attack from the more orthodox party-line critics, wrote: "It is a ring of allegorical and symbolic tales, mutually intertwined, expressed in a rich, rhythmic language.... It is a kind of confession, a renunciation of the idealistic view of the world..." Except for the last phrase, obviously mistaken though intended, no doubt, as a protective device, the editor's description was a helpful one. For it leads us into the labyrinth of the story, into the actual experience of it rather than a misconceived attempt to reduce it to an intellectual jigsaw puzzle. The important thing, we believe, is not to look for detailed one-to-one equivalents of meaning for the rendered events, but to yield oneself to its phantasmagoria and thereby gain a general sense of its implications. So we offer here not a worked-out interpretation, but a few notes that may be helpful.

The story begins with a confession by a middle-aged scholar. Obviously a man of some achievement and stature, he tells his daughter about his debasing involvement with Lili, a circus rider, and his seeming drunkenness after being rudely thrown out of the circus. As the daughter attends her sick father, he confesses to having been unworthy of his calling, and this ends the initial episode, or narrative frame, of the story.

Then comes the substance of the confession, staged (hence the subtitle) as a "revue." What follows apparently has to do, in various grotesque forms and through the imagery of dream symbolism, with an experience of guilt— the scholar's guilt before his pupils (his literary disciples?), the trial where he is punished by burning, etcetera.

The scholar, writes the Yiddish critic Khone Shmeruk, "sees himself as an accused man, completely losing his bond with his 'real' self. He is now an ex-hermit in circus leotards. He is tried by the senior judge, his former teacher Medardus, of the school of hermits, along with his own pupils.... During the trial, the hermit tells about his transformation."

A phantasmagorical figure, the "dustman," appears. This figure tells the scholar-hermit that all of his creatures—father, mother, child—are made of "straw." They are, that is, useless, obsolete, ready for destruction.

The dustman, writes Shmeruk, "is the actual cause" of the scholar's guilt. "It is he who brought him to the circus and led him to Lili. . . . He is capable of subjecting the hermit's values to public ridicule. . . . At the same time, however, he is highly intimate with the hermit and solicitous about him. . . . This is undoubtedly a personification of that part of the hermit's self which embodies a number of satanic, Mephistophelian attributes."

The name of Lili "is similar in sound to and hence associated with Lilith—the traditional female demon who makes men stray from the path of righteousness." As for Medardus, the scholar-hermit's teacher or master, Shmeruk traces a complicated genealogy from a story by the German writer, E.T.A. Hoffmann, where the figure represents a literary tradition of seriousness and autonomy—the very tradition the circus denies.

"The scholar, the last hermit, represents an intelligent man, an artist or perhaps even a writer. . . . External pressures and internal doubts pursue him ceaselessly. His daughter—his one creation up to now, his very own—is betrayed and harmed because of his attraction for Lili—an opposite creative principle, whose place is in the circus, and whose essence is tricks. External pressures are expressed by the loneliness of the hermit, which inclines him and readies him to accept his own doubts, symbolized by the dustman. He begins to believe in the strawness of his former path."

This story is a complicated but extremely powerful and moving revelation—a kind of symbolist outcry—of the agonies experienced by a gifted writer who has been forced, in part, to submit to the demands of a repressive external authority. Obliquely, it tells us a great deal about the feelings of Soviet Yiddish writers as the inquisitors grew more demanding. And in a way, the party-line critics were "right" in denouncing the story.

"Even so," concludes Shmeruk, "the issue is not too simple for Der Nister. One cannot ignore the opposition between the lonely tower of a last solitary hermit, filled with doubts, and the security of a seasoned circus actor in a packed hall. There remains the gnawing question: Is this, then, the way? Is it, after all, only for select individuals? There is no definite answer to this question. Insecurity coupled with hopelessness and with the necessity to submit, out of 'hunger and joblessness,' to the transformation, increase the depth and horror of the tragedy of the man undergoing the test.

"Despite all of the doubts, Der Nister's judgment is, nevertheless, unequivocal. The feeling of guilt is stronger than the doubts, and the threefold punishment appears justified." °

° The full text of the Shmeruk essay appears in the volume, *The Field of Yiddish.*

Der Nister closes the story's frame on a poignant note: the scholar-hermit, "drunkard and ashamed," is wept over by his daughter while he had "nothing to comfort her with and couldn't lift my head up to her."

I AM SICK to death with grief.

And only you, my daughter, will feel it and understand me. For tonight your honored and respected father could be seen at the circus, not among the clowns or in the audience, but on the narrow, twisting stairs that lead to the dressing rooms. There, with a bouquet of the last flowers in my garden, the last of my money, and all the love left in me, I went up to a small room and knocked softly, like a puppy, with a trembling heart, and waited.

"May I?"

"Yes," came from within.

And I went in to the bareback rider, dressed in her flesh-colored costume, ready for her entrance. She held the whip in her hand and slapped it against the tops of her riding boots as she looked at me and my presents. She considered me a pest. She took the bouquet, said it would be beautiful on her horse's head, and filled her mouth with my sweets, but wouldn't let me tell her that I loved her. All the while she slapped her boottops with the whip.

"Lili," I said shyly.

She looked at me with pity and held herself away from me, and I could see that she would never let me near her, no matter what might happen.

Then the door opened, and another circus performer came in from another dressing room. An athlete with gigantic legs and huge calves. His pectorals were like two anvils, festooned with medals; his arms and legs were bare; his face was a barrel; and his features were like a moon. When he saw me with Lili, he asked, "Who is this?" and Lili, sucking the sweets, answered, "He's a professor in the city. He's famous, and he's one of my admirers. Ha ha. . . ." And she showed him my presents, the bouquet, all that I had brought her, and he looked at them and, my daughter, at me, your father.

He looked me over with contempt. He found me insignificant, but he pretended to be angry at Lili. Lili went along with the joke and pretended to talk back to him, to be afraid of him, and begged him to forgive her for my visit. He forgave her, but not me. He went up to me and pushed my hat down over my ears. And he took the whip from Lili and struck me on the side. "Out!" he ordered. "And don't let me catch you here again! Professor!"

And I went out and retraced the labyrinth of dark little corridors that smelled of horses and stable and circus. Such was my reward for going there, for my presents and my love for Lili.

I came home, changed clothing, and sat down in my usual armchair, and one of my students knocked and with great respect asked:

"May I, sir?"

"Yes," I answered.

And he entered and sat down with great deference, and I began to talk to him—not as I usually do, not about the things that he expected of me—but about something entirely different and irrelevant—about love.

My student looked astonished, and only his great respect for me made him listen without interrupting. I warmed to my subject, spoke of love and how it misleads us, turns our heads, how we grow foolish and set out on childish and dangerous paths. "And yet"—I added—"however bitter its fruit, the man who tastes love is lucky."

My student stared at me and listened to it all—he thought I intended a parable, that I would soon come to the point, and would then proceed to the things that concerned us both.

But I went on, and spoke of how love is sometimes rejected and ridiculed, of how miserable it is for the rejected, of how he comes with his arms full of good, and the good is thrown back in his face, and they stand and laugh at him while he kneels and gathers his crumbs up off the floor.

My student listened and pretended to be interested, and agreed because he wanted to comfort me.

"Yes," he said, "and the ones who refuse to love aren't worthy of the love they reject."

"Do you think so?" I said. "And should the rejected be comforted by that? What if they aren't? What if they fall in love again and are rejected again?"

And in innocence my student answered:

"In that case, they deserve what they get. If they don't have the pride to look down on the worthless people they love, they get what they deserve."

He was naive and he held firmly to his opinion, but in the end none of it really mattered to him. Only out of courtesy had he allowed himself to be drawn into the conversation. I could see that he was hoping for me to finish as soon as possible so we could turn back to the proper subject, to the things that he had come for.

But I didn't. I went on as I had started. And I warmed to my theme even more. I rose from my armchair and paced around the room and spoke about worth and worthlessness in love. As if I were arguing excitedly with myself, I said:

"Really, what is 'worth'? Does the word 'worth' apply to love at all? Don't we lay all worth at her feet? Don't we give love gifts of all that we have? Do we deal in reckonings and bookkeeping with love?"

My student would have answered me but, as I have said, none of it really mattered to him. All the time I could see the questions in his eye: "What do you mean, sir? Why are you saying all this? Surely you must have something else in mind . . ."

But I had nothing else in mind, nothing else in the world. The only thing in my heart was the memory of how I had been insulted. It burned inside me, the story of the circus and what happened to me there rose before my eyes, and most of all I saw Lili before me— mounted and riding or sitting among the clowns and acrobats, surrounded by performers, with so much charm in her lips and so much sweetness in her mouth. The acrobats taking her, lifting her up. Poor or rich, each of them would have given all he had, all his body and life for one kiss.

I don't know how, but somehow I ushered my student out. I didn't speak to him about the things that interested him. I just wanted him to go. I don't even recall whether he said "goodnight" or not. I was alone.

I wasn't able to turn to anything or deal with any students that night. I opened one book and immediately put it aside, then another, with the same result. I couldn't concentrate on anything or think through a single thought.

And suddenly: I forgot who and where I was, my position in

society, and instead I was a performer myself, dressed in flesh-colored tights, with a whip in my hand like a circus rider. I was in the center ring of the circus. A beautiful horse was brought and I mounted him. And just ahead of me an even finer horse was in full gallop, and Lili rode it, balanced on one leg, her other leg stretched out behind her. The packed audience passed dizzyingly before my eyes. All around us the circle of seats and the crowd, all eyes and enthusiasm. Each pass of Lili's took their breath away. Each "Hup-hup!" each shout excited and enchanted them. And I, too, was excited, and I stood on the back of my horse and rode, as Lili, weightless in her light costume, rode before me.

And suddenly she turned as her horse galloped. Now her back was to his head and she stood facing me. And the crowd burst into applause as Lili stretched her hand out to me and I reached out to her. We couldn't touch because the horses were between us, but we felt just as though we had. Lili's success was mine too, and I had my share of the crowd's excitement and applause.

Then Lili turned her back to me again and rode on, cracking her whip in the air, around the ring once, then a second and a third time. When we came to where the horses make their exit, I leaped down, and as Lili rode up, I gave her my hand. She sprang to the ground, and the horses were driven out by her assistants. We went after them, but the crowd wouldn't leave us alone. They called us and we turned to them and bowed. That was our first number.

And the second time we rode out, I don't know how, or where you came from, but suddenly, my daughter, you were there too, in the arena, where the clowns and acrobats and animal trainers perform.

As Lili and I rode by, you met us. You were waiting for us en route. We had arranged among us that you were to leap up on one of our horses as it galloped by.

And you did. Lili was the first to ride by, and you leaped up on her horse. You were young and agile and amazing to the crowd. You leaped to a standing position on the horse and rode holding on to Lili, and I followed. And then suddenly (but again as agreed among us) you were to lean on Lili's hands, lift yourself, and balance on her hands as you rode.

And I was to keep my eye on you and the horse, to see that it didn't alter its pace, and on Lili, to see that she maintained her balance. I wasn't to miss anything, not the slightest movement of the horse or Lili. If I did, it would be a circus scandal, or worse. There might be an accident. Lili might slip and both of you might fall.

And that is exactly what happened. Lili rode before me holding you balanced on her hands, and she had only done a half-circuit of the main ring when, either because the crowd suddenly began to applaud or for some other reason, the horse dropped his head, and Lili slipped just as you were passing the barrier that separates the public from the arena. And you, my daughter, fell, and I heard your skull crack on the wooden barrier.

The audience was horrified. All at once everyone cried out "Ah!" Lili leaped down from her horse and left it where it was, and I came over to you and did something, and suddenly the entire circus, the arena, the audience, and the uproar that followed your accident was gone, and we were alone in my room. You were wounded and lay on my bed, and I applied ice and wet towels to your wound. You were delirious. I gazed at you, full of guilt for what had happened. Your pain was my shame; your delirium, my great grief.

As I sat by you, you kept saying over and over, "Father and I, father in the circus, my father a performer in the circus . . ." and I felt both pain and shame, though your eyes were closed and you couldn't see me.

It was late, but I thought I heard someone knocking at my door, asking "May we?" "Yes," I said, "you may," and the door opened and my student came in again.

"Good evening, sir!" he said.

"What's happened? Why are you here at this hour?" I asked.

He said, "I heard what happened at the circus, sir, that your daughter was hurt. . . . I came to see whether you needed help."

"Ah, really!" I leaped to my feet. "Does that mean that people know about the circus already?"

"Yes, the whole town is talking about it. People can't understand what you were doing on a horse. They say that the circus owner must have disguised one of his people as you, but they don't know why. Was it just for publicity or is he angry at you and trying to get back at you in some way by ruining your good name? Your students and other people who were there say that it wasn't you, and my friends chose me and asked me to go to you, in spite of the late hour, so that we could be sure that it isn't true."

And at that, he looked around the room and saw you on the bed, and he grew confused and began to stammer:

"But I see, sir, that what they say is true. What does it mean? What can I tell my friends?"

I looked at him and had nothing to say. I only stammered back:

"Say? Yes, say that ... it's the truth, and my daughter is the proof."

And he looked at the bed, my daughter, and there was pain in his eyes, and he looked at me accusingly though with great sympathy for my fall. He stayed awhile, turned to go, turned back again, then finally went out and closed the door behind him.

And I was alone with you again, sitting beside you, gazing at your bandaged head.

And suddenly: the walls of the room opened. There were holes and cracks in the walls, and in every hole there was a head, and at every crack I saw eyes and faces. Some ground their teeth and mocked me, some gave me ugly looks, and others stretched their hands through the wall. And all at once, stones showered on your bed, meant not for you, but for me, and voices called out, "Old lecher. You sold your daughter for a circus whore, sold your daughter for a whore. . . ."

And, my daughter, the stones fell like hail. People threw them with murderous intent, and if I hadn't jumped up, at once, the stones would have shattered the other side of your head. But I jumped up quickly and bent over you to protect you and made my whole body into a target for the falling stones. One especially pointed stone struck me in the head, and I lost consciousness. All I knew was that I was bleeding and growing lightheaded with the loss of blood and feeling somewhat empty and yet somehow relieved.

And suddenly: I was no longer in our room, but in a court of justice. There was a felt-covered table with chairs and benches around it, and on the chairs and benches all my students were seated. They were the judges and I stood before the bar of justice. And at the center of the table sat the oldest judge, at first unfamiliar to me, but when I looked closely, I recognized him. It was *my* teacher, whom I had studied with at our academy, whom I hadn't seen or heard of in so many years, Medardus.

He gazed at me with pity, and so did my students. There was no one in the hall but my judges and myself, no witnesses or spectators. I was asked to step up to the table, and I did.

And I was glad that my own were judging me, that I stood before my own students and teacher, for I expected them to be both understanding and just.

Medardus waved his hand and a wall opened, and you, my daughter, were brought in on your bed, meaning this was my guilt, the trial would concern you, and I would have to account for your fall and the injury to you.

Then Medardus gave me a sign, and I felt as if I were his student again, a scholar among scholars in the academy, as I had been, as my students were. And all of them were dressed as scholars. I was the only one dressed for the circus, in flesh-colored tights. Shyly, I began my defense.

"You have permitted me to defend myself," I said, "but I don't know how I can. Standing before you now, I feel like a turtle without a shell: completely naked. Medardus, my teacher, I left my shell, our tower, and I grew cold. And when we are cold we hug anything that can keep us warm, any garbage or filth, as long as it covers us. And we wear anything, even rags or flesh-colored tights, as long as it's clothing. And when we are hungry and have no work, being a clown is work, after all. And when we have no home, the circus can be home. And the circus is as it is. Your life is cheap. You are there only to gratify others. Your soul hangs by a thread, and your life is unimportant, so is it any wonder that your child is unimportant too, and that you can sell her to the tightrope for a trifle, for your breakfast?

"And don't be amazed, my teacher, Medardus, that I left our house. You know better than anyone that if our house flowered in your time, it withered in mine. In your time, the light from our tower was dazzling. It glittered like gold, and was visible for miles around. But in my time, not only was the light gone, but the house itself was in ruins, and no one came to it except the dogs that pissed against the walls. And in your time you still sat secure on your seat and directed us, but in our time the seats were falling apart, and the legs were about to collapse under us.

"And you should have foreseen it, Medardus, my teacher, and told us to abandon the house. You should have written that into your will when you left us, so that we wouldn't have had to stay behind with the walls and ruins and rusty keys. We stayed and, out of respect to you, we observed the order established by you. But no one supported us, no one came to study with us, and we no longer served as an example.

"We sat down to our own poor meals by ourselves, and it was melancholy at our tables. There were no visitors to us, as there had been to you. No one brought us gifts. Our cellar and storeroom were empty, and our bread was dry, and there was nothing to dip it in. We washed for our meals without joy and said grace in sadness, and one by one our servants began to leave us, and after them, the weaker students as well, and the ones who stayed couldn't blame the ones who left, because all of them felt that staying was useless. No one could condemn the ones who gave in to temptation and went away. And in the end, when we were very few, my turn came. I want to tell you what happened to me, and I ask you to listen.

"Once I was alone in our tower and heavy-hearted because the streets outside were full of life and our house was deserted, except that once in a long while a teacher would bring schoolchildren to see how poor we were. The children would ask about our tower and its history, they would want to know who used it and what it was for. And the teacher would tell them that it wasn't for anything, that it could have been torn down, but it was left standing because of its age, as a reminder of the way things had been. And when the children sometimes saw me or a student or a servant in the courtyard and asked who we were and what we were for, the teacher would answer that we were useless and we were also only reminders of the past, but there were things to be learned by observing us too.

"On one such day I was alone in our house. Everyone else was away, and I sat by myself staring at a corner of my room. And suddenly something strange happened. My vision wavered, and I saw a dustman coming out of the corner. He was frayed and nearly bald, with dusty eyebrows and clothes that were so worn out it was impossible to tell what color they were. He still had a few hairs on his head, but no beard, and at first glance his eyes looked half-dead, as if they were coated with dust. But hidden somewhere in the corner of his eye there was a sharp, thievish smile.

"The dustman was a surprise to me, but apparently I was even more of a surprise to him. When he shook free of some of his dust, he looked all around him and then at me and asked me who I was and why I was there. I said, 'What do you mean why am I here? I belong here. This has always been my place.' But who was he and what was he doing here?

"He answered, and there was that hidden smile at the back of his eyes, that he came from the corner, which had always been his place.

"Then why hadn't I seen him before this? Why hadn't he shown himself?

" 'Because,' he answered, 'I had no one to show myself to.'

" 'What do you mean? What of the scholars who live here?'

" 'No,' the dustman said, 'if I had come to them, they would have taken me to be an illusion or an apparition, and they would have spat and turned away.'

" 'What of now and myself?' I asked.

" 'Now isn't then,' he said. 'And you aren't the others. You are not a scholar to me now, and I am not an apparition. You are the last one here. Your teacher is already dead, and your students are leaving you. Any day now the rest of them will go. I have nothing to do in my corner anymore, and soon I'll have no way of making a living, so I came out to introduce myself to you. You and I are the last ones. Let's get acquainted. I know you and your work, since I am used to seeing you through the wall, but you don't know me. Let me invite you in to me. You have nothing to lose and I have nothing to lose. We are both in the same situation. Maybe after we have become acquainted we can look for a new place and a new livelihood together, eh?'

" 'And your work?'

" 'Come in and take a look.'

"The dustman beckoned, and I followed him through the wall into a tiny room where a wick was burning in a can though it was daytime, and there was a bed and a rusty dipper at the foot of the bed.

"It took a long time before I could see anything else, and even then there seemed to be nothing but a stool, a little table, and a few worthless utensils. But when I looked closely at the bed, I was suddenly amazed to see that there were three people lying there: a father, a mother, and a child. The father was in the middle, the mother was next to the wall, and the child was on the outside of the bed. All three were made of straw, and they had all lain there a long time and smelled moldy. The mother was dried out, thin, and flat as a board, without breasts for the child, but the father was fuller, and he was the one with breasts, and the child lay at one of his breasts and sucked. The straw child had a little straw mouth, and the little mouth apparently pained and bit the father as it sucked at him, for he twisted and grimaced while giving the breast.

"And the dustman pointed to the bed and told me to look, and I saw that the father had nothing left to give and that the straw child was sucking the marrow out of him, and the father twisted like a snake, and groaned and cried out.

"And the longer I looked at him, the more his pain became my pain, and the more he twisted and turned, the more I twisted and turned as well.

"And suddenly I found myself in the father's place in the middle of the bed, with the mother on one side of me and the child on the other side, and the dustman stood and looked at me. And when I asked him, 'What is this, and what's happening here?' he said, 'This is my work. This is what I always do: the father is made of straw and has no milk to give, the mother has no breasts, and the child wants to eat, so it sucks and bites, and I have to feed and sustain all three. In the rusty dipper you see here I draw damp and mold from the walls for them, and I gather hair from the beards and bald heads of scholars and make wicks to give them light.'

" 'But what am I doing here?' I asked again. 'How did I get into this bed and what do I have to do with the straw mother and child?'

" 'But this is your straw,' he said, 'your straw work. It belongs to you and all your brother scholars. These are the children of your straw lives. You suckle them, but you have nothing to give, and so you twist and turn.'

"At this I jumped up and moved away from my wife, but I pulled the child close to me, and I put my feet down on the floor and sat there with my head bent and my eyes to the ground, and my eyes grew wet, and my tears began to fall.

"And I cried, and at first my tears fell on my hands, then on my knees, and then on the floor. They dripped like rain from the roof.

First they made the floor wet, then they formed a little stream, and all the time, the dustman stood over me. And when I had cried a lot, and the stream of tears had risen, the dustman told me to put my feet into it, and I did.

"And immediately I saw a wheel of light on the opposite wall. It was small, like the circle of light cast on a wall by a lamp, but the light grew and the wheel kept opening and growing larger until it filled the whole wall, and then the wall opened, and sitting on the bed with my feet in my tears, I saw a great open space out of doors. After the tiny room lit by a wick, the light was blinding, and I thought I was looking at a sea.

"And it really was a sea. I could see the shore from my bed. Groups of people were standing on the shore. They looked like they were there for someone's burial, and in the midst of them, there was a person who was very familiar to me. He was taller and paler and more impressive than the others, but he seemed to have been sentenced, and the people seemed to have gathered on account of him, to throw him from the high shore into the sea and dig a grave for him in the earth.

"And suddenly the people on the shore lifted him up and held him on high for a while, as though holding him up to the sun, and all at once I could see that the person held on high was you, my teacher, Medardus, and I also was helping to hold you. Then all the people flung you, I along with them, and you flew down. And as you flew, you turned into a bird, and you cawed and laughed and flapped your wings and laughed again. And when I looked at the bird, I saw the dustman's face, and at each caw and laugh he snorted and sneezed dust. The bird flew over to each group of people and circled them, laughing and sneezing dust, and then my dustman came over to my bed and laughed and said:

" 'Laugh too and let your dust come out of you.'

"And I laughed and a bird flew out of my mouth. Again, and there was another bird, and again and again, and birds flew out of my ears, my eyes, my nose, even out of my head, and we all laughed together, and I felt relieved and happier, and I thought that I would now do whatever the dustman or the birds told me to do.

"And the dustman appeared again and waved his hand, and the sea and the people disappeared; another wave of his hand and the birds were gone; and a third wave and the walls closed again before my eyes, and there was the bed and my wife and child on the bed and the can and the burning wick that lit them both.

"And the dustman pointed to the can, meaning that I should take it and pour the kerosene over my wife and leave her there and that I should take the straw child and put it under my belt. And I did. I put the child under my belt and poured the kerosene over my straw wife, and what happened after that I don't know, because the dustman led me out of his room at once. And I don't know how, but he and I and the straw child were suddenly outside our house, and I held a bunch of keys in my hand and turned a rusty key in the door and locked it.

"Then," I continued telling my judges and Medardus, "then the dustman and I left the courtyard of our house and stepped out onto the street. And as soon as the first passers-by saw us, they looked at us in amazement, and I wasn't sure who it was that amazed them so; the dustman, or me, or the straw child sticking out of my belt, or all of us together.

"Then I looked around, and I found that I was wearing the clothes I had always worn in our house, but the dustman looked altogether different now that he was out of our house. He looked richer and more important than the richest people on the street. He shone in a new hat, a black frock coat and tails and patent leather shoes, a pressed shirt and deep-cut vest, and in his hand he held a stick of some sort—not a walking stick, but the kind that orchestra conductors and magicians carry.

"And when people saw us together, the dustman in his new clothes, and myself so typically a scholar in clothes worn out, shiny with age, and tattered, with my child in my belt and the straw poking out of it, they were amazed. Some stopped and stared. Others, who had already passed us, turned back. Some of them smiled and some assumed that this was publicity for the circus or some other show, but we weren't carrying placards, and they weren't sure what we were trying to publicize.

"The dustman saw their interest and wasn't at all uncomfortable. Unlike me. I felt very uncomfortable. But the people saw that he was interested in their response to us and that he wanted it.

"When we went further down the street and came to a busier

spot, people surrounded us at once, and the dustman made us stop in the thick of the crowd. The people here were also amazed and questioned us, first with looks and then with words: who were we and what were we publicizing? And the dustman waved his baton, meaning, 'People, listen to me. I have something to say.'

"And they waited, and he let them wait a bit longer, in order to awaken their interest even more. He stood there in silence for a moment, and then he said:

" 'A public announcement. The scholar who stands here before you has lost his livelihood. He has nothing to do. As you know, the scholars are all shut out of their shops these days, and so is he. And he has no home because he lived in his shop. In addition, he broke up with his family. He had a wife—a sack of straw—and when he left his home, he poured kerosene over her, and if you care to see it, ladies and gentlemen, turn in the direction of the tower, and in a short while, you will see smoke and flame rising out of the chimney.'

"They did care to see it, and when he pointed, they all turned to look. Our chimney had been cold for a long time, but now there was smoke rising out of it, and then a flame, and within the flame there was suddenly a woman, who didn't last long, but disappeared in the fire.

"And when they had seen the brief fire that came out of the chimney, and there was nothing more to see, they turned to the dustman again and said, 'What more?' and he said:

" 'The scholar who stands here before you—I am about to help him. I am going to lead him out into the world. When he was a great and important man, I was a hanger-on in his house. I lived off his wealth and importance. And now that he has fallen so low, I can't just abandon him. He is alone and helpless. From his long years of isolation in the academy, he has lost his good sense. You can see that he is impractical and that he has hardly any strength left. It took all he had just to leave the building. He could hardly lift his half-dead feet over the threshold. And here he stands before you, aimless and good for nothing. Something has to be done for him. He has to find some way to make a living, and who should help him if not I? After all, I lived the same life, ate with him, and was close to him for years.'

" 'Of course,' some of the people said, nodding and agreeing with the dustman. 'Of course. That's only just.'

"And the dustman seized on the nodding and agreeing of those few, and he continued and said:

" 'I have had him on my mind for a long time, wondering what to do with him. He has no work, and a scholar's hands are no good at all, and there was nothing to take along when we left the house, except for what you see in his belt, which he had by his wife, who just went up in flames. When I decided that we would have to leave the house, I realized that there was nothing to hope for from him, he wasn't good for anything, and there was no use hoping for a miracle or luck or coincidence to help us, so I began to prepare myself to go out into the world. I poked around in all the corners of the house and searched all the cupboards in case there might be anything valuable left, but there wasn't. Everything had already been taken before our time. There was nothing left for us but dust and rags and torn books covered with mouse droppings. Since I had no other choice, I picked over the rags, but I couldn't get anything for them. The rag dealers wouldn't take them. They were worthless. However, among the torn books I found something useful, a fortunetelling book, without covers and pages yellow with age, and I began to read the prophecies in that book. And there was one prophecy—if you care to hear it, ladies and gentlemen, I can read it out to you now.'

" 'Yes, we want to hear it,' some of them said.

"And the dustman put his hand into his breast pocket and pulled out the little book he had referred to, yellow and without covers, and he turned the pages and found his place, and no longer looking at the public, read from the book.

" 'This is what the prophecy says:

" 'First,' it says, 'he will be poor and capable of nothing, and he will get his living from a basket of mockery which he will carry around with him, mockery of himself and his former teachers and his work. Second,' it says, 'all paths are closed to him but one—to go into the circus and onto the tightrope. Third,' says the prophecy, 'let him take to it in time, and let him seek the companionship of tightrope walkers and magicians and learn their work from them, because his fortune can only be mended by them.

" 'And fourth,' says the book, 'let him be ready to pay for these things with the shirt off his back and the eyes in his head and everything dearest to him, and unless he does, he would do better to dig his own grave at once and not even bother to leave his house.

" 'Who? The last of the scholars!'

"Here the dustman finished reading from the little book and put it back in his breast pocket. Then he turned to the public and added:

" 'After reading these prophecies, I saw what had to be done. I saw that the academy had come to nothing and that this man who stands before you would finally turn the key in the door of the house and no longer return to it, that the little book was speaking about him, and the prophecies would provide him with a way of earning a living. And since I was close to him and he was close to me, as I have told you, I used to come to him and urge him to think about it, but he was lazy and heedless, as people usually are when they are going down and no longer know what world they're in. They stand teetering on the edge of a ditch and don't see it.

" 'So I gave up on him, but out of gratitude to the house, I took pity and did it all myself: visited performers and pledged brotherhood with clowns and tightrope walkers and sleight-of-hand artists, and I learned from all of them.

" 'And look,' and here the dustman raised his hand and pointed to my belt, 'here is our first trick, and I hope it will please you and that you will come to see our shows. Look!'

"And the dustman grabbed my straw child from my belt and all at once: the audience and I saw a real child before us. We saw you, my daughter, spring to the ground in front of us, dressed for a performance, in a short skirt, with arms and legs bare, poised and ready to dance.

"At first the audience was stunned by the trick itself and then amazed at my daughter—at her beauty, her easy, graceful bow, and her poise. Even after they had recovered from their surprise, they kept praising her. The dustman held out his hat and went around with it, and the audience gladly threw coins into it, and the dustman thanked them and invited them to come and see us again, and they promised to come. And then my daughter and the dustman and I said goodbye to the crowd and left them and went to an eating place. And so, the first day after leaving my house, I had my first taste of circus tricks and of showing off my daughter to the crowd.

"And, my judges and teacher," I continued telling Medardus and my students, "while eating I suddenly began to cry bitterly. Looking at my daughter, I drowned my head in tears, and the tears ran down my cheeks and into my bowl. I wanted to wipe them away, and I looked for a handkerchief in my pockets and couldn't find any. Instead, I found the keys to our house, and I don't know how, but suddenly I found myself back at our house, standing before the door I had locked that day, and I opened it and went into my room. In the corner where I had seen the dustman, the wall was broken. A draft blew in from behind it, and the air smelled of burnt straw. It was like a ruin after a fire, and I grew sad, and as always when I am sad, I leaned against a wall, and I cried again and couldn't stop crying.

"And suddenly someone was shaking me, and when I lifted my head to see who it was, I found myself back at the table, and it was the dustman rousing me: What was it, why wasn't I eating, why did I drift off in the middle of the meal? I should finish, since we had to go somewhere after we ate.

" 'Where?' I asked.

" 'To the circus,' he answered. 'After all, we invited the public to a performance.'

"And I obeyed the dustman and finished eating, and we left the restaurant and in a little while we came to the circus.

"And when we arrived, the dustman introduced himself to the circus manager first of all, and then my daughter and me. We stood behind the dustman's back and he spoke for us. And he explained that my daughter had made a big hit on the street, and he expected that she would do the same in the circus, at dancing or riding or whatever the circus manager asked her to do.

"The circus manager asked my daughter to come closer, and he looked her over and was obviously pleased with her. Then he glanced at me, and it was clear that I didn't please him. He said that he was ready to take on my daughter, but I was useless to him, he had no work for me.

"But the dustman argued for me and convinced him that with a little training I would be ready to do anything. And more to the point, he added (and gave the circus manager a knowing wink), was that I would be good for publicity, for if they announced on their posters that so-and-so, the well-known scholar of such-and-such academy would be appearing in the circus, the circus would certainly fill right up, and they would run out of tickets at the box office.

"Then the dustman bent down and whispered my story in the manager's ear. 'And ... since he's a scholar ... he understands, of course ... that he gets no pay ... just let him meet some of the circus people, in particular, a woman.... He is starved and he will certainly fall in love. Scholars are hotheads and stop at nothing. The woman can easily take him in hand. He'll do anything for her, and he'll serve the circus well. Perhaps he'll even be a magician, a tightrope walker or a trick rider....'

"The circus manager liked this suggestion, and he agreed that my daughter and I could stay and, of course, along with us the dustman who sold us to the circus.

"And it was just as the dustman predicted. The next day during the riding lesson, I saw Lili on her horse, and I couldn't keep my eyes off her. She let me get close to her and pretended that she wanted me to ride with her and be her partner in her act. The circus manager apparently persuaded her to agree to this so that my lessons would be successful. He knew that if I had Lili before me, I would work hard, and it would be to his advantage. We would put on a good show, there would be something to announce on the posters, and my appearannce was sure to be a sensation.

"And I rode after Lili and loved her, and my daughter rode with us. All three of us practiced together. And the dustman was also given circus work to do, so that he would be earning his bread too.

"The dustman was full of ideas. He suggested to the circus manager that since the last academy was locked now and the last scholar had come to work in the circus the public might be interested if we did a number based on this.

"A trial of the scholars. And I, the scholar turned circus performer, would be the chief judge, and other circus people would assist me as fellow judges: clowns, acrobats, and sleight-of-hand artists, and the sentence would be carried out openly before the entire audience. Some of the circus people would have to be the accused, and among them an older one, who would be a teacher of the scholars, and younger ones, who would be his students, and when the sentence was pronounced, a bonfire would be built, and they would be burned up then and there.

" 'And,' the dustman said, 'the clowns would have plenty of

opportunity for humor and ridicule. The theme was current, and the people would love it. They hate scholars, ridicule of scholars would give them pleasure, and it was sure to be a success.'

"The circus manager heard him out, and he liked the idea, and they immediately started to work on it. I had the main responsibility, because, as I have said, I was to play the main role. I was to be the head judge.

"And when everything was ready, all the roles distributed and the texts learned, the circus manager had posters made announcing the first number in the biggest print. It was to be:

The Judgement of the Last Scholar

on His Teacher and Students.

In addition, it said, the assistant judges would be the world-renowned clowns, Jack and Mack and Shlim Shlimazl. And, it said, the public would greatly enjoy this number because all the guilty were sure to be sentenced to be burned. A bonfire would be built on the spot, and Lili the circus rider would put the first match to the dry wood.

"And it all went exactly as the dustman predicted and as the circus manager calculated. As soon as the posters were put up, there was a great crowd at the ticket office. People stood in long lines, and the cashiers' hands grew tired of selling tickets, and there weren't enough for everyone.

"And when I made my entrance as the head judge, along with my assistants, the clowns Jack and Mack and Shlim Shlimazl, the audience began to howl with laughter just looking at us, because we were dressed like real judges. We sat down and the accused were led in, an old scholar, who looked like you, my teacher, Medardus, since I had had him dressed and made up like you, with long hair and a long gown, and his feet got tangled in his gown. And after him the younger ones, who looked like you, my students, in long gowns and droopy velvet skull caps that came to a point on top. And when you, Medardus and my students, were led in, the entire audience let out one resounding roar of laughter. Everyone held their bellies, it hurt so much, and the plain public and the gallery let out belly laughs and snorted like horses, because the clowns who were made up like scholars looked so serious. But then, turning around to the audience, they made funny faces and winked, and the audience razzed them and shouted wisecracks at them.

"And the trial didn't last long, only as long as a circus number should last, but the whole time the circus building was full of laughter that resounded up to the roof at the accused when they defended themselves, at the judges when they questioned them, and at me, the chief judge. And I don't know how so much insult and abuse came out of me. But I suppose that I was influenced by the clowns and the circus air in general and the huge audience that I was performing for, and I plunged into the hubbub, and I mocked more than any of them, and when I told the scholars off, I was wittier than anyone. And finally the sentence was pronounced: dirt and garbage that had to be burned. And assistant clowns came in dressed like executioners and axemen, and set up a bonfire, and they brought in straw effigies of the people sentenced, laid them on the woodpile and skillfully lit the fire, and the flame shot up, and the straw effigies burned. It was Lili who lit the fire, and she invited the audience to come down and light their cigarettes at the flame, and the crowd laughed again; and for some time after, whenever they thought of the number, they laughed out loud, and they had a fine time at the circus that day.

"And that," I continued telling Medardus and my students, "that was my first number. And I prepared myself for more. I continued my riding lessons. At times I rode alone, at times with Lili or with my daughter, and sometimes all three of us rode together.

"And I saw that Lili was jealous and couldn't bear to share billing with anyone else or to have another woman nearby. Though she knew that the woman was my daughter, it still bothered her, and she was always angry at her and worked against her whenever she could, in riding and in other things as well. She spoke against her to the circus manager and belittled her riding ability to the other circus artists. And I felt that she was capable of worse and that she was just waiting for the chance. Lili was the sort who would stop at nothing. If she felt she had to, and her jealousy overcame her, she would do physical injury to her rival, even cripple her.

"But I loved Lili, and for her sake I bound myself to the circus, and I felt the force of all the years of ungratified needs, all the time

that I had spent in our house with my straw wife. Now when I saw
Lili, I fell in love with her and went crazy for her.

"But she never even noticed me. She loved everyone else, the
athletes, the clowns, and all the other circus people, but not me. For
what was I to her, what could I bring her but my moldy, scholarly
past? That was the truth. She would certainly have driven me away
the first time I came to her if it hadn't been for the circus manager
and the dustman. The first, to promote his interests, because a
scholar-rider meant money to the circus, and the other, for my own
sake, because he was loyal to me and wanted to see me suited to
circus life, persuaded Lili not to do it. The manager asked her only
to let me hang around her and not to send me away, and the
dustman asked her to love me because I deserved it, and he told her
about my good points.

"So Lili let me near her, but she made a fool of me, and though
to please the circus manager she often allowed me some small
liberties in a corner, I felt that it was all a joke to her. In the middle
of it she would smile at me coldly and mockingly. Also, often while I
was making love to her, she would complain that I didn't love her
with my whole heart, because I gave most of my love to my
daughter.

"The truth was that I loved my daughter very much, even
though she came from straw and from a wife I didn't love. All my
past was bound up with my daughter. How could I deny her? I saw
my life through her. She was my reminder of it and of how much I
regretted it now.

"I was always with her, and Lili couldn't bear it. It was no longer
a joke to her, especially since my daughter showed great talent for
circus riding from the very beginning. The riding master and the
circus manager praised her, and the circus people would come to see
her riding lessons and couldn't take their eyes off her, her body, her
skill, her speed, her great mastery in riding.

"Lili saw it and she was envious of the praise that was showered
on my daughter by everyone. My daughter was a thorn in her flesh. I
could see that she regarded her as her rival, that my daughter's
successes gave her no rest, and that Lili planned to do my daughter
harm one day.

"And that," I told my judges and pointed to the bed where you, my daughter, were lying, "that is what happened tonight. Lili managed to carry out her plan. And surely it wasn't the horse's fault or my daughter's lack of skill at riding. It must have been that Lili didn't give her her hand at the time arranged between them, and she lost her balance and fell and injured herself.

"And it is my fault, my judges. This is what happened to me after I left our house. I betrayed my teachers and made my only daughter a cripple. And it all came about in the course of time because the corners of our house were broken up, and dustmen and those who lived off our mold got control of us, and we were good for nothing and completely unprepared for the outside world, and they took over and led us where dustmen have to lead us, to the street and the market place, to tricks and the circus and to giving up the shirt off our backs, the eyes in our heads, and the daughter of our loins, for a piece of bread. Sentence me and do what you want to with me. Deny me, just as I denied you, and just as I injured my daughter, do me injury too, and carry out your sentence on me."

With that, I finished speaking to the court, and they heard me out to the end, but in Medardus' eye I read "guilty," and in my students' eyes there was pity and sympathy, but they agreed with Medardus. They also found me guilty.

And suddenly: the hall where the trial took place and my daughter had been brought in as witness of my guilt and had been constantly before my eyes, began to change and grow larger and higher. The walls dissolved, and the ceiling lifted, and there was a high space overhead, and I recognized the circus and felt the circus air.

And there it was, the whole circus building, the benches and seats, the arena and the galleries, but they were empty. No one was in the seats or on the benches, but in the center was the judge's table, exactly where it had been during the clown show, when I was the head judge and Medardus and my students were on trial. Now it was exactly the opposite, Medardus and my students were the judges now, and I was the one on trial.

The building was lit by one little lamp. All around it was dark and empty except for that little light at the judges' table, and I stood before it with my head lowered, and Medardus began to question me.

He said:

"Did I know that the last one is obligated to the end, and to the end means until the ship goes down and the captain goes down with her?"

And I answered: "Yes, he is obligated."

And Medardus asked further:

"Did I know that dustmen and similar creatures are not persons or living creatures at all, but only illusions, born in the sick minds of scholars, and to allow oneself to be led by them and to do as they do is a disgrace?"

And I answered: "Yes, I must have been sick, and I took illusions to be reality."

And Medardus asked me further:

"Didn't I know that we scholars had no wives and of course no children, and that my child of straw that was brought to life by the dustman was illusion and magic, and that magic must be burned along with anyone who uses it or has the slightest connection with it?"

"Yes, I know," I answered.

Then suddenly I heard laughter in a dark corner of the circus, and I looked around and saw Lili coming down dressed like an executioner in blood red, down to me at the judges' table. And when I turned back to the table, I no longer saw the people who had been there before. Instead of the table there was wood laid on for a bonfire. Medardus and my students stood to one side. Lili didn't wait to be told by Medardus, but went over and took hold of my daughter, who was light as straw and allowed herself to be taken, and laid her on the bonfire. Then she came over to me and told me to go up there too, and I went.

Then Lili struck a match and held the flame to the wood, and the fire caught in the wood and in my straw daughter, and the whole circus was lit up immediately, and it was silent in the circus, and my daughter had already burned up, and I began to burn, first my clothes, then my body, my hair, my hands, my feet, and my face, and I burned briskly.

I burned and illuminated the circus for a long time. Then the fire began to burn down, and the circus grew darker. The coals settled, and I had turned to ashes, and the light of the bonfire burned lower and lower.

And then I noticed that Medardus took his shoes off, and my students did the same. And when the circus was dark again and there was only a little heap of ash and coal where the bonfire had been, Medardus and my students sat down on the ground and mourned for me, while Lili stood by the fire and lit a cigarette on one of the coals. And when Medardus and my students had sat in grief for a while, and I had burned up entirely, I spoke from the ashes and said:

"Stand up, my teacher and students. I deserved what was done to me. I brought you to shame, and you turned me to ash, and we're even, all equally brought to nothing. There won't be any grief at the circus. What kind of circus person was I really? If you hadn't forced me out now, the circus manager would have shown me the door later. He only kept me because of my daughter, and if my daughter can't perform because she was injured, why would he need me? What good would I do him? And Lili won't shed any tears for me. I was never anything to her, and now that she's free of my daughter, why should she bother with me? Stand up, my teacher and students!"

And saying that, I suddenly woke up, as if from a dream. I was cold, and I was lying somewhere, and a person stood over me and shook me. For a while I resisted him and wanted to lay my head down again. Why wouldn't he leave me alone? But he was stubborn. He woke me gently at first. Then he shook me harder and harder. He had a strong hand. He turned me and rolled me from side to side, and finally I couldn't get away from his hand, and I was forced to open my eyes.

And when I did, I didn't understand where I was. I thought I must be lying on the ground outside, and when I looked up, I saw that I really was outside, with my head under a fence, and the ground I lay on was filthy, like a place where drunks throw up.

And that is exactly what it was. There was filth all around and some straw near me and my hands were filthy. When I lifted my head higher, I recognized where I was. I saw the circus and the wooden steps that lead up to the galleries, and I immediately understood and remembered: this was where I came out after my disgrace with Lili and the athlete. I couldn't bear the pain of it, and I went right into a tavern near the circus, and I must have gotten drunk and set out for home and passed out near the fence and dreamed everything that happened up to now, and now it was morning, and a man stood over me, waking me, telling me to get up and go home to sleep.

And I obeyed him. The policeman helped me to get up. He supported me for a few steps until I was a little surer on my feet, then he left me, and I went on alone.

I came home and dragged myself up to my door and rang, and the housekeeper came down to open for me, and I went into my bedroom, fell into bed in my filthy clothes and slept most of the day. And when I opened my eyes again, I saw my daughter standing over my bed, looking down at me and crying for me, and for all of that day and the following night, her eyes were red from crying, and I— drunkard and ashamed—had nothing to comfort her with and couldn't lift my head up to her.

Translated by Seymour Levitan